LOVE & COWARDICE
The Nick & Greg Books #5

LOVE & COWARDICE

John Roman Baker

WILKINSON HOUSE

Love & Cowardice
Part 5 of The Nick & Greg Books
Copyright © John Roman Baker 2021
The moral right of the author has been asserted.

Published by Wilkinson House Ltd, July 2021

FIRST EDITION
978-1-899713-68-4

Wilkinson House Ltd.,
20-22 Wenlock Road,
London, N1 7GU
United Kingdom

www.wilkinsonhouse.com
wilkinsonhousebooks@gmail.com

Cover image: *Scène d'été*, Jean Frédéric Bazille
Cover design: Rod Evan

British Library Cataloguing-in-Publication Data
A catalogue record for this book is available
from the British Library.

*"If we want things to stay as they are,
things will have to change."*

– Giuseppe Tomasi di Lampedusa –
The Leopard

CONTENTS

PART ONE:

NICK

Nick's bookshop was both a haven and a prison. Sometimes he felt comforted by the books, and at other times oppressed because the millions of words that surrounded him alienated him from life itself. Then there was the silence—except for when a customer would come in and converse for a while. But when the door closed behind them after their browsing or purchase, he would face the walls of silent words and stare at the spines and realise it would take hundreds of years for him to read every sentence of every book in the shop.

He looked at his watch. It was four-thirty on a Friday afternoon in February 1973. It had grown dark outside, and the interior of the shop was dimly lit. He wiped his right eye with the back of his hand as if hoping that somehow it would brighten his vision. Already he was wearing glasses for reading, and he wondered if one day he would lose his sight. This was the prospect that depressed him most. Physical pain was possible to endure, or so he thought, but not the loss of his vision. He picked up his glasses from behind the desk: a simple writing desk that he had bought cheaply at a second-hand furniture shop. It was dark brown, and some of the drawers were difficult to open. He had placed it in front of a shelf of first editions he intended to keep for himself, and it was there in a space between the books that he kept his glasses. It was a ritual he maintained every day when it grew dark outside. Once his glasses were on, the shop appeared larger and seemed to breathe more. He laughed at the thought of it breathing, but that was how he perceived the relief of sharper vision. He had an hour before closing time, and he occupied himself as he usually did, tidying the counter, adding up the money, and putting back books that customers had taken down and not returned to their temporary homes. He had his back to the door when he heard it open, and a deep masculine voice say, "Hello." He did not turn until he had finished his job. The last book to be placed was a leather-bound edition of Thackeray's *Pendennis*.

"There," he said aloud, "that's done," and as he turned, smiling his usual smile, he saw a solemn scowl and two rather angry eyes looking at him. "People leave books lying around. I had to put them back," he said as if excusing himself. The young man, for very young he was, intimidated him.

"This is the last street I expected to find a bookshop on!" the youth explained.

"Clearly, you don't come down the London Road often," Nick replied, irritated.

"I do, but I don't often come down the side streets."

"It's usually there that you'll find the most interesting places, away from the usual shops."

The young man shuffled his feet awkwardly on the wooden floor and stared down at his boots. They were black and solid and caked with mud as if he had just returned from a long walk across the Downs.

"I'm dirtying your floor. You keep it neat in here, don't you?" He looked up, and there was a smile on his dark-skinned face. Nick rather liked the look of the youth, whose deep-set brown eyes attracted him. "I'm looking for a book. I don't suppose you will have it." The words were said almost as a challenge, and his smile widened at the same time.

"Try me," Nick said.

"*Homosexual: Oppression and Liberation* by Dennis Altman."

There was an awkward silence, and now it was Nick's turn to look down at the floor.

"I'm sorry, I—" Nick broke off the sentence, then moved behind the shop counter.

"You haven't got it then?"

The scowl on the face had returned.

"I do have a gay section. It's at the back of the shop."

10

"Always is," came the reply. Then came the questions. "Do you know the titles of all the books in that section? I mean, this isn't your shop, is it? I imagine it's run by an old person."

"I am that person."

The youth laughed.

"You? No. You're only in your twenties."

Nick felt he should be flattered by this, but he wasn't.

"Isn't that a rather ageist thing to say for someone looking for such a radical book?"

"Have you read it?"

"I haven't even heard of it, but I know it's not in the shop."

"Pity."

"Perhaps."

With the fussiness of someone much older, Nick started to dust the counter. The youth laughed again. Putting down the duster, Nick stared at him defiantly.

"Why don't you try that alternative bookshop in Little Preston Street. It's a bit far from here, but if you run, you might catch it before it closes," Nick said.

"I'm in no hurry. I'll take a look at what you do have. You said at the back? How many shelves?"

"Three," Nick replied crisply.

"All old books?"

"If you want to call Marguerite Yourcenar, Mary Renault and Angus Wilson old, then perhaps they are. I prefer to call them timeless."

"Sorry to offend, but I am looking for mens' books, written by men, hopefully gay men."

"I did mention one: Angus Wilson."

Nick was handling this unexpected customer badly, and he knew it. Now was the time for him to soften the hardness in the air, to be more complicit, and to counteract this defiant youth with friendliness.

"I am gay myself," Nick stated.

"Oh!"

Nick smiled at the open-mouthed youth.

"We are supposed to be everywhere, aren't we?"

The youth shuffled his feet again.

"I just wouldn't have thought it, that's all. I've just *come out*."

Making light of this, which he should not have done, Nick retorted, "For a long muddy walk?"

"Smart! I mean, have you ever heard of the Gay Liberation Front?"

Nick walked from the counter to where the youth was standing. "I am sorry," he said. "You just sound so defensive. Yes, I know about GLF, but I have not joined it, and I also know what it means to come out. I'm not usually so flippant. My name is Nick."

"Nicholas?"

"I prefer Nick."

"I'm Nathan." A muddy hand stretched itself out, and Nick shook it. The grip was firm and strong. "As it happens, I have just been for a walk. Stanmer Park. That accounts for the mud. It was fucking depressing, I can tell you. The grass was full of hidden dog shit, and the trees were dripping with yesterday's rain. I live in a bedsit. It can get pretty gloomy and smelly there too."

Nathan reminded Nick of Greg: the Greg of what was now long ago. His language was just as vivid. He was not sure if he desired Nathan, but he was beginning to warm to him.

"You look as if you need a cup of tea," he said impulsively.

"Great, but where? Aren't you supposed to be running the shop?"

"Yes, but it's my shop. I can close it when I want."

"Look, if you're thinking I'm up for—"

"Don't go on, Nathan. I am not thinking anything of the kind. I have a cubby hole where I make tea at the back."

"Next to the gay books?"

Nathan was laughing now—a soft and pleasant sound. Nick had wished for the silence in the shop to be broken, and like a minor miracle, the right sort of person had come in.

"Most of my customers are older. I quite often shut early and have a cup of tea with them at the back. It's part of this shop's charm."

"Do they think you're special? I mean, do *they* come on to you?"

"No one comes on to anyone. We talk."

"Sorry." The brown eyes once more looked down at the brown mud covering the boots. "It's all pretty new to me," Nathan said, "being gay. I'm seventeen. Some people say I look in my twenties."

"Well, you're safe here. I could almost be your father, and I'm certainly not going to risk jail for you."

Nathan stared at Nick then, a glint of impending tears in his eyes. He looked genuinely hurt.

"Everyone says I'm too young when I tell them the truth."

"Just wait while I close up the shop. I've got biscuits too. I bet the tea shop in Stanmer Park wasn't even open."

"You're thinking of Preston Park," Nathan replied with a laugh.

The laughter broke the ice, if there was any, and Nick locked the shop door and led Nathan to the small back room. They talked for a couple of hours, a sweet and gentle couple of hours that had its consequences.

When Nick arrived back at the empty house in Islingword Street, phantoms of the past returned to haunt him. He recalled the days of the three who were now elsewhere. He thought about each in turn and wondered what they were doing at that precise moment. He sat in the wicker chair he had found abandoned a year before in the street. It was his safe place: his place of memories and past desires. He told himself that at twenty-nine, going on thirty, it was too early to reminisce like this, but all his rationalisation and rejection of memories didn't prevent them from coming. The chair in the large basement faced out into the garden. During the dark months, he sat and imagined the three others talking outside, laughing, and above all, loving. He would spend a good hour like this before making his meal. And after eating and washing the dishes, he would return to the chair, and with the light on, pass the rest of the evening reading. Few people visited him. Anna, who had come so often, now came less and less, and out of respect for her secretive need to be alone, which was similar to his, he only contacted her by letter. It was their new relationship, letter writing, and it seemed to be a safe way of contact for both of them.

After his encounter with Nathan, he made his meal as soon as he came in and paced the room as he ate his pasta. Over and over, he thought about what they had said to each other in the shop. He recalled his nervousness as he opened the biscuits, conscious that it must have appeared a very *old* thing to do, especially to a youth of seventeen. But Nathan was hungry and managed to eat half of the packet. He had also joked as he munched on his eighth biscuit, saying that the walk had made him hungry. Nick had wanted to invite him to dinner but had resisted the temptation. He listened more than he talked as Nathan explained his home situation and how lucky he was to have a family who accepted his sexuality. His father had said he hoped he would perhaps marry later on in life and that there would be a grandchild, but this wish was not often mentioned. Nathan had made it quite clear that he had no sexual inclinations towards women and was sure he would not develop them. His mother occasionally asked if he had met anyone he liked, but despite his desire for a youth he had met during his exams for university, he was hesitant to confide in her. He was 'gay', but he felt a sense of repugnance at the thought of going into details of either physical or emotional desire with her. Nick listened and added comments that he thought appropriate, and became more verbal when they turned to the subject of books. Nathan was polite in asking what gay books Nick liked most, but when told, he replied that he had heard of none of them. Finally, they talked of the Stonewall riot, of how GLF had developed in the UK, and how interest seemed to be falling off as people were tired of both the theory and the practice. Nick, who was somewhat ignorant of both, did not pursue the conversation, and Nathan eventually stood up and said he had taken up too much of Nick's time. As he was about to leave, he asked for Nick's phone number, but Nick hesitated. What if the police were to find it if Nathan got into trouble? Nathan, taking this hesitation as a sign of rejection, shrugged his shoulders and made his way to the shop door. As he put his hand out to open it, Nick quickly jotted down his address and phone number for him. Nathan called back with a "Thank you," before disappearing into the night, adding, "I will ring you. I promise."

Nick put down his half-eaten pasta and felt suddenly elated that he had dared to elicit the possibility of further contact. *Did he desire Nathan?* The youth was handsome—of course he did. And yet, it was not a powerful desire. Later in bed, he masturbated, conjuring images from an old *Physique Pictorial* magazine. He ejaculated to the mental image of a young man with black, curly pubic hair, visibly aroused beneath his jock strap. He reassured himself that the youth from the magazine bore no resemblance to Nathan and soon fell asleep. His sleep was dreamless, and he awoke refreshed.

It often happens that after a dry spell of near solitude, friends return, and life becomes more social again. This was what happened to Nick, who had led a fairly lonely life for quite a while, hearing from Greg at reasonable intervals but otherwise in contact with very few people. Sarah had not been to the shop for at least a year, and further invitations to her house in Hova Villas had ceased. There were other regulars who came in to chat, and quite often he went to their houses to view or buy their collections, but none of the people he saw in this way pursued a further acquaintance, and he no longer received dinner invitations. Despite his youthfulness, he was not quite young enough for affluent gays to open their doors to him. He accepted this unwritten law of the gay world with resignation.

He recalled a song sung by a drag queen many years before: *Nobody Loves a Fairy When She's Forty*. The sentiment's basic cruelty was tacitly accepted as gospel truth by most, including himself, yet he still had more than ten years before he would reach that deadline.

The first rain that ended the dryness of his life was an unexpected call from Anna.

"My darling," she said, "I am quite ashamed at the long silence between us. It has been a bad time for me, and you know how much I loathe sharing bad tidings."

"What about our letters?" Nick reminded her, and the peal of laughter he had missed rang out so loudly that he held the phone away from his ear.

"You excuse everything, Nick. That is why you are so dear to me! But no, It has been unforgivable of me."

"Won't you tell me what's been going wrong?"

"I will, but only after you have eaten one of my meals and spent a whole evening with me. I also want to ask you a special favour—"

"Of course," Nick interjected.

"But you don't know what it is."

"Dearest Anna, you are not someone who makes heavy demands."

"Well, I am now. I want you to sit for a portrait."

"Again?" Nick asked, surprised but not displeased.

"The other one was years ago when you were practically still wearing nappies! No. This time I want a real adult face from you."

"Can I ask why?"

"I have been asked to exhibit some of my work at next year's Brighton Festival. Just a room in a hotel or somewhere equally ghastly, but it is flattering all the same. And it has broken my artistic block."

"I don't understand," Nick said.

"Oh, to hell with it! I was going to tell you over dinner, but I might as well give you some idea now. I didn't mention it in

my letters, but I've had a long patch of ill health. No details."
She paused. "I have not been painting. This has caused me a lot
of distress. The health business was a bore, but not having the
desire to put paint on canvas has been the giddy limit! I have
no idea how I managed to survive each day."

Nick remained silent. She was being deliberately reticent
about her health, but he couldn't ask her more unless she gave
her permission. Knowing her so well, he knew she would not.

"Are you still there? You are annoyingly quiet!"

"How long would you want me to sit for you?" he asked.

"Once every couple of weeks. I am working slowly. That is
why I am asking so far ahead. I want what I give them to be
good. Really good. Show them I have female talent, which as
you know is sadly underrated."

"Why have they requested so early?"

"Oh, you know how it is—long-term planning. They also
know I've been around for quite a long time as well and feel
they have to rectify a mistake made years ago—some cock-up
where they initially invited me and then switched to some artsy
male bastard from the University instead. All cubes and circles,
adding up to strictly nothing!."

"You never told me that," Nick said, with a slight note of
reproach.

"Well, one keeps one's failures to oneself, Nick. You are old
enough to know that."

"Don't be waspish, Anna. It doesn't suit you."

"Oh, no?" she laughed. "But enough of this waffling on.
Will you do it? Sit for me?"

"I certainly will."

"Then let's talk about it over dinner. A week today. Would
that suit you?"

"Of course."

"You are a lamb, my darling. It's a wonderful reason to paint
you again. I mean it. No flattery. You just have a face that is
actually worth painting. Not everyone does, but I shouldn't say
that, should I? I used not to believe it before." She paused. "Do

you know, the seventies somehow don't appeal to me? How a decade can make a travesty out of Herman Hesse's work by reinventing it for morons is beyond belief. But it is true! Remember that documentary about his work? Adding motorbikes in it, and God knows what else. Just an excuse to add him to the list of awful new books out there."

"I remember," Nick laughed.

"Now I must go. Nature calls as they say. So, see you around seven-thirty?"

"On the dot," Nick replied, and with a brief goodbye, the phones were put down.

A week later, he was with Anna and saw for the first time how frail she looked. The rather plump figure was gone, and beneath her long, billowing dress, he saw, if vaguely, the outlines of a body that was fast becoming emaciated. Anna noticed his questioning look and, by remarking on it, indicated that no further discussion of the issue was needed.

"I've had to diet—doctor's orders. Blood pressure was getting too high. You know me and the bottles of wine, well now they have to be a fond luxury of the past. Don't miss it really. Everything you give up for a good reason is right. So stop dissecting me with your looks. That's the problem with us not having seen each other for so long."

Nick joked about how he was getting too fat (which he wasn't) and that he was addicted to biscuits (which he was), and this reminded him of Nathan. He held out the bottle of wine he had brought with him and mimicked a guilty look.

"Shall I take this back?" he asked.

"Let's make an exception tonight. I see it's a good one. How can I resist? Next time though, bring nothing but yourself and that dear face of yours that I want to paint."

She took the bottle from him, and fetching a couple of glasses, uncorked it and poured them both a drink.

"Here's to—oh, here's to whatever happens," she said, laughing, and held up her glass. The deep red of the wine glowed in the light of at least twenty candles that were lit in the room.

"Exactly," Nick replied and was the first to bring his glass to his lips. He watched Anna over the rim of his glass and saw that she took only the smallest of sips before putting the wine down on the table. She lounged back on the sofa while Nick perched on a round stool he had chosen to sit on. He looked around the room, taking in the few paintings that were on the walls. Against the far wall of the room, unframed canvasses were propped up, all of them facing inwards. Anna followed his stare.

"You are using your x-ray eyes," she said. "Nothing new there, and these on the walls are just a few I have to keep me company. One is a portrait of an old friend who died a month ago, literally of old age, and then there are a few of what I call my 'sea' pictures. The sea has become my closest friend during this recent period, reminding me of that great and fantastic cliché that it will always be there. Each wave a friend, waving to me as it hits the shore. So, to underline it all, these are all my companions."

She laughed again, but Nick sensed an underlying sadness. Then with a chuckle, Anna smiled at him and asked him to relate all the juicy details of his life that he had left out of his letters.

"Not much to tell," Nick replied as he bent forward to a bowl of cashew nuts and popped a couple into his mouth. "My favourites, these," he muttered as he chewed.

"Are you trying to tell me that you have been wasting away all on your own in that delightful house that reminds me of the Orkneys?"

"Yes. It's true," he replied. "But you are wrong. It's nothing like the Orkneys. No, for me, the solitary life encourages a lot of meditation. I am getting so much better at meditation."

"You are too young!" she replied. "I cannot imagine you in isolation. I recall only too clearly the night when we were all together, that charming boy, Bart. I really took to him. Heard any news? I mean letters from him from Paris?"

"None."

"No letters at all from any of them? I know Karel has a good reason—Czechoslovakia, but Greg, and especially Bart?"

"Why especially Bart?" Nick said as he reached out for more of the cashews. He felt hungry and longed for what she had prepared for dinner.

"Because he has a kind soul," Anna replied softly. "I cannot imagine him ignoring you."

"I told you in one of my letters that he and Greg had parted in Paris. He has gone his own way."

Anna sighed, and picking up the wine glass, took another sip of wine. It was clearly not an act of desire, just an action to not force the subject of Nick's departed partners. "I guess even the most loved must leave us," she concluded, and then turned to the subject of the meal she had prepared. "We're having roast chicken and golden, crispy potatoes with fresh peas, followed by a mystery dessert."

"Anna, you have no idea how starved I am for this meal. I have longed for it, along with your company, all week."

"Silly Nick," she said. "Starve indeed! I know damn well you can cook."

"It's a bore, just for myself, so I eat basic stuff. Pasta usually. And my sauces are not worthy of description."

She got up and led him into the dining room, where the table was elaborately set as if for Christmas. Once more, a seemingly endless supply of candles surrounded them in every available space.

"You know, Nick, I find this the best light of all. Above all, I love reading by candlelight. Fortunately, my sight is good. I sometimes get through a book a night, and then I am very, very tired and capable of sleeping. I have just finished *The Sound and the Fury*. Faulkner has always defeated me. Don't really take to the Southern States style—do you?" she asked as they were cutting into the crisp exterior of the chicken.

"The style is certainly *Southern Fried*," Nick replied,

laughing at his attempt at a pathetic joke.

The conversation steadily waned as there appeared to be nothing to say. Whatever had happened in her life, she was not going to divulge, and Nick, poverty-stricken for inspiration, could only have talked about meeting the mysterious Nathan, but he resisted. Nathan was like fresh paint: too new to spoil by touch. It was only after the dessert, a chocolate pudding with cream, that Anna spoke about her creative work.

"Nick, I want to tell you something I am rather ashamed of. It's partly why I asked you over. I couldn't put it in a letter."

Raising his eyes from the black coffee in front of him, Nick glanced at Anna.

"I sense something is wrong."

"It is."

"Tell me."

"Let's go back to my waves—my sea friends. I feel calmer in their presence. I also get a lot of comfort from the portrait. The woman's name was Alice. She lived nearby. We were friends for years, but recently she had to die. It was a tough blow."

Nick looked at her and said nothing. She had never spoken of Alice before. Why? Had she been the closest person in Anna's secretive life? He did not want to ask. He also did not want to say the pitiful words, I am sorry. Once seated as they had been before dinner, Anna opened up.

"I am not sure I can paint anymore," she said slowly.

"I don't understand."

"The gift seems to have gone. I rang you in one of those moments when you think it will return, but I am not sure it will. I've lost my touch."

Nick looked at her in silence. Why did he feel so impotent with her? Why didn't he probe more? Was it the death of Alice, or was it her health? He felt the cowardice of one who cares too much but cannot show it.

"But surely, all the inspiration you had still exists? Don't tell me you've lost that, or is it that you fear losing it?"

"I don't feel the paint on the canvas is real anymore. Paint to me is like words to you. Those words must glow sometimes in your poems. They really must. Otherwise, you couldn't write."

"I don't write much anymore."

"You are still young. It will pass. I am not young, and—well, it's quite simple, the paint does not shine for me anymore, and I have tried! God knows I have tried. Yet each time, I see daubs of nothingness. A void. A colourless void that has sucked all my attempts into the depths of the canvas and lost it. Like a hole in the darkness."

"But this exhibition—?"

"I know. Over a year away. I tell myself I have to try. I have to make one last attempt. It has been a long time coming, this offer from the Festival. As I said, it was mooted years ago, back when the Festival first started, but then the clever boys took over. I was out of date. I knew I was at my peak then, but they didn't see it. I was pushed aside."

Nick felt furious at the Festival for its lack of vision, but he wanted to comfort her and said the first thing that came into his head.

"I may have an answer to this," he said. "Don't use colour. Use blacks and whites and greys. Begin again. Form will help colour to return. Blacks and whites and greys really bring out form. I know that from how I use words in my work."

Anna leant back on the sofa and looked at Nick for a long while in silence. Then she picked up her glass of wine and downed it in two swallows.

"That was a toast to you," she said, laughing. The same wonderful laugh had returned. "I knew it. I knew I had to see you. You are right. Absolutely right. That is how it should be. No letter could ever have expressed it as simply as you did."

"But I said nothing."

"You said everything, Nick."

Anna got up and approached Nick. Her face was radiant.

"The greys," she said. "The beautiful greys. Why didn't I

have the intuition to know that was where to begin again. Now we are really going to finish off that bottle, doctor's orders or no doctor's orders." She paused then, and after a short while added, "I am such a fool. I was even going to cancel tonight. I thought I couldn't dare to tell you. Somehow I must have known you would use *your* intuition, and you do have it, Nick. Intuition is at the heart of your work and the way you look at life. And yet, I am sure you never think of it like that."

"No, I don't," Nick replied quietly.

"All the better. The best of us is best not known. It stays truer then."

She returned to the sofa, and bringing the wine bottle close to her, poured out a large glass for herself. She then took Nick's glass and poised the bottle over it.

"Only a little," Nick said.

"Your glass is almost full. Drink half of what's there and let me top it up. I have an idea, and I want us to be merry when I tell you about it."

"But Anna—you're drinking too much."

"No buts. Come on."

To humour her, Nick drank as much as he could. The red wine had a heavy flavour to it, a darkness in its taste, and he was afraid it might go to his head. He seldom drank alcohol now and didn't want to start needing it. He knew well how a semi-solitary life could lead to alcohol dependency.

"There," he said and placed the near-empty glass on the table. "But only up to halfway."

"It's a small glass as it is," she said with a laugh, and despite Nick's request, she filled it.

Anna leant back again on the sofa, and Nick looked at her in silence, remembering her robust figure and reddened cheeks. Her once-black hair had streaks of grey, and her complexion was pale. She had also put on make-up which she had rarely done before.

"Stop staring, Nick. You have a way of doing that. I share it with you. I call it my dissecting glance. But I feel you are asking silent questions."

"I am sorry," he said and looked down. "I led you to believe I do not hear from the others. It's not strictly true. There've been no letters, but Greg calls me every few months."

"The wayward one," she laughed. "How is the rascal?"

Her use of outdated terms to describe Greg amused Nick. He looked at her and smiled.

"He *was* a rascal," he replied, "long, long ago when we were adolescents."

"Hasn't changed, I'm sure," she murmured, drinking at the same time, which made her cough. After she recovered, she added, "But he is the most important one to you, isn't he?"

"Yes, Anna. He is."

"Then all love is not lost. I am glad. That boy needs a happy ending to his life. And he will live to be very old. I predict it now. I don't need to throw my I Ching coins for that!"

Nick got up and walked over to the portrait of the woman who had died, hoping that Anna would tell him more about her, but she made no personal comment, only an observation.

"I wasn't sure about the orange dress," she said. "I hardly ever use the colour, well certainly not in that shade, and yet it works. Don't you feel that it works? It should clash with her complexion, but somehow it doesn't. It is such a risk, the choice of colour, in a garment so near the face. I think I used green for you. Yes, I know I did."

Standing with his back to Anna, he heard a slight slur in her words and knew that the wine was taking effect. If only it would open up the floodgates of emotion she possibly felt for this woman. What held her back? What is it that holds us all back from letting go of our emotions, shouting them aloud if necessary? What shame, cowardice or fear? He did not reply to her observations but looked even harder at the eyes of the woman. They were blue, pale blue, and fixed in their stare as if incapable of blinking. Was she staring at Anna as she painted, or was it at the middle distance that makes so many painters feel more comfortable when at work on a portrait? Eventually, he asked.

"Was Alice looking at you?"

There was silence as Anna fumbled for something on the cluttered table in front of her. As well as the bowl of cashew nuts, Nick had noticed a couple of books on Paul Klee and various large, coloured balls, like enlarged marbles. They looked cold, and he had briefly wondered if they were held to relax or soothe away some fevered heat. He listened to the fumbling sounds and imagined her clutching at one of them. He did not want to turn around to find out. Instead, he waited for her reply and continued looking at the pale blue eyes and taut skin of Alice's face.

"I can't remember," Anna said eventually. "I only know she was very patient with me."

Nick moved on to look at one of the sea paintings. It was a stormy blend of rising waves and flecks of white, suggesting the tattered wings of seagulls in flight.

"This, I love," he said and turned at last to face Anna. She was leaning forward. Her hair was longer than it used to be and almost covering her eyes.

"Then it will be yours," she said, and lifting at once her head, smiled a weak smile at him. Her eyes, he noticed, were very red, slashed by lines that showed the pressure of blood. "Now for my idea, Nick," she began.

"It's late, Anna," he said. "I have to open the shop early."

"Must you go?" she asked.

"Soon, yes."

"It won't take long. I promise. Just come and sit on the sofa. We'll move the table. I want to do a brief sketch of you. No need for an easel."

"But—"

"It will only take a little while."

Anna got up unsteadily, and acquiescing to her wishes, Nick sat in her place on the sofa. He sat there in silence while she left the room. When she returned, she was wearing her painting shift and holding a dark brown board and a sheet of drawing paper. In silence, she placed a chair at a distance from him to sit on, and retrieved several crayons from her pocket. After a short while, he heard the sound of crayon meeting paper. The whole process took around half an hour.

"Finished," she said, and getting up, went to a desk drawer and took out some pins and fixed the drawing to a wall. "Come and look."

Nick did. Delicately, very delicately, she had achieved an exact image of him, as precise as a photo, a grey photo with a precision of detail that took his breath away. She had seen *him* much more clearly than when he was younger, seen him with a clear inner sight that made the drawing live. To the right of his face, held in the air in a gesture of magic, was one of the glass balls from the table. It hung like a small planet, coloured with two shades of green. The blend was so startling in contrast to the grey that he gasped with pleasure. From precision, she had returned to that imaginative sphere of colour, a planet of promise, not only for the figure depicted but also for the promise of her own return. Her promised return to painting and all the richness that was her inner being.

"I love you very much," he said and kissed her.

Anna moved away as if embarrassed by his show of affection. She sat beside him on the sofa, leaning forward this time, and she looked worn out, exhausted as a person looks after a great deal of strain and effort. Nick knew it was time for him to go but was unsure of what to say. Anna turned and looked at him with the hint of a smile on her face.

"The word love, Nick. It must be used with care. With great care. I know how much regret can come in one's life from using it unwisely. Not that you did. I know how much you think of me and always have, but please, my dear, reserve those words so tarnished by the marketplace for someone who—" and here she trailed off, and picking up the near-empty wine bottle, poured the last of it into her glass.

"I have offended you," Nick said.

"No, no." She put the glass to her lips. "Just be careful with words. After all, they provide our only means of expressing how we *think* we feel?"

"But—"

"You meant it. I know. Your thoughts were on the pleasure I gave you by producing a work that is quite good. Not perfect. What is? But good. And I want to show my feelings to you, without words, by giving it to you."

Nick did not want to take it. He thought she might need it to induce her to further work, but he knew he could not refuse her.

"I don't know what to say," he replied, and realised how limp and feeble the words sounded.

"Nothing. Take it off the wall. Somewhere in this near-abandoned studio of mine, I have a tube to put it in."

She got up and moved with difficulty. At one point, she lurched as if she were going to fall forwards, but she regained her composure, found the small tube, and rolled the portrait into it.

"Here," she said and handed it to him.

"When do you want me to come again? For the portrait? The one you want to do for next year's exhibition?"

"I will write. I will explain more. Now I need my bed, and so do you."

She patted his face affectionately in a subtle gesture of dismissal.

As Nick walked away from Anna's place and the studio he had grown so fond of, he questioned whether she would have the courage or even the physical strength to build up a collection for the following year's festival. His body shuddered, and not because of the cold, for the air was almost warm. He shuddered as a dark thought crossed his mind, and he clung to the poster tube as if for support to get home.

In the morning, two days later, the sky was blue, and the air was refreshing. He had the door to the garden open, and he glanced at what appeared to be a triangular object just beneath the wicker chair. He bent down to pick it up, thinking it was a piece of bread or some other food he had dropped there, but his hands met nothing solid. He glanced again. The triangle was a trick of the sun that had cast its light on the kitchen floor. His hand covered the glow, and when he drew back his hand, the triangular shape disappeared. Looking out of the door, he saw that clouds had gathered. The object he thought he had seen would never appear again in the same way, and a fierce emotion of unwanted solitude ripped at him.

The day was dull in the bookshop. Customers were scarce, and he sold only a couple of books. He tried to read but could not focus his attention. Solitude was draining him of all response, and he knew it.

"Greg, why don't you call?" he whispered.

The books looked too solid and meaningless around him. What sentence in any of them could relieve him of the pain he felt? He imagined a dying man trying to read a book he had loved in his past but, instead, putting it aside. Books, he thought, were best for life's hope and ambitions, not for times of inner pain or suffering. He had read that Elizabeth Taylor had written her final novel *Blaming* while she was dying of cancer, and he wondered how she had been capable of doing that.

"I will close early," he said aloud.

Annoyingly, a customer he did not like came into the shop. It was an elderly gay man who liked nothing better than to relate his experiences with rent boys to Nick.

"Hello Alan," Nick said with a forced smile.

"Not busy today? Good. I wanted a little natter with you."

"Alan, I don't feel well. I was just about to close."

"Then you need a drink. Close the shop, and we will go for a drink."

Alan, who was in his late sixties, looked at Nick with forlorn eyes. Rich as he was materially, Nick knew that he had few friends and that most of them were straight. He often told Nick how much he had wasted his youth, that he had not lived openly until 1967 for fear of imprisonment. His sex life until then had consisted of rare and furtive encounters, mainly on dangerous Hampstead Heath where he had lived. Freedom for him had come too late. Since the 1967 Act, he went with young men he met at parties in London and Brighton, young men he paid for. He had once said jokingly to Nick, "I am like Karen Stone in that wonderful film of Tennessee Williams' novella *The Roman Spring of Mrs Stone*. But I am *not* going to move to Rome or end up in Tangiers, which is probably what happened to poor Karen." He talked of her as if she were real, and always described her in detail with memories of Vivien Leigh's performance in mind. He joked how much he would have loved to have met dear Vivien. "So sad," he would say, finishing the eternally told story.

"I've had a mishap, Nick. Let me buy you a drink. You understand my situation in life so well."

Nick felt yet again that Alan was talking to him as if he too were in his late sixties.

"Only for a short while," Nick replied.

"How good you are. In return, I will sign a cheque and buy up that lovely *Pléiade* of somebody or other that you have in the shop."

"I'm afraid I sold it. I cannot even remember the author, and I don't have many books in French at present."

"Not one?"

"A first edition of Gide—*La Porte Étroite*."

"Oh, that is too narrow for me! But I will buy it. Is it a fearsome price?"

Nick told him.

"My overused chequebook can bear that."

Nick found the book, wrapped it securely, and handed it to him. "You really didn't have to buy this," he said hypocritically.

Alan's cheque was generous. He had thrown in a few extra pounds, clearly forgetting the price Nick had stated. This happened quite often with him, but Nick never commented on it. If he had, it would have somehow questioned Alan's memory (which fluctuated, to say the least), and perversely, he was quite happy taking a bit more from a man so rich. He thought unkindly that many of the rent boys probably felt the same. Alan always paid with cheques. He had a horror of physical money. Nick knew, therefore, that he would have to pay for the drinks; it was cash that was needed in a pub.

"Shall I tell you about my mishap, my catastrophe, call it what you like, now or over a drink?"

"Over a drink, Alan, please. This shop is getting on top of me today. Right now, I feel I don't want to see another book ever. I've had the impression today that they own the place and not me!"

"How dreadful. Sell. Get another occupation."

"Yes, Alan, what a good idea." Nick laughed as he said this, and once out in the street, Alan insisted on getting a taxi to East Street. He wanted to go to a newish bar that had just opened up there, close to the police station.

"It's tacky, but I quite like it. I am sorry to say, that's where I met my catastrophe! A redhead! Never, ever go with redheads. They simply adore money and will commit any crime to get it. Sadly, I know."

The taxi took a long time to arrive and then refused to go to East Street for a reason not explained, so they had to wait three-quarters of an hour for another. Alan was chatty and talked about his next favourite thing after bought young men: the cinema.

"I saw a re-run of *Sunday Bloody Sunday* recently in London. The audience hated the moment when Peter Finch kisses that boy, whose name I cannot remember. When I felt that hatred in the audience, I thought, quite right too! Elderly men should not be seen kissing young men on the screen. It looks sad and unnatural."

"But Alan, that is so wrong."

"It's not wrong! It's not aesthetic. It's ugly."

"Then what about you and the young men who—"

"That is different," Alan interjected. "I cannot see myself.

On a big screen, everyone can see how tragic the whole thing is!"

The bar, tucked away in a corner of the street, was reasonably full and seemed well run.

Once settled with a drink in front of them, Nick hoped Alan would get to the point of his mishap so he could cut short the evening.

"Okay, tell me all about it," Nick said.

"About what?" Alan replied vaguely.

"What happened to you. Your misadventure. The thing that upset you."

"The redhead! Yes, I dragged you here for that. Can you believe it? I have come back to the scene of the crime: the place where I met him. Beautiful red hair, and he—"

"Yes?"

Alan paused for a long time and then said dramatically, "He beat me up! On our sixteenth meeting. Yes, I am sure it was the sixteenth. I jot each visit down in my diary."

"Did you go to the police?"

"What?" Alan almost shouted.

"The police, Alan. They are there for getting people who abuse others."

Alan shook his head.

"Not people like us."

"Yes, Alan, people like us. They *can* charge the man without charging *you*."

"Too much of a risk," Alan mumbled, "even now the law has changed."

"So, where did this man attack you?"

"Well, it wasn't exactly brutal, what he did, but he did chase me around my living room with a—firearm."

"A firearm!"

"Yes. A poker. You know what a poker is. It pokes at fires." Nick wanted to laugh at this but restrained himself. "He said he was going to crack my skull in because I was seeing another young man. He said the young man knew him as well. What a nest of vipers!"

Nick let the last comment pass and replied that perhaps it had been rather foolish to have two men on the go, when inevitably, in a town like Brighton, one rent boy would know or know of the other.

"He said I was unfaithful, Nick, that I was going to ditch him for this other boy. I protested that it was all nonsense, but he persisted, making me run around that room until I fell over with exhaustion and nearly had a heart attack. Then, while I was near to death on the floor, he handed me my chequebook and demanded, demanded, can you imagine it, for me to pay him five hundred pounds! He said he would use the poker if I didn't."

"So you did?"

"What choice did I have? My heart was hurting. Pounding with fear. I couldn't breathe. It was a terrible assault. So I wrote out the amount, and then I am ashamed to say I started crying, and do you know what he did? Do you know what this evil redhead did? He laughed in my face. He jeered at me. And then he threw the poker aside and called me a stupid old queer. Can you imagine the horror of all this? Me, lying there in my dying state, with that horrible poker beside me?"

"Couldn't you have stopped the cheque?"

"How could I? I was ill in bed for days. I couldn't even get to a phone. No one called me. I was quite alone."

Clearly, this story was true, but up to what point, Nick wondered. He reached out and patted Alan's now trembling hands. The whisky that Alan was drinking had made him maudlin, and he cried silently. He rambled that he had been in danger of falling in love with the redhead, and so to prevent that happening, he had started to go with a blond, similar in physique and sexual prowess. Nick spent a long time listening to intimate details about them and how they compared with each other. As far as sexual organs went, the blond won, apparently.

"By at least two inches," Alan clarified as he dried his eyes.

"Will you continue to see the blond?"

"I don't know. I'm so wounded. I can't believe I've just lost five hundred pounds. I cannot afford anyone."

"I still think the police should be contacted."

The repetition of the word *police* obviously jarred on Alan, and he buried his face in his hands. He gave out a quiet little wail, but not quiet enough to prevent a group at the next table from looking over.

"Alan, people will think I am breaking up with you or something. Please try and pull yourself together."

"But I can't go to the police, don't you understand? I am more afraid of the police than anyone?"

"Times have changed. Trust me."

"I'm old," Alan said, lowering his hands and turning to look disconsolately at Nick. "I can't change the fear."

"You realise this young man will continue what he is doing—that he will extort money from others?"

"I know."

"And you won't do anything to try to stop him?"

Alan shook his head, and Nick knew that nothing more could be said on the subject. He was about to say that he really had to go when Alan clutched his arm.

"Quickly! What's the best way out? I must go the best way out." He looked desperately at Nick.

"I don't know the place."

"The emergency exit! Where is it? Where is it? *He* is here! The redhead is *here*!"

Alan shuffled to his feet, upsetting a half-full glass as he did so. Bent double, he was almost on all fours. Nick laughed aloud and received a loud *hush* from Alan as he crawled towards the exit. Caught up in this ridiculous farce, Nick followed, and within minutes the seedy pink curtains were parted to reveal a door that led out into an alley. Once there, a bedraggled looking Alan got to his feet and stood with his back to the wall. Even in the semi-darkness, Nick could see that Alan's face was white.

"The redhead. The terrible redhead," he mumbled, shaking his head. For a few minutes, they remained facing each other and then Alan lurched forwards. "My breath! My heart! I should have known this would happen." He then opened his mouth and spewed out a mess of vomit. Nick jumped away just in time not to be hit by it.

"For God's sake!" Nick said and waited as Alan reached for a handkerchief in his jacket pocket to wipe his mouth.

"I'm not sure he didn't see me. He may follow me home. Nick, will you come back with me, or better still, may I come to your place for a couple of hours?"

"This is totally irrational."

"I know, but I can't be alone for the next few hours."

"Alan, you see too many bad films."

"I'm serious, Nick."

Clearly, Nick had to help, and he said that Alan was welcome to come with him to Islingword Street. "We'll get a taxi in East Street."

Once more, the ritual of the taxis began. The first driver had just accepted another call. The second was heading for Woodingdean, and the third was equally busy. It was by pleading with the fourth that they got underway. Alan kept nervously looking around him. Nick thought of the chase scenes in *Some Like it Hot*, and in his imagination, saw a good-looking rentboy with a gun approaching them from the shadows. Although he tried to deny it, he was enjoying the farce and even wondered whether he was Jack Lemmon or Tony Curtis. He chose Tony Curtis. As the taxi headed towards his house, he tried to suppress the moans coming from Alan's mouth by whispering *hush* into Alan's ear. A couple of times, the man who was driving looked around. Nick knew that he thought they were just a couple of stupid queens who had had too much to drink, and he did not like the image.

"Here we are," Nick said at last, and the taxi stopped with an abrupt judder that threw Alan forward. Nick caught Alan's body and helped him out of the taxi. He paid the driver and opened the door of the house. In the hall, Alan's face got its colour back, and he said excitedly, "I have never been in one of these little houses before! How *bijou*!"

Without replying, Nick led him into the small living room and settled him on the red sofa he had bought recently at Habitat.

"It's all so modern," Alan said, looking at the white blinds and the walls decorated with paintings that were incomprehensible to him. "Do you have more rooms?"

"A large basement downstairs and a couple of bedrooms upstairs."

"Well!"

Nick said he would make some coffee and left Alan alone. As he descended the stairs to the basement, he felt giddy and knew that he needed food. He drank half of a pint of milk too quickly, and soon he was feeling sick as well as giddy. He wondered how long it would take to get Alan out of the house. The so-called farce had worn off, and he made a silent vow to never go out for a drink with Alan again, to discourage him from recounting his *adventures* and to treat him solely as a customer. Then the phone rang, but just as Nick had giddily crossed the room to reach it, it stopped. He thought at once of Greg and stared at the phone for a long while, waiting for the ringing to return. He imagined Greg having trouble calling from a café, or perhaps he was at home. He knew he was living with a man called François, and he knew they had a phone in their apartment somewhere in the north of Paris. He could never remember the name of the district, which distressed him. He *should* be able to remember it. It was where Greg lived. But this is Greg's home, he thought. Yet even as the thought crossed his mind, he knew it was no longer true and that it would never be true again. Never! What a terrible word; a word that has the resonance of death, of fading out, of no longer knowing, also of disappearance and of no longer existing. *Never* was the eternity of time; a word that really had nothing to do with death, for Nick felt there could be no awareness of words after that final frontier had been passed. Never, in itself, was just another word in the dictionary.

"Nick, I've been waiting here for ages!"

Nick did not respond immediately to the call from the top of the stairs. He wanted the phone to ring again and to hear Greg's voice; to know that he was alive, but then maybe it was not Greg. So few people contacted him at the house now. It could have been Anna, and after three rings she had changed her mind. Yes, that was probably it.

"I'm coming," Nick called back.

"This is such a small room. How could you have a party in a room this small? It must be so claustrophobic. Do the guests ever pass out?"

"Don't stay on up there, Alan. Come down."

Nick was inured to the slight insults that came out of Alan's mouth. His patronising comments about the house and the living room would have hurt others, but Nick felt nothing. There was truly nothing to feel about Alan. He then turned to see Alan clinging onto the bannisters as if there were a thousand steps to conquer, and realised he was being callous towards him. The man was old, old and tired from what he had been through, and it was not right or human that he should feel nothing for him.

"Come on, it's not that far down. I'll make you a cup of tea."

Alan, at last, reached the bottom step and stood there, gazing around him as if he had come out into the light after having been imprisoned.

"My dear, I don't like places that are underground, but this space is so much better than above. I am sure you could have a party down here, and look, you have a garden. Why don't you have lamps outside to show it off?"

"Because there is not much to show off."

"But guests! When they come, as they must, why keep them in darkness in the garden? Even in summer, the light fails an hour earlier than abroad, so lamps are needed. It's not good to have drinks and chatter lit only by reflected light from a room."

Nick laughed. The absurdity of Alan's obsession with parties was touching. He wondered how many people Alan really knew and how many parties he gave. And yet, he knew that with lots of money in the bank, people could be bought; whole room-fulls of them with, in Alan's case, rent boys stealing from every one of them.

"I don't have parties," Nick said at last.

"No?" Alan's face looked haggard under the harsh central light of the room, and hurriedly, Nick turned on some side lamps.

"I should have stayed upstairs. It was rude of me to barge in down here."

"Not at all. Sit down."

Alan sat awkwardly on the wicker chair as Nick made the tea. He said nothing, and Alan was silent as well. The atmosphere in the room was akin to that of a couple who have nothing of interest left to say to each other. It was only when he handed the tea to Alan that the older man said, "I really am grateful, you know. You have saved me from loneliness this evening. We have known each other for quite a while now in the shop, but we are still sort of strangers, aren't we? I mean, how rude of me not to have invited you to one of my *do's*, but then, one forgets. One forgets these important things."

Nick smiled and sat on a chair facing Alan. He said, "Personally, I think our relationship probably belongs to the shop and the occasional drink in a pub, don't you? I mean, that is what we are used to, and it can be a mistake to blur borders."

"What borders?" Alan asked.

"The borders that we all make for ourselves. You have your territory. I have mine. It is best we meet on neutral territory."

"I suppose so, but I wouldn't have thought you would consider your shop neutral," came the wistful reply.

"As it happens, Alan, I am waiting for an important call. There were three rings and then the phone went dead. I have a friend who is abroad and probably trying to get through. You know how difficult it can be to call in another country."

"Only too well," Alan said, sipping his tea. Then putting his cup onto a side table, he murmured, "I suppose it is time for me to go." The way he said the words reminded Nick of a child realising it is time to leave and go up to a lonely bed.

"We still have time. I expect he will go back to his flat to make the call." Nick said, attempting to make amends for the note of dismissal in his voice.

"Is there still time?" Alan asked, looking at Nick.

"Yes."

"What I really need to know now is how long taxis take coming up these hills? Would you ring for one?"

"Of course."

It all became very formal after that. The taxi arrived promptly, which amazed Alan, and once departed, Nick closed the front door softly. He went back down the stairs to the basement and was washing up Alan's cup when the phone rang again. He paused to let it ring, just in case it was Anna, to let her decide if she really did want to speak, but when the phone reached its fifth ring, Nick snatched up the receiver, greedy to hear Greg's voice. Who else could it be?

"Hello? Have I got the right number? I want to speak to Nick."

Realising it was Nathan, Nick said his name, and there was a moment's silence.

"Is this a convenient time? I know it's late, but—"

"Of course."

"I mean, you are sure I'm not interrupting anything?"

"Quite sure."

How long was this eternal politeness to go on?

"I wondered if you were free? I'm ringing from a pub in Gloucester Road. I mean, if you would like a drink—"

The voice trailed off, and in the background there was complete silence. It certainly didn't sound like a pub.

"That's not far from where I live," Nick replied. "All you have to do is walk up a couple of hills. The Islingword area is all hills," he added.

"Good for the legs."

Nathan was laughing, and Nick, to encourage, laughed with him. Then he repeated his address twice.

"Got it," Nathan said. "I will only be a few minutes."

"I hope you like warm white wine," Nick said.

"It should be me bringing the wine," Nathan replied.

"Don't be silly. I can't think of an off-licence near you, and the bottle has been in the cupboard for weeks. It's about time it had some air."

Nathan laughed again: a soft laugh that sounded a little forced and nervous. Then without another word, Nick heard him replace the receiver. For a moment, he felt dazed as if suddenly his home had become a revolving door. It was a bit of a shock to his system, this bombardment of two strangers. He looked around him and, for a second, disliked the idea of his place being judged again. Would it be to Nathan's taste, he wondered, and then conscious that he needed to change his clothes, he dashed upstairs to his bedroom. He exchanged the grey clothes he usually wore in the shop for something brighter and more youthful, and he combed his hair. Then the bell rang. "Oh, God, I'm not up to this," he said aloud as he went back downstairs to the front door.

"Nathan?" he said as he opened the door.

The rest was a blur. A figure emerged out of the darkness and took Nick into his arms. Nick felt his mouth being kissed, and he responded. It was a long kiss, and the door was wide open. Then they drew apart.

"I do have neighbours," Nick murmured as he closed the door. Turning to face Nathan in the brightly lit hallway, he saw a smile, almost of satisfaction, on the sharply cut dark face. His hair was tangled, and once again, he looked as if he had just returned from a long hike over the Downs.

"I wanted to see how it felt," Nathan said.

"You mean that was just an experiment?"

"Yes."

Nick laughed at this frank answer and, gently pushing past

Nathan, asked him to come downstairs. As they descended, Nick added that this was where he mainly lived. They stood side by side at the bottom of the stairs, and Nick studied Nathan's face closely to see if he could gauge a truthful response. Not that he expected a polite one. He knew perfectly well that what the youth said, he meant.

"It's good," Nathan whispered as if the room were full of people. "I like the quiet down here, and you have a garden! Can I go out and have a look?"

In silence, Nick opened the garden door and went out. Nathan followed. A light emanating from the house behind lit the place sufficiently. Along the dividing walls separating garden from garden, the brown soil, preparing to display its spring flowers, attracted Nathan. He bent down and touched the earth and whispered how soft and moist it was and how much he loved it. As he stood up, a few pieces of earth fell from his hands.

"Beautiful," he said in a louder voice.

It was at that moment that Nick felt emotion. He *was* attracted to Nathan. He wanted to kiss again, to feel again that lean and strong body against his own. Should he make the move this time? Out here in the semi-darkness where everything was silent and still? He tentatively moved forward, but instinct told him to hold back. Nathan was not ready to be approached in such a way. Intuitively, Nick knew he would take flight, and this thought made Nick cautious. Maybe the kiss he had received would never come again, and if so, he would accept it. Further to this thought was the realisation that as he had not had any sexual contact for so long, any desire for the physical was questionable.

"Are there any chairs for out here?" Nathan asked.

Nick replied that there were and retrieved a couple of deckchairs stacked against a wall.

"I'm not sure if they're clean. They've not been used since last autumn."

"Do you think I care?" came the gently mocking reply.

"No, I don't think you do," Nick replied as he opened them out. He watched as Nathan immediately sat down. "Wouldn't you like a drink?" Nick asked.

"Not really. I'd prefer for the two of us just to sit here and get to know each other a little bit more. It's kind of private here, despite the people opposite, and the light, which I think comes from their bathroom."

"You're spot on. It does."

The deckchairs were more or less aligned, and as Nick sat down, Nathan reached out with his hand.

"May I hold yours?" he asked.

Without replying, Nick reached out with his, and in the grasp, he felt the remnants of earth still attached to Nathan's fingers. He also smelt the closeness of the earth, and this too was unique for him and pleasing. There was an innocence in the touch that he did not want to betray.

"That kiss—" Nathan began.

"We don't have to talk about it," Nick quickly replied.

"I enjoyed it. I really did. I dared myself up the hill to do it, to get an impression of how two men's mouths meeting can be. And before you reply, I don't mean that to sound clinical. True, it was an experiment of sorts, but you were the right person for it. Like holding hands with another man. It's all new to me, and so far, it is good, but I am not sure about anything else physical other than what we have done so far."

"That's okay by me."

"Do you mean that?"

Nathan turned his head to look at Nick, who returned the look, and Nick noticed how fiercely dark, almost black, his eyes appeared in the garden.

"We don't even have to say anything," Nick said.

"I would like to tell you certain things about myself and my family," came the slow reply, and each word seemed separated from the other. Nick sensed hesitation and a kind of fear. He made no response to this other than squeezing Nathan's hand. He wanted it to be a sign of total assent. "My parents had me late in life. My mother was in her forties, and my father was in his mid-fifties. He is an old man now, and I don't want to confuse him with my homosexuality. They seem in their way to be more like grandparents to me."

There was a pause, and the light from the house behind went out, leaving only the muted light from the side lamps in the kitchen. Somewhere in the distance, a fox made itself heard; that strange sound that always seemed to Nick to be unique. But then, like Nathan, it *was* unique.

"There are so many things of my generation that I cannot talk about with them. But recently, they have been open with me about a subject that I believed was almost taboo."

"Which is?"

"Our Jewishness."

Nick immediately thought of Karel, but this was different. He could not as yet identify in what way, but he sensed that it was so. Perhaps it was Karel's love for Czechoslovakia that made the difference, but he did not want his mind to try to explain it.

"Go on," he said gently to Nathan.

"First, I want to make a couple of things clear. We're not a practising family. No prayers. No candles. Nothing of that kind. Totally secular. But the truth is, we are Jews. And I don't know if you quite understand this, but Jews in Brighton and Hove don't exactly have an easy time."

"Can you explain?" Nick asked.

"My parents came here in 1947. They survived the Holocaust despite both of them being in concentration camps. They were scarred and bitter, and to make it easy on themselves—or so they thought—they changed their surname so they wouldn't be perceived as Jewish. It was a decision made on impulse, my mother told me. Before moving to Hove, something happened while my mother was walking along Hove Lawns. She loved the town and the Lawns. She sat down. Rest, for her, was so necessary, after what she and my father had been through."

42

"I'm trying to imagine her feelings," Nick said, aware of the lameness of the statement.

"Don't. It can't be done. I can't even imagine it. All I know is, if there is a God, he was absent. But to return to my mother, she was sitting there enjoying the sun, and the rest and the peace, when a woman came and sat beside her. She was in one of those shelters that face both out to sea and towards the Lawns, near where that useless angel stands." He paused. His voice was shaking, and he seemed near to tears. "The woman was chatty, and my mother was too polite to move away. And then came the assault. Before my mother could respond or say anything, this woman opened up a tirade against the Jews. How they had taken over the town, how they had come like leeches to suck up flats and houses that good Christians needed. It was all spewed out over my mother like vomit. Why didn't they scatter themselves elsewhere? Why didn't they go back to Europe, where most of them belonged? Europe was different from England, and would welcome them. And my mother told me she said nothing. It was like a paralysis. She could not move her limbs. She had *come* from Europe. She had *originally* come from Poland and had met my father, who was German, in Baden-Baden. It was a holiday romance in the mid-thirties when the warning signs were already written everywhere. And as the woman ranted on, oblivious to the effect it was having on my mother, my mother said she remembered both her and my father learning English. They had hoped to go to America."

Nick heard Nathan's voice crack, and his hand released itself.

"You don't have to continue," Nick said.

There was a silence for a while, then Nathan continued. "They moved in together in Berlin where my father lived and thought they had everything ready to go, but a few days before departure came the knock on the door. They had misjudged time. It was too late. They were among the first batch of deportations."

Nick watched as Nathan went back to the earth border and

knelt to knead the brown, night-smelling soil. He went over to him, laying one hand on his shoulder.

"You'll get cold," he said.

"I like it here. Let me stay for a while."

Nick knelt beside him on the concrete, and quietly and with determination, Nathan continued his story.

"After encountering this woman, my mother doubted Hove would be any good for her. She told my father that only by changing their names would she consent to live there. He agreed, and when I was born, the only concession to their Jewishness was my first name: Nathan. They held their Jewish heritage inside them. I had an ordinary education at an ordinary Christian promoting Grammar School. I had no Bar-mitzvah, and I am not circumcised."

He kneaded the soil more fiercely now and demanded, "Were they cowards? Tell me! Were they cowards?"

"I don't know enough to say anything," Nick said gently.

Calming down, Nathan continued. "The years between '46 and '55 were the worst. The Jewish population doubled to over 4,000, and the open hostility was hard to bear. People said the concentration camps should have continued until they'd got rid of all the Jews. I even heard this remark recently from the mouth of a young man. I was quiet. I said nothing. I did not speak out. I let him say these things."

Nick remained silent, but as the night air grew cooler and Nathan began to shiver, he suggested they should move inside.

"I said too much," Nathan whispered.

"You said what is important to you. I'm glad that I was the one you chose to tell."

Once inside, Nick made tea and a plateful of hot toast. Nathan sat and watched him, and Nick wondered what could and should be said next. Nathan hungrily ate half of the toast, and after drinking down two cups of tea, he asked Nick where the toilet was. Nick told him, and while he was away, he wondered how he should continue with the youth. Something had started between them, but his intuition told him that he should not be Nathan's first sexual experience. He hoped they would continue seeing each other as friends, but there was a vulnerability in Nathan he felt he could not handle in regards to emotional and physical intimacy.

"You do have a nice house," Nathan said as he came down the stairs. "You live here alone. Am I right?"

"You are."

"Have you ever lived here with anyone?"

Nathan sat on a chair, his youthful voice sounding as it had consistently done, mature beyond his years.

"It has been a long while now, and even I cannot believe it, but once this house was full. I lived here with three others."

"As friends?"

"No, Nathan, as lovers. We were all of us, in various ways, in love with each other. It worked for a time until one of the three had to break away and go to another country. The other two followed him to try to bring him back, but so far, none of them has returned."

Nathan shook his head in astonishment.

"That is what GLF has been proposing," he said. "A commune! Not bonding between only two people. It's incredible, and yet you have never read Altman or any of the GLF Manifestos."

"You clearly have."

"A few, but GLF started when I was too young. Work it out."

Nick laughed.

"I have, Nathan. But please do not confuse the Gay Liberation Front with how we four lived together. It cannot be explained simplistically. Just as what you said about yourself and your family cannot be explained away. Easy words trivialise. Some of the dots cannot be joined. Maybe they are meant to not be joined." Nick paused. Now it was he that needed to talk. "Your parents, for example. You never mentioned their financial situation or how they managed to relocate to this country. You did not go into the horrors of the camps. These are things you left unsaid because some things either do not need to be explained or are too personal or painful to talk about. Am I right?"

"Partly," Nathan replied. "I know my father was tortured in the camps twice. He also just escaped selection for the gas chambers. The same for my mother, only for her it was psychological rather than physical torture, but torture all the same, and she too nearly died. All I know is that, despite the horror, they survived, and from what I can understand, their survival was due to a combination of their youth, their strength, and luck. They worked hard in the camps, and as workers, they were kept alive—that was the sole reason."

"The sole reason," Nick repeated slowly. "It's not even thirty years since, and most of us think we live in a civilised world. Like this place—a town of fun and pleasure, and yet as you described, certain people have patterns of thought that are despicable." He paused, then said slowly, "I don't think anyone can talk, write, or think about Brighton without taking into account the Jewish population. To any decent person, it should be obligatory not to add torture to torture, and any vile anti-Jewish talk is simply that—vile."

"Have you ever had a Jewish lover?"

The question was asked calmly, and Nathan's dark eyes stared intently.

"Yes. One of the three who lived here. A Czech. His name was Karel."

"Where is he now?"

"In his country. I said one of them left. It was him. He stayed a short while in Paris before going, and the two others, Greg and Bart, went there in the hope of bringing him back. We all loved him."

"I won't ask anymore. As you said, it's not necessary to fill in all the dots. Clearly, you are no stranger to us Jews." He looked down at his watch. "It's really late. You have work in the morning. I don't."

"What do you do? Are you studying?"

Nathan smiled, and shaking his head, stood up.

"Me? No, I'm not very good at studying. I'm just trying to work out what I want to do."

Nick asked cautiously, "It is easy to waste time. Have you thought of that?"

"Yes." The word was said with emphasis. "I am considering my life extremely carefully." He made as if to go towards the stairs.

"Stay just a while longer."

"I don't want anything physical—"

"I have guessed that. I am here as a new friend. I would like to be that."

Nathan paced the room, and then after a while, went to the garden door and opened it to breathe in the night air. "I am attracted to you," he said as he looked out into the garden. "But am I ready to get involved in that way? It is something else that I have to work out. Seventeen is, as the cliché goes, a difficult age. Part of me wants to get involved in the gay community, go on marches and *do* things to make life better for us. I've talked about being Jewish, but being gay is far more important to me. I will always be Jewish, but I need to *become* a responsible gay man—a man who is willing to fight for our further rights. I mean, what sense does it make that a sexual relationship between us is illegal in the eyes of the law? I have the body of a mature man, and I believe I think like a man. And yet, if we became lovers, we would be criminals."

He was still facing outwards into the dark night. Nick wanted him to turn to face him. He wanted to see the expression on his face.

"I'm not involved enough in gay rights myself," Nick said quietly. "I could have gone on the gay pride marches, but I didn't. I have become a sort of hermit in my bookshop. Maybe you could inspire me to change."

Nick was not sure he really meant what he said. The thought of demonstrating and shouting slogans of defiance to a mainly hostile crowd did not appeal, and yet, he felt suddenly ashamed as if he were failing both himself and this youth.

"Please turn and look at me," Nick said.

Nathan turned. His face looked tired. The evening had taken its toll on him. Explaining and striving for explanations always does, and Nick now regretted they had talked of such serious things.

"I have tired you with too much talk," Nick began, taking full responsibility for the course of the evening.

"Rubbish. It started with me saying I was Jewish. I'm the one to blame."

"Can we meet again?" Nick asked.

Nathan looked hesitant. He moved awkwardly, his body suddenly appearing gauche and very young. He looked as if he were not able to make that decision, or any decision. He no longer gave the impression of being a mature man. He looked like the seventeen-year-old he was. Too young to be bombarded by adult dilemmas and demands.

"I'll ring you. I'd like to say yes, but I am not sure. Can I be really honest?"

"Of course."

"I want to have sex with another man so much. So very much. I want to experience everything the body can give. I have dreams. Sexual dreams. So strong. I take every physical position in them, and I enjoy it. I know that I will when I—" and here he stopped, embarrassed perhaps at this declaration of desire.

"When you meet the right person?" Nick murmured.

"Not necessarily. Why should the first be right, as you put it? I kissed you out of desire, but as I said, it was also an experiment. I wanted to taste your saliva, breathe your breath. Several times before I gathered up the courage to ring you, I masturbated thinking about you. I know I want you. Looking at you now, I feel stupid—stupid saying all this. Saying things ruins things. I am talking us out of letting go, and *you* do desire me, don't you? You responded to my kiss, my hands—"

"We are both tired."

Nathan sneered at the words, "No, it is not only tiredness. It is a lack of nerve. I am sensitive about what I will feel in your embrace, and you—you are sensitive about the age difference and committing an illegal act."

Nick responded quickly.

"Then come upstairs to the bedroom now. I do desire you. It might work for us, and it might not. How will we know until our bodies express our needs?"

There was a long silence. The room felt electric with tension as if both were waiting for a wire to snap, a barrier to fall. Nick knew all this. He had to make the first move. He had to take Nathan in his arms, but time ticked by, and he did not make that move, and with every second lost, he knew the possibility of it happening was lost.

"I—" he said.

"What do you want to say?" Nathan replied. "Do you want to say that you are afraid? That you lack the courage? Moments ago, you said come to the bedroom now. Why didn't you make a move? It's all bloody words!"

After this last sentence, which came out more like a sob, Nathan leapt up the stairs, and before Nick could react, he heard the front door slam. To his astonished surprise, he felt nothing but fatigue, fatigue that had begun with Alan and then continued with Nathan. He told himself he did not need or want to see either of them again, and his inner words were petulant and accusing as if it were entirely both their faults and not his. Slowly he made his way up to the bedroom, and once there, he angrily ripped off his clothes. This act reminded him that Nathan had been dressed entirely in black, and as he got into bed, he thought how beautiful he had looked; the severity of the black matched his dark looks perfectly. "I am fucking stupid," he said to himself. "It was not his fault." And then sleep began to draw him under. His last conscious thought was, it was not Nathan's fault.

The days and the weeks passed with monotonous regularity. Nick worked hard in the bookshop, rearranging categories and sorting out volumes he thought he would never sell. These he put outside the shop for a minimal price. But even discounted, the world was no longer interested in Samuel Butler or Sir Walter Scott, so in the end, he gave them all to a dealer who specialised in what he called *the unsaleable*. Instead, in the window, he put copies of Hermann Hesse and Carlos Castaneda, and more younger people began to come into the shop. The young, however, spent less than the old, and some of Nick's older customers stopped coming. It was his friend Sarah who pointed out this folly.

"I know," she said as she entered the shop. "You thought I was dead. Well, I am not, and I have to say you are making a dog's dinner of this wonderful little place. Aren't you ashamed?"

She smiled, and Nick felt safe with her at once.

"I have missed you," he said.

"Illness and distance, my dear Nick. From Hova Villas to here is quite a distance for me nowadays. I even get taxis and not buses. I have changed."

It was true that she had. Her body looked frail. Her hair was white, and her features were pinched and drawn-in as if she wanted to retreat from existence.

"But no self-pity," she added. "I have recovered, and I have taken a taxi expressly to come and see you. But the shop, the shop! Please change it. You look as if you no longer care. Take out that dreadful man who advocates drug-taking. Even I have heard of him. He has no right to rub shoulders with such a master as Hermann Hesse, and well you know it. And what is that ridiculous *Zen and the Art of Motorcycle Maintenance* doing so close to it? Soon you will be putting pornography in your window."

She laughed as she said this.

"I'm not sure I could find pornography if I wanted to," Nick replied.

"Of course you could. You are young, aren't you? Not yet thirty?"

"Almost."

"Almost is not thirty. It is young. But young as you are, you're not here to appeal to the minds of morons. And they are not going to be terribly attracted to the fine first editions you must still have somewhere in this shop." She paused. "I do watch television. I keep up to date. More than you, obviously. Anyway, I haven't come to scold, but to see how you are. I must say that you look peaky and run-down. Sentimental problems? Anything fit for an old lady like me to hear?"

Nick remembered her near aversion to personal problems, especially those concerning homosexual issues.

"You were the one who brought up pornography," Nick said.

"In my youth, I read what was considered to be a clandestine copy of John Cleland. He writes well. That is all I know and all I want to know about explicit sexuality. And I would rather see *him* on display in the window than what you have now."

"Then give me some guidance," Nick replied, and he put the *closed* sign up on the door. She looked as if she needed tea, and he was determined to make her sit down and relax.

"It is nowhere near closing time," she said.

"For you, my friend, I will always have time for a private chat and a cup of tea. You took a taxi, after all, to come here. What finer honour could you pay me?"

"Don't be silly. You will end up like a stuffy old bachelor if you continue to talk like that. It's precious, and I do not mean that as a compliment. It's like something out of that awful Firbank who mocks people of my age so much."

"And Ivy? Do you still read her?"

Nick led Sarah through the piles of books to the cubby-hole that he had fortunately cleared out only the previous day. Sarah cautiously sat down on a new chair. It was small and upholstered in red, and she said she quite liked it.

"I just hope my bottom does too," she added.

Tea was made, and a few rather tired biscuits were put on a plate.

"So, how do you want me to guide you?" she asked.

51

"Sarah, this shop needs overhauling. It needs a new look."

"Not the one you have given it!" she interjected.

"My regular customers have dropped off recently. There seems to be a lull in antiquarian books. I think my customers may go more to Holleyman and Treacher in Duke Street than traipse all the way over here."

"Well, like me, they are old or have become older. Life is not such an adventure anymore, and let's be honest, London Road is less and less appealing with every passing year. The problem is, your shop is no longer the flavour of the month. I know how fickle people are. Even of my generation. Never mind the ones who came after."

"I'm not as good-looking as I once was," Nick said frankly. "For a lot of—how should I put this politely?—older men, it was an attraction."

"What a dreadful thing to say. Even Ivy Compton-Burnett would have hesitated in making such a judgement. She would definitely have avoided the subject."

"Perhaps, Sarah, but reality is reality, and it is true. And I'm not speaking out of a sense of narcissism."

"Yes, you are, and you resent the three and the 'O' that comes after it. Everyone does when the first blush of youth has faded. And if I am not mistaken, you *did* blush."

"I can't remember," Nick replied and poured more tea.

"If it is true, and you, Nick, think it is, then these so-called gentlemen should be ashamed of themselves. It is not a circle I have ever moved in, and neither did my beloved sisters. Oh, dear, the older I get, the more I miss my sisters. What a household it used to be in Hova Villas, and it is rare for siblings to get on. I know that from Ivy's books. Mind you, with some of my sisters, I—but no matter about all that. You want me to advise you."

"If you would, Sarah."

"Art, Nick. Art. Art books. Second-hand art books. You like the visual arts. What about a window full of books on Rembrandt or Goya? Not to mention my beloved Constable."

Nick suddenly visualised a window display of Rothko and Egon Schiele, but he kept quiet. They may not have been to Sarah's taste. Nevertheless, Sarah was perhaps right. He thought of the unlikely success of the Caspar David Friedrich exhibition at the Tate Gallery the previous year. His work had been a revelation to many. Nick himself had seen the exhibition and had been overwhelmed by the artist's vision. A painter from a previous century who caught the contemporary imagination. It had been an event. The near abstraction of *The Monk by the Sea* looked as if it had come straight out of the Twentieth Century.

"What about modern art, Sarah?"

"Do you mean all that Op Art, or Pop Art and squiggly lines that mean absolutely nothing?"

"No. I mean artists of our century that the world now considers to be really great."

"Oh, my dear, you are putting me on the spot. My mind sort of ends with Turner and Constable. Does Sickert count?"

Nick laughed (not unkindly) and asked Sarah if he could talk about something she might consider controversial.

"Dare me," she cried." As long as I can have a last biscuit and a drop more tea."

"Have you ever heard any anti-Jewish comments being spoken in this town? Things that are hurtful?"

"But Nick, I'm not Jewish!"

"I know that, Sarah, but among the people you have known or knew. Especially from the mid-forties to the mid-fifties."

"My memory is poor, Nick, and I have no idea why you are asking me this. Have you a friend who is being persecuted or something?"

"In a way, yes. Let's just say it's a part of his life's legacy. A legacy, even though he hides the reality that he is Jewish."

Sarah sighed at this and paused. Then like an imitation of a great actress on a stage, to give herself time, she patted her hair into place and brushed invisible crumbs from her dress. Each gesture was slow and self-conscious, as if the audience in the stalls were taking note of her every movement. He had seen Edith Evans adopt a similar technique in the film version of Enid Bagnold's *The Chalk Garden*. Sarah bore no physical resemblance to Edith Evans, but there was a distinct similarity of measured approach.

"Yes," she said finally, looking at him, her eyes flashing as if stoked by hidden anger. "It was in the very early fifties. A young couple had moved into a house further down the street. Hova Villas, of course."

"Of course," Nick echoed.

"The wife, and I think she even had the same name as me, Sarah, that's maybe why I remember. Well, anyway, she had run out of sugar. Or something like sugar. Rationing was still on. When she knocked on our door, she was very pale, and she was shaking when she asked. I invited her in, and she was reluctant to do so. 'Am I really permitted?' she asked, and frankly, I was amazed. I assured her that she was welcome and being *permitted,* as she put it, meant nothing to me. Anyway, to cut a long story short, she had gone to two other houses before ours—I knew the people well then—and at both doors, she had been insulted. The first was what I would call impoliteness. I can't remember the response exactly, but like saying you have to go elsewhere, but very rudely. The second house—and the woman who lived there I knew very well as being a staunch Christian—to the point of practically being an imitation of the Virgin Mary—shouted at her, 'I don't give anything to Yids. Go to Israel, where you belong. You are not welcome here.' I was shattered, of course, when I heard this. I could not believe that a woman who had such extreme religious beliefs, bordering on blasphemy, could be so inhuman. 'Are you sure?' I asked her, and then I made her smile and tried to put her at her ease by telling her we shared the same name. I also added that we were not at all like those other people. I asked her in for tea, and yes, it is all clear to me now, she sobbed on the sofa. Just below that Constable that you like. I tried to make excuses for the woman, saying she was over-fervent in her beliefs, but I knew I was wrong to make any excuse for her at all. Sometimes we are not very brave in situations like this, and I'm afraid I was a bit feeble. 'I don't understand,' she kept on saying. 'I don't understand. To be called a Yid! I do not even speak Yiddish, and the hatred. The terrible hatred.' She kept on repeating the line about the hatred, and I felt so sorry, so sorry, not only for her but for us as human beings."

"I feel like that too," Nick added.

"But why? Has this friend of yours been called names like that?"

"No, but his parents changed their names so as not to appear Jewish and brought him up in a way that neutralised his heritage."

"You mean, his being Jewish disappeared?"

This word *disappeared* hit at Nick. He felt an urgent need for Nathan to call him, for Nathan to see him again, to talk, to know how he was. He realised that he cared.

"Disappearance is the right word, Sarah. People like that want people like him, or rather, people who are open about themselves, to literally disappear. Six million killed, and they want more annihilation."

Sarah patted her hair again and coughed. Nick got her a glass of water.

"It's a lump in my throat when I get upset," she said as she drank slowly.

"I apologise if I have upset you."

"No, don't. It brings it all back. Those years after the war when there was so much hatred. The Jews. The Germans. It was all so horribly confused. And all these people, victims of hatred, trapped in a world that did not want them." She paused. "You must comfort your friend. Tell him we don't all think like that. My sisters and I had no disrespect for all those who were displaced. It was just not in us to talk like that. Aren't we all on the same path?"

Nick wanted to kiss her; he felt such tenderness.

"Sarah, we are all on the same path. I will certainly remind him of that."

"I've not been of much help."

Nick reminded her she had given him a great idea for his display. "Art, it will be, Sarah. And I will try to put your beloved Constable in the centre, just for you."

"Forgive me if it is a while before I come again. I trust my affection for you, but I don't trust my health."

Nick called for a taxi, but could not know as he helped her into it that he would not see her again. Six months later, she moved into a care home, and the Hova Villas house was put up for sale. He was told this by a neighbour who could not recall her new address. Sarah disappeared out of his life.

As he was about to close the shop one day in late March, he noticed Nathan standing at the end of the road, waiting to cross and not looking in Nick's direction. Nick had hoped he would see him again, and now he was here. As Nick approached him, he saw that Nathan was looking downwards and that his limbs looked limp and weak. His whole posture spoke of misery and to Nick's mind of desolation.

"Nathan?" he said, and Nathan turned to face him. There were tears in his eyes. "What is it? What has happened?"

"Nothing. I slept badly. I wasn't sure if I should come to you. Maybe I had better go."

Nick reached out and put his hand on Nathan's shoulder. He wanted to hug him but was conscious of the passers-by.

"Come on, we must go somewhere else."

"I ran out on you—" Nathan began, a look of panic on his face as if he wanted to flee again.

"There's something wrong, Nathan, and you have come to me. What other reason for being on this street corner. Come back to my place. Are you okay to walk? There is no bus or taxi in sight."

"I'll walk," Nathan said, accepting Nick's offer.

Nick locked up the shop and re-joined Nathan. The walk

seemed endless. Nathan was silent, totally withdrawn into himself and dragging his feet as if in pain. Halfway up this first hill, they sat down on a bench. Blankly, Nathan looked around him.

"I'm glad you're with me," he murmured. "I have thought about you. I should not have run out of your house as I did. I regretted it as soon as I was on the street, but pride—"

"Pride ruins everything," Nick replied. "You used the word *ruin* that night also, but in a strange way. I can't recall it exactly."

Nathan stared down at his large hands, placed awkwardly in his lap.

"I am strange," he said.

"No more than any of us," Nick replied.

"Did you miss me?" Nathan looked sideways at Nick as he asked.

"Come on, let's get to the house. Only a couple more hills."

"Tell me."

"I have worked hard. Too hard. I was trying to forget the need I had to see you again. I am still not sure what we can be to each other, but I know there is some destination in our meeting—some goal to be reached, and that it should not be spoiled."

"Aren't you using too many words to express something very simple?" Nathan got up as he said this and stretched in the late afternoon light. The bench had been cramped, and his body appeared relieved to be free of it. He glanced down at Nick. "I feel better," he said and looked up in the direction of Nick's house. "It isn't exactly the seven hills of Rome, but it feels like it might be seven hills of Hell. Do you believe in Hell? Catholics and Jews alike believe we all go there. I wonder if it's a bit like Brighton."

Nick laughed and got up. "Probably," he said and then joked, "but where are the devils?"

"In all of us," Nathan replied, the seriousness of his tone dispelling the joke.

Once inside the house, Nathan went directly down to the basement, and after the few moments it took him to hang up his coat, Nick joined him. Inevitably, he saw that Nathan had gone out into the garden and was inspecting the slow advance of the spring flowers.

"The soil is too shallow," Nick called out as he prepared a drink for both of them.

"It's rich enough," came the reply.

"Hungry?"

"I could eat a biscuit."

"I think it would be better if I made some sandwiches."

Standing at the kitchen table while cutting the bread, Nick positioned himself to watch the stooped figure of Nathan bending over the shoots. Some had flowered early, and he was touched by the intensity of Nathan's caring hands as he reached out with his fingers to almost embrace them. Nick knew he wanted him. Yes, wanted him. But love, or any emotion resembling it? He was uncertain. The thought weighed itself in the balance for a while and then fell in the direction of denial; no, he could not love this youth. And why? Because although in many ways he was unlike him, Nathan reminded him of Greg. The brusque manner Greg had as a youth, the roughness and the tenderness conjoined. There were too many resemblances in this, and yet the comparison ended there. Nathan seemed trapped within himself in a way Greg had never been, even in adolescence when Greg had battled with his homosexuality. Nathan was clutching within him a great rock, which like Sisyphus, he kept on pushing up only to have it roll down again within himself.

"I am almost ready with the food," Nick said loudly.

"It's okay. Take your time." His voice was sincere. Nathan was clutching at his struggling aloneness. The stooped hunch of his back showed the effort.

Nick took the food out. It was still warm enough to sit on the concrete, and they sat with their backs to the house and consumed their sandwiches and coffee.

"All you need is a cat," Nathan said.

"Do you think so?"

"Definitely. A big fat one. I can see it now, playing happily by itself in front of us. It would complete the garden."

"And perhaps destroy the flower beds."

"Nonsense. Cats are—"

"What?" Nick asked, surprised by the pause.

"I was just going to say, more human than us."

Nick looked where Nathan was looking and tried to imagine this large cat, but it was not what he wanted. He wanted a human being in the house again to end his solitude, not a cat.

"I think I'd prefer another human," Nick said truthfully. Then he got up and returned with the empty plates and cups to the kitchen. Within seconds, Nathan was beside him.

"Show me the rest of the house," he said.

"I've lots of books in the second bedroom. There's not much else to see. Even the views from the windows are not that great. The house isn't high enough to give any sense of distance."

"Is the second bedroom your bedroom?"

"It is now," Nick said softly.

"Take me to it."

With trepidation and yet excitement, Nick led Nathan up the stairs, and on the way, Nathan commented on various prints and paintings on the walls. Nick responded to a couple of them and paused in front of the bedroom that faced onto the street.

"Open the door," Nathan said. His voice was very deep, and in his face, Nick saw a look he could not determine. It was a look that denied desire, and his features were blank. The look of a killer, Nick thought, and was immediately ashamed. The next thought was worse. No, not a killer of others, but of himself. He shuddered and pushed open the door. The room was all white, with just a few pieces of furniture. Only the books made a splash of colour in their newly bought but sterile Habitat bookshelves. These rooms, these bedrooms, were not the same as when the other three had lived in the house. All the splendour of chaos had gone; all sense of joyous mingling.

Nick had changed the decor to make it look neutral and not remind him of them

Nathan was the first to cross the threshold, and he went immediately to the books. "How do you keep them?" he asked. "In what order? By author? By size? Subject?"

This barrage of questions came out without any real interest. Nick knew that by the thin sound of Nathan's voice, all depth of tone gone, just a strangled questioning that meant nothing.

"I don't have any order."

"*Giovanni's Room,*" Nathan commented and held up a battered hardback. "I've heard of it. James Baldwin. Is he good?"

"I prefer *Another Country,*" Nick replied. "I used not to, but I do now."

"Does he write well?"

Nathan's questioning was insistent, and Nick realised he was wrong. Nathan *was* showing a passion for something, showing a need.

"He is a great writer. I discovered that last year when I read all of his books one after another. *Go Tell It on the Mountain*. Beautiful. No, that's not the correct word. A fierce need to express, and he does. Others pale beside him."

"May I borrow—?"

"Start with *Another Country*. Here. I have another copy. Take it. Keep it. Even if you don't like it now, keep it. You will like it later, I promise."

"You make me sound like a child, not yet ready to read a *difficult* book."

"I didn't mean that."

Nick came close to Nathan and reached for the copy of the book. He handed it to Nathan, who took it without a word of thanks. The action done, Nick retreated back to the white writing table. It was here that he wrote, sometimes late into the night, the endless poems, the endless struggling to write words he knew would fail. They tried too hard to succeed, and that is why they failed. Lost for a while in his thoughts, he was not aware of the creaking of the bed, the single bed by the window. He heard nothing, but when he turned around, he saw Nathan's naked body sitting on the edge, his legs wide open, his clothes piled next to him. There was no expression on his face as he spoke without intonation, robotic, void.

"I've been with someone. We lay on a bed and sucked each other off. Sixty-nine, he called it. We did not kiss. I only wanted the taste of his cock. That's all, the sperm, not the saliva. And I thought of you. I thought that I only wanted the kiss from you."

Nick did not move. He could not respond. He looked at the body, at the dark hair on the chest, the thick bush of hair around the penis, the shrunken penis, with its foreskin, a wrinkled blob in the dark shroud of hair.

"I wanted your kiss, and then I wanted you to get a knife. I imagined you cutting my skin, this skin that hides the slit of my cock, that hides the opening. I wanted you to slash at this meaningless flesh that makes me a gentile when I am really a Jew—when I should be a Jew, part of them, and part of their guilt."

Nick now felt frightened. Nathan's face remained blank as it mouthed these terrible, and at the same time to Nick, ludicrous words. What had happened? What had made this youth he cared for crack like this, expose himself like this, and wish for the unthinkable. But Nick knew one thing for sure, what he had thought as he had entered the bedroom was true. Nathan was seeking to kill, to kill the part of his body that was the most vulnerable.

"Why?" Nick asked. He could say nothing else. He also felt cold. He wanted to run from the house as Nathan had run before. He was not so much afraid as in shock. He wanted to wake up out of this nightmare. Eventually, he said, "Please get dressed."

"Don't you want it?"

"You think of a knife—of me cutting into you? How can I *want* when such thoughts have gone through your mind? I am not here to be used in that way, even in fantasy."

"You think I am sick in my mind, don't you?"

"No. It's confusion. It's something else. I want to know about that something else."

Nick perched on the edge of the table and said nothing more. After what seemed like hours but was only a matter of minutes, Nathan reached for his clothes and slowly began to put them back on. He stood and tucked his shirt into his trousers. The blankness on his face broke, creased, and tears began to fall from his eyes. Nick made no move to comfort him. He then stood, and with a motioning gesture, made his way to the bedroom door. Nathan hesitated to follow.

"Pick up the book I have given you, and we will talk downstairs in the living room."

Nathan eventually joined him and asked, "So you want to know about that *something else*, do you?"

Nick watched as Nathan looked around the room as if searching for some special object. It turned out to be a simple black wooden chair with a rush seat and an armrest incorporated into its back. Nick had bought it from an antique shop and was told quite blatantly that it had been stolen from a church in France. Awkwardly, Nathan sat down on it, stretching himself out. He had long legs, and they touched the coffee table nearby. Nick remained standing. The room seemed suddenly too small for both of them. Nathan's posture was almost threatening; like a sexy spider, he dominated the space. He was, in that position, all arms and legs.

"As well as trying and succeeding in getting my first sexual experience, I spent a lot of my time in the reference library."

Nathan paused, and Nick was at a loss for words. What was Nathan about to reveal? To lengthen time, he asked clumsily, "Are you sure you're comfortable sitting there? I mean, there is the sofa."

"Well, we're not going to cosy up to each other, are we? Anyway, what more inappropriate place for me to sit than a chair for praying Christian prayers. I guess that's what it is."

"You look awkward."

"I'm Jewish. It does not like me. It is tolerating me. And its roughness on my arse feels like a chastisement." He laughed and then tried to straighten out a bit.

"I had never thought of it as a flagellating chair," Nick replied tersely. Although he had calmed down since the bedroom, he now felt exhausted and inwardly very angry. He no longer cared about Nathan's state of mind or his concerns. He just wanted to see him out of the door.

"I read in the library about the Palestinians and how my so-called people are treating them."

Anger drained away from Nick. He knew he had to listen. He sat on the floor as close to Nathan as he could. Clearly, what had happened upstairs was a prelude, a prelude, in its brutal and immature gestures of self-loathing, perhaps mixed in with desire, that had brought him to this opening declaration. The objectification of his body had by a certain necessity led him to the point of clear and meaningful words.

"The fact is, Nick, that I cannot want to be a Jew any longer. I cannot accept that a rounded-up people, who experienced what they experienced in the death camps, could force another people from their land and put *them* into camps. How could the race I come from have so little empathy with others, to see them crushed and defeated and to cage them in a limbo place?"

Nick looked at Nathan's clenched features and his dark eyes. "More than six million Jews were killed," he said. "The number can never be accurate. There's a book in the shop that's been there for years, a first edition of a novel no one seems to want. It's called *The Last of the Just* by the French writer André Schwarz-Bart. This novel is a history of Jewish persecution, and if you read the last pages without crying and then shaking with anger at the perpetrators, you are not human. I read it a year or two back over a couple of afternoons when the shop was quiet. It engulfed me."

Nathan looked defiantly at Nick and murmured, "I don't want to read novels about my people. I hate my foreskin. It makes me look innocent. I am not innocent. Only with it cut off can I bear the badge of shame that is being a Jew."

Nick tried to avoid the excess of these last statements and said as gently as he could, "You are wrong, Nathan. It is as important to relate Jewish history in novels as our history of what it has been like, and is still like, to be homosexual in this world. Both Jew and homosexual are linked in a man-made atrocity of mind—yes, *mind*. The Jews, because of Christ's death, but that's only part of the reason. It is a primal hatred, a hatred, almost beyond history itself, to scapegoat, and it joins up with men going with men. You see, the Jew committed the worst crime of killing our so-called Christian saviour, and we, Nathan, as homosexuals, spill our seed on dead ground, killing life by rejecting our sperm and choosing to reject that sperm as the means for procreation. It is all there in the Bible, the old and the new. And you, Nathan, have the heavier burden of being both Jew and homosexual. Damn it, Nathan, all this has been said before, but it needs to be permanently said, written on stone—the stone of our words. We, Jews and homosexuals, are the eternal victims of a necessary hate. Christian normality and sexual normality need it."

"What do you mean, even beyond history?"

Nick sighed and remained silent, then he said slowly, "We have been the *shadow* since life began, since any record was made, and even before—victims of being driven into the wilderness, of not being allowed a home. The Jew murdered, the homosexual burnt at the stake and later imprisoned. We are married, Nathan, homosexual and Jew, in a hell of normality's making."

"The shadow is our voided self, isn't it?"

"It is everything that needs to be hidden from the eyes of ordinary men; everything they put in the dustbins of their hearts, they are the white souls, we the outer night. Andrei Biely, the Russian writer, expressed it well when he said, 'The biology of the shadow has not yet been studied.' It never will be, and I believe we will always, always be just outside permissible vision. Neither to be seen nor to be seen persecuted—even after periods of relative freedom, for both Jew and homosexual, the darkness will return. It is in the nature of things. And you, as Jew *and* homosexual, have it doubly. As Jew, you are willing to cast a shadow on yourself for what the Jew has done to the Palestinian, but just think, Nathan, the Jew is human. There has to *be* a shadow to be sent into darkness. As gay men, we too scapegoat others within our tribe—the drag queen, the effeminate boy or masculine girl, the ugly because we fear the loss of beauty, and even these have their own scapegoats. Why? We are all human."

"But I am responsible," Nathan insisted. "I am responsible for the Palestinian camps. I am responsible for not knowing enough, also for being a Jew in denial, of wanting, along with my family, to create a safe self."

Nick reached out and touched one of Nathan's hands as it rested on his leg.

"Nathan, we are all responsible, and we are not. All we can do is try to make life a little better for all of us. To speak the truth about hatred and replace that hatred, if possible, with as much love as we can."

Nathan smiled for the first time during their meeting, a *true* smile, and he replied, "I want to love you, Nick. I want to."

"Yes," Nick replied, "but one day, you will be *in* love, and it will not be with me."

Nathan was silent, then stood up.

"I don't know how you can foresee that," he said.

"We will give each other everything except hatred. That, my dear Nathan, is all I have left to say."

Nathan's eyes filled with tears. He stared at Nick and said, "Jews can hate homosexuals, and homosexuals can hate Jews. Is that how the shadow falls as well?"

"Yes."

There was silence in the room.

PART TWO:

KAREL

It was the beginning of April, and one afternoon while in the bookshop, Nick cracked. He had felt it coming for days, that inner sensation of crumbling, of falling into oneself. He knew that the human building of his body was about to crash, to break apart. There was no way of stopping the destruction, and yet he tried; he tried very hard, rearranging the shelves yet again and doing what Sarah had recommended, dressing his window with books on art. Recently he had bought a whole batch, volume after volume of Impressionists and Post-Impressionists, and they had sold, slowly, but with enough regularity for Nick to accept that the idea had been good. Good, so long as he kept to the artists that people knew, and that had what he defined as a chocolate box attraction. He had started with Paul Klee and Jackson Pollock, but the customers he attracted were not interested, and when he put a rare French book on Yves Klein in the window, an art student came in and asked him why he was showing off this man's 'rubbish'. His nerves, taut, reacted badly.

"Who are you to say what is rubbish," he asked.

"It is. Everyone knows it is. Nothing but blue! How many times can you look at blue? The man is a charlatan."

Nick laughed at this rather quaint word coming out of the mouth of someone so young.

"I adore charlatans," he replied. "Dali is a charlatan, and it seems he does very well."

The student's eyes became bright with fury while his face turned white, repressing it.

"Clearly, you know nothing about painting," came the reply, delivered with a chilling coldness that almost defeated Nick in its ferocious contempt. "It is absolutely clear that Yves Klein is a fool, and while his work may fool the French, I doubt that it will in this country. I went to the Slade School—"

"Oh, I see," Nick jumped in. "That bastion of dull brown portraits and grimly painted vistas of the backsides of buildings."

The student left, slamming the door so hard that it shook a couple of books off a nearby shelf. The young man's craziness added to Nick's feeling that he was losing control, and his hands and then his whole body began to shake. He sat down, locking the shop up for the day and picked out a volume of Georg Trakl's poems in translation, a slim book he often read, and many of the poems he could recite to himself without even opening the book.

"Daily the yellow sun comes over the hill.
Beautiful the forest, that dark beast.
And man: hunter or shepherd."

After reciting this, he opened the book to the page the poem was on and realised that he had partly done his own translation. He had substituted the words 'Each day' with 'Daily' and preferred it. He felt calmer as if the words had been an actual balm. He then put the book back on the shelf and left the shop for the day.

When the afternoon of his crack-up came, there was no holding back the storm. He fell to the floor and lay there for a long while, too paralysed to move. The attack came without warning. In fact, he had felt relatively peaceful before the invisible force felled him to the ground. He looked up at the ceiling and saw that the white paint was dirty. He realised that it had never been cleaned, perhaps in all the years he had known the shop. I must clean it, he thought, with sharp clarity. I must get up and clean it. But when he tried to move, not one of his muscles responded. Tears came, but no cry. He wanted to cry aloud, but the muscles in his throat would not work. He felt as if he had a large pebble lodged there, and in his state of heightened awareness, he imagined his tears falling uselessly into his open mouth and his mouth overflowing with salty water that he was unable to swallow. I am going to die. His mouth tried to move and say the words, but the paralysis was too great. His mouth gaped open and was fixed like his eyes. This attack lasted for hours, and no one came in. Night shadows filled the room, and as he started to scream out in his mind that he *wanted* to die, the movement of his limbs returned. The pain was terrible, as if each part of him was reassembling itself, knocking itself together with a hammer and nails. He felt the nails in his feet and hands first, and then a creeping sensation accompanied the hammering back into life of the rest of his body. He could not stand, but he crawled. He crawled across the dusty floor to the cubby-hole, and once there, curled himself up into a tight ball and fell asleep.

He awoke the next morning and found his limbs now moved quite easily. He stood up, and there was no shaking or giddiness, just a dullness of sensation covering his entire outer being like a sheath. But within this sheath, he acted normally. He poured water. He filled a kettle. He made tea. He then reached for a stale packet of biscuits and began to munch on them mechanically. He ate the lot and then drank his tea. Still within his sheath, he went into the shop, put up the closed sign on the door and decided the time had come. He would have to give up his work and get someone to work for him. And with that decision made, the sheath fell from him, and he was *himself* again. He took in long breaths of air, gulping them down, and the pebble had gone. The air was good, and he was alive. He had survived the storm.

For a week, he did not answer the phone, nor did he open the letters and junk mail that came through his letterbox. He did not go out and subsisted on tap water and the contents of his food cupboard. It was only when he had eaten the last dried bread and opened the last tin that he knew he had to brave the street. Slowly he walked down the hill until he reached St

Peter's Church, and there, a sudden attack of giddiness made him clutch onto an iron railing. Fortunately, this turned out to be a minor storm without further consequence, and he continued his way to the centre of town, where he bought a few provisions. Before returning to Islingword Street, he decided to walk up Trafalgar Street. He remembered, long ago, going to a shop there and being Greg's accomplice (or was he also a thief?) stealing magazines and comics. During the past week of total solitude, the phone seemed to have rung more than usual, and he wondered with a sense of loss whether he had missed one of Greg's calls from Paris. He promised himself he would answer the next ring of the phone. From Trafalgar Street, he wandered through the network of streets until he found himself outside the Unicorn Bookshop. It was not a shop he often visited, as he was frankly not particularly interested in the so-called alternative culture it represented. He had an antipathy towards the Beat writers, having tried Kerouac and Burroughs and failing with both. Like the ardently bigoted student who damned Yves Klein, he saw no merit in either *On the Road* or *The Naked Lunch*. He especially disliked the homosexual imagery in Burroughs, which he found superfluous and, in a word, fake. He realised, with a wry smile to himself, that he was no better than the Slade School student, and that like the browns of the portraits he had mentioned to him, he had better return to the subdued hues of George Eliot. Suddenly, he was determined to address his bigotry and made his way into the shop. Jarring paperback covers assaulted his eyes, and there behind the counter was the man who ran the place, Bill Butler—big gruff Bill, as Nick thought of him. In front of him was a short but good-looking young man with fair hair.

"I've told you, I don't think it's good enough. It's too fuzzy, too mystical," growled big gruff Bill.

"Many have read it, and they have liked it," came the defiant reply.

"Well then, let them go and publish it. You have written two good opening chapters, and then you have gone off into all this pseudo-religious crap. Do I look as if I would publish a book that has raided its imagery from the florid prose of Dion Fortune or others of her kind?"

"It's not like that at all. Why not let someone else here judge?"

"I have."

Bill Butler stood tall and determined, like a frontiersman in a Western. He had not yet fired all of his guns, but he looked ready to do so.

"Then maybe I could rewrite—"

"No. Wait a few years, then write yourself another book. If I am still alive, bring it to me, or send it to someone else who is more receptive. And for shit's sake, read other kinds of writers."

"You don't know what or who I read!"

"Course I do. Take me for an idiot?"

The combat here was so close and personal that neither of them had noticed Nick enter the shop. He coughed loudly, but still the ping pong of defiance and defeat continued. Nick pretended to look at the books but kept looking at the young man at the same time. His cock was getting hard, and he wanted to rush in and come to the youth's defence. He wanted to defend this slight, fair body and ward off the larger beast that was threatening it. But like most smaller beings, this young man had a strong voice.

"Okay then, Bill, tell me who I should read."

"First, a question."

"Yes?"

"Do you want to be a professional writer, or do you want to be an artist?"

The young man laughed.

"I'm curious," Bill Butler replied.

"An artist," was the strong reply.

"Wrong, wrong, wrong!" Bill slapped his big hands down on the counter. "Where do you think being an artist—a wanky artist—gets you?" Silence. "Strictly, and I mean this, kid, nowhere."

"That's just your opinion," and it was then that the young man turned and saw Nick.

"I've said my say," his now rather bored assailant retorted.

"You still haven't said who I should read."

"Oh heck, read Michael Moorcock if you want to be popular and a bloody good writer and if you want the right marriage between artistry and professionalism. Pär Lagerkvist. Read his novel *The Dwarf*. The best book ever written. My opinion, and it *counts*." He slammed his hand down again onto the counter. The showdown was drawing to its end.

"So this is definite, is it? You're not going to publish my book?"

Before Bill Butler could reply, Nick picked up the first paperback that came into view, a William Morris novel that he had no desire to read, published by Unicorn Bookshop, and placed it on the counter. Staring at Bill Butler, he asked, "Isn't *this* badly written?"

"Seemed good to me," came the simple reply, and Bill Butler looked at the price. "I think we did well with the cover."

"I'm talking about the book, the text," Nick persisted.

The fair-haired young man retreated behind him. Nick was conscious he was being stared at, and he hoped the youth knew he was coming to his defence.

"The best thing is to judge for yourself. Want to buy it or not?"

Nick put the book back from where he had taken it.

"No, I don't," he said, and with a brisk, "Goodbye," he walked out of the shop. He browsed the shop window. Unicorn Bookshop was important to Brighton, and he knew it, but why did he feel alien to the so-called *underground* material that the shop sold and produced? He knew that Butler was interested in the occult, so why had he been so caustic about the mystical content of the young man's book? He knew too that he had been the subject of a traumatic and useless obscenity prosecution, but he had not taken much interest in it at the time because outer revolution against Brighton's staid attitudes was not his way. True, he had cohabited sexually with three people, but it had not been a public gesture. It had been for himself and for the other three—an individual choice, not an outward fist against the standards of the time. But simplification was too easy; Butler was a brother of sorts, and he did respect him. If Nick's way was the more withdrawn one, then Butler's was one of open challenge and defiance. Maybe Butler's way was the better way. No one sees revolutionary actions that take place behind closed doors, but a clenched fist against society, as Butler's was, changed things, and things in Brighton did need changing.

The young man came out, glanced at Nick and smiled, saying, "He says Herman Hesse is just a bandwagon people are jumping on. That Hesse is a soft choice whereas Burroughs…" and then he stopped and sighed.

"You had a rough time in there," Nick said.

"I've known him for quite a while, and when I told him I'd written a short book, he was interested. But that was a year ago, and I hesitated too long before showing it to him. I don't think he's happy at the moment. He is not in the shop much. I think he'd like to leave. Go and live in Wales or somewhere. But I can't ask direct questions. He's certainly not here full-time."

"I'm Nick," Nick said and held out his hand.

"I'm James. Call me Jim. Do you feel like a coffee? I could do with a chat."

"After all that?" Nick joked.

"Yes, even after all that. He's a good guy. We just don't get along. I'm not really his kind, and he's not mine, but underneath what you heard, there's a strange but mutual respect. But he definitely won't publish what I wrote."

"I guessed as much."

"I got the manuscript back though. Now all I have to do is destroy it. I was playing devil's advocate. It is bloody awful."

They had begun walking up towards Queens Road, but Nick stopped when he heard this and stood in front of James.

"Don't do that. Let someone else read it. I write myself. Maybe I—"

"No, he's right. It's wishy-washy. I'll start again from scratch in a while. I can be defiant with myself as well as with him. I knew he was right, but I wasn't going to let him see that."

Nick asked, "What if he had relented and offered to publish?"

"Bill? Do that? Oh no. This was one of his days for definite gestures. No way would he have budged even if he had been wrong."

They began walking again, and James pointed out a café across the main road just before the station.

"It has seats in the window. We can watch the parade go by."

With brisk determination, James crossed the road, dodging the traffic. Nick joined him on the other side.

"You seem very sure of yourself," Nick said. "I thought you might be upset. That's why I waited."

"That was a nice thing to do."

Once seated, James asked, "What do you do?"

"I have a bookshop."

"You mean here in Brighton?"

"Yes."

"Where?"

"Off the London Road."

"So you must know Bill as well. Why did you act as if you didn't?"

"I don't know him at all. I've rarely been to the shop. It's not my style."

James laughed and sipped his coffee.

"He's put up a good fight in this town over the years though, hasn't he?"

"Yes," Nick said and looked out of the window. A boy of about eight years old was sitting on the pavement, misbehaving. His mother was trying to pull him up, but he was screaming at her and saying that he wouldn't. People passing by were laughing.

"Even he is making his protest," Nick remarked.

"And you don't believe in protest?"

"I do, but not in the same way as Unicorn. How can I express it? I find the shop garish and, in some ways, vulgar. Most of the writers he responds to, I don't, and the book covers are too much of *now*—they scream at you like that child."

"Aren't you ever childish?"

"Enough of Unicorn," Nick replied, avoiding the question. "Tell me about you."

"I've just finished university, and I need a job."

The kaleidoscope shifted in Nick's mind and what fell into place was beautifully clear.

"I've just had to close my shop because of personal problems," he said. "I need space from it—someone to run it for me. You seem to know about books, and I think we could get along on a professional level. The pay wouldn't be brilliant—"

"Stop," James said.

"You're not interested?"

"I'm overwhelmed. From bad news I expected, to good news I didn't! When do I start?"

Nick gulped down his coffee and put any physical desire he felt for the young man to the back of his mind. He knew it was never going to happen and was not disappointed but relieved. He didn't even want to know James' sexual orientation. The young man had come into his life by accident, and Nick felt a sense of release that the shop would no longer be entirely his responsibility. James was also attractive, and maybe the old clientele would return, charmed by his face and charisma.

"My bookshop is a mixed bag," he added.

"You mean from Thackery to Iris Murdoch?"

Nick smiled, and to celebrate, he ordered more coffee and some cakes for them both.

"May I ask what the personal reasons were?" James asked.

"Nothing you need to know," Nick replied with a dismissive gesture. "Just the recent past and a few too many other problems. That is all I need to say, plus a thank you."

"But, I should thank you. You've saved my financial life."

"And you have given me freedom." Nick paused and then, munching on a piece of cake, said, "You are right about Thackery and Iris Murdoch. The place really needs sorting out, and if you do it in the forthright matter with which you addressed Bill Butler, I won't be unhappy."

"I will do my very best."

Dates were made, and telephone numbers and addresses exchanged. James was to start work in a week's time. As they shook hands outside the café, Nick thought, I know he is enthusiastic and capable. I don't need to know anything else. He smiled to himself as he walked away, wondering what Bill Butler would have made of this outcome.

Exactly a week later, Nick's bookshop reopened with James looking very smart on his first day. Despite his good looks, Nick felt detached and totally at ease as he handed him the keys and showed him around the shop, and life, which had been waiting patiently behind a door, prepared to charge in.

On a warm night in mid-April, Nick decided to take a walk along the seafront. He made his way down to the Old Steine and to the Palace Pier, where he turned left onto Madeira Drive. He knew exactly where he was going and walked underneath the arches until he reached Dukes Mound. There was a bright moon, and it was light enough for him to see clearly. He entered what he termed the jungle, passing several benches hidden by overhanging shrubbery and noticed several men, either in couples or alone. One couple were openly fucking, and as he passed them, a hand reached out for him—a blind hand of sexual need wanting more, greedy for extra touch, extra sensation. The hand grasped at his face as if wanting to pull him in, and looking, he saw two eyes, wide open, yet not seeing, too far gone in the throes of sex. He moved away from the touch, recalling a distant past when he had entered a room and joined two men with such a need. But tonight, he wanted only one body, one contact. As he passed a lamp, he saw a youth who appeared to be a very young teenager. He was standing close to the lamp in full view with his jeans lowered to his knees. He was not wearing underwear, and Nick noticed how thick the hair was around his groin. He had the face of a boy who had barely started to live and the body of a man. The impact of this collision of ages was too strong for Nick to pass by. The boy's hair was cut short, which set off his childlike features. Even in the obscurity of the place, in the pale moonlit darkness, Nick could see the face clearly—the small snub nose, the wide eyes, open as wide as the sky and just as vast in their intense depths. As he approached, he saw the boy's lips were wet with need, the saliva visible on his open mouth.

"Kiss me."

The plea was as intense as the eyes.

Nick moved forward, and in a moment, he was pressed against the warm body and felt the boy's cock against him. He undid his trousers, and immediately his underwear was pushed down by the boy. He kissed the mouth and then lowered his head to take the boy's penis in his mouth. He sucked on the round, uncircumcised head and stroked the foreskin up and down over the glans with one hand, while with the other hand, he reached for the boy's mouth and felt his fingers hungrily drawn in. Before long, the boy groaned, and hot liquid spurted into Nick. Drinking it down, he tried to bring himself to climax.

"Wait!"

He looked up at the boy, startled by the word, which was more of a plea than an order.

"Fuck me. I need to be fucked. I can come again. I promise."

Even the words were childlike. Nick ceased to pump at his erection and stood to face the boy.

"Here?" he asked gently.

"No. In the bushes. I know a place. More hidden."

He followed the boy, who had hoisted his jeans up again, and entered a space that was big enough to stand in and yet totally enclosed for privacy.

"I want to know your name," Nick whispered.

"Ben," came the reply, and as Nick repeated the boy's name, he felt his cock being pulled out and squeezed.

"I want it inside as far as it will go. All the way." The boy said, looking at Nick. "You are handsome."

"So are you," Nick replied. "Beautiful. Do you realise how beautiful you are?"

"No."

The boy's light voice trailed away, and within seconds he was bending over, his hands opening himself up for Nick. In the darkness, Nick felt how hard and thick his penis was. He was fearful of causing the boy physical pain and hesitated, afraid he would make him bleed, that his anus would be too tight and that he would hurt him.

"Have you done this before?" he asked.

"Yes. Put it in me. Please."

Nick entered him, and the youth's body writhed as if it were indeed in agony. It seemed more like a death struggle than passion as the boy screamed and thrashed against Nick. Within minutes Nick came, and quickly withdrew, fearful that he had violated this tight and too youthful flesh. The boy flopped forward, and Nick grabbed him, thinking absurdly that he had collapsed. I raped him, his inner voice said, and he drew the boy into his arms. Wasn't it the same with me once, in gardens similar to this? he thought.

"Are you alright?" he murmured. The boy's flesh moved in his arms, and Nick felt himself being hugged. "How old are you?" Nick asked.

"I'm—" and the voice stopped.

"Tell me."

"No problem. Don't worry about my age. I've done this since I was twelve. At school. A boy who looked like you. In the moonlight, you reminded me of him. I chose you for that."

"And you reminded me of someone when I was young."

"Was he like me?"

"Yes," Nick said, imagining a composite image of himself and Greg. "Tell me your real name," he asked, stroking the boy's dark blond hair.

"You knew I made Ben up, didn't you? It's Edward." Then there was a pause before he added. "Isn't it ridiculous? My mother called me after a king I didn't even know about until I started school. Her obsession. Some king who left his country for a woman he loved. The kids at school call me Eddie."

"You're not even fifteen yet, are you?"

Eddie withdrew from Nick's touch and said he didn't want any trouble with the law. These words made Nick shudder as if the full impact of the world's gaze was waiting outside this enclosed, secret place. He too was afraid of the law.

"I'll go out first," Nick said, then gently added, "Be careful. Don't do this too often. You could be—"

"Caught? I know. I'm scared, but I need this. I need it."

"Goodbye now."

Eddie did not reply, and Nick left Duke's Mound as quickly as he could. He had been an idiot to do what he had just done. He knew the place was dangerous. And yet, his flesh denied this as it still glowed with the pleasure of the experience. If only Eddie had been over twenty-one, but he was not. The law would be pitiless against him for the acts he had committed. And what of Eddie himself? He saw in his mind another night when he would meet the wrong man—a policeman pretending to be gay, or a queer-basher. The tragedy of their mutual desire was the cobweb of persecution that surrounded them. Nick made a promise to himself never to go with a boy that young again. He had known this from the start, and he was now running from the act, afraid that he had been seen and was being pursued. The naked seafront afforded him no protection, and the expensive houses of Kemp Town glared whitely down at his hurrying figure.

The day after his sexual encounter with Eddie, Nick, at last, went through his letters, a pile he had forgotten and put aside.

Among the pile, he noticed one that made his heart beat faster. He recognised the handwriting. It was Karel's. The stamp was English, and the postmark London. He held it in his hand for a long while and remembered, of all things, how it had been watching Greg fuck Karel, and how Karel had stared at him with the longing of desire. That longing, Nick had felt as well, and as he held the letter, he felt it again. How much Karel had been loved by all of them! By Greg first, then Nick, and then Bart. The golden light within Karel had touched them all with its mystery, with its gentle and passionate force. It had been a magnet for them, and when he disappeared, the light had dimmed. Nick thought of the glass collection he had left behind, the glittering forms crafted by Karel's people—the Czechs he had returned to. Karel had taken none of them with him, and going upstairs to the bedroom where he had made love to Karel, Nick stared at a tall, crystal vase, so pure in its beauty that even among the beauty of the rest, it seemed the most perfect to Nick. He had Karel's letter in his hand, and now he was ready to open it. It was tightly written in Karel's distinctive style.

I am arriving on April 22nd. Brighton Station at three. I hope you will be there. Love Karel.

If he had not gone with that boy the night before, and if his depression had not been lifted by the very necessary relief of physical desire, he would not have opened the avoided letters. He knew perfectly well that he may have taken weeks to open them—probably well beyond the date of the 22nd. Nothing, it seems, happens by accident. He reasoned that if he had not met Eddie at Duke's Mound, he would probably not have gone to meet Karel, who would have taken this as a sign and returned to wherever he came from—probably London—and Nick might never have seen him again. Now there were only a few days before he would be there at the station! Nick longed for that moment, and the light in the room brightened as if Karel's presence was already there. The simple words came to his mind: the return of the light.

He spent the following days wandering around the town. He wanted to ring Anna to tell her the news but held off, as he feared he would be tempting fate by doing so. This return of Karel's was to be for himself alone. Then by chance, he met Alan in a perfectly ordinary pub on Ship Street. Alan was sitting at the bar, looking down with a disconsolate expression on his face. Nick could have avoided him and left but instead went up to him. He felt strong enough to talk now, filled as he was with renewed hope. He touched Alan on the shoulder, who turned and looked at Nick blankly.

"Who are—?" he began, then without finishing the sentence, Alan returned to his drink.

"It's me. Nick."

"Nick? Who's Nick?"

The words came unsteadily out of Alan's mouth, and gently Nick touched him again. Alan winced.

"Sit down, whoever you are."

Puzzled by this reaction and alarmed at the state of the man, Nick sat on an adjoining stool. He had not been vital to Alan's life, but surely he had not forgotten their going for drinks together after the closure of the shop and how that night he had come back to Nick's house.

"I am Nick. Don't you remember?"

Alan shook his head, then, turning slowly, stared at him for a few seconds, with the same blankness, the same lack of recognition.

"Nick, Nick," he repeated mechanically. The words were said with a searching sound, the sound that can be made when something not remembered has to be remembered and found.

"Yes. Me. The shop. The bookshop."

"Oh, yes," came the casual reply. "*La Porte étroite*! I remember signing a cheque. You overcharged. The novel was, *is*, worthless. Have you ever read such rubbish? That denial of love? All that cowardice? All that self-torture and denial?"

"Gide," Nick said and felt suddenly helpless.

"André Gide! What an idiot! One book lusting after Arab

boys, and then this so-called narrow gate or way or whatever you want to call it, such great suffering and renunciation. From the Primrose Path to the Narrow Way. Fuck all that religious stuff. I suppose he wrote about the Arabs with a hard-on and had a crucifix on his desk at the same time. What a cunt!"

"You may be right," Nick replied and at the same time felt guilt for not realising before that Alan was a real reader. He had not just bought rare books to put them on shelves to impress others but had bought them for his own knowledge. Alan liked books, and rare ones, but the rarity of the edition was secondary to the words inside. Nick had not seen this clearly in the man before because of his outer mannerisms and camp ways. He had misjudged.

"I am sorry," he said.

"Sorry for what? That you asked too much for the blasted thing?"

Nick tried to laugh it off. "I don't think so."

"Don't you? Well, you did. Someone in the know told me. It was worthless, outside and inside. A tale to make you weep at human stupidity and that high elevation of love. Fuck love and all lovers. We are born, we fuck, and then we die. That's all there is to it. We invent love and God to make the whole awful mockery of creation bearable. Now, what will you drink?" He smiled at Nick, but the smile was forced. Nick meant nothing to him.

"Whisky please. Nothing in it, Alan."

"Strong stuff. A man's drink." He laughed. "What men we are, aren't we?"

Alan stretched his ample body over the bar counter, nearly knocking several bottles and glasses to the floor at the same time. He shouted at the barman. "I want another for Nick. Whisky. Nick is someone I am supposed to know. He likes whisky. Nothing with it. No rocks!" He laughed, but it was more of a growl, then he seated himself back on the stool. "I am drunk," he said. "Do you mind?"

"I just want to know if you remember me clearly now."

"Why should I? Why should I? Raiding my chequebook like a rent boy. But you didn't mean it. I know that. Better to overcharge on books than overcharge on the body."

There was silence between them, and after a while, the whisky arrived. It was the first drink that had come to mind for Nick, but he had not drunk any for a long time and could not remember how it tasted. As he drank, he felt its taste attack the back of his throat—an attack of burning warmth.

"Drink it like a man, in one go, and then have another," Alan said. "You cannot imagine how many gins I have had."

"I'll just have this one."

"Sissy boy!" Alan said with an unexpected look of disgust on his face.

"Alan, please. Don't," and Nick reaching out a hand, touched Alan's arm.

"Take your fucking hand away. I don't want men to touch me ever again, do you hear? I don't want their stinking smells and their farts and their fancy Eau de Colognes. I'm for nobody now in the touch department. Been had by too many. Far too many. Could make a list, but it would take too long. Oh, but I can remember them alright! The weasel faces, the foxy faces, the 'I am innocent but corrupt inside-out' faces. I can remember the slobbering kisses given without real desire."

"I don't understand," Nick said.

"I told you. I don't want to be touched by any man again. No one, but no one, lays a hand on me again. No one asks for money from me again. I am not available anymore." He paused for a moment after this outburst, then whispered, "I am sixty-nine today. The doorstep to seventy and hopeful oblivion."

"Happy—"

"Cut it out," Alan shouted and glared at Nick. "Who are *you* to wish me a happy anything? You're just a man I know, with whom I've had a few drinks, told stories to, and no doubt behaved like a sickening faggot with! I am a sickening faggot because I like to be fucked."

"Alan, what's happened? I want—"

"Nothing to give! I can't even explain myself properly anymore. Being fucked made me into a mincing, silly pastiche of myself. Do you know I am passionate about Latin and Greek? Do you know I can recite whole passages of Seneca and Euripides? I was a thinker once. I also loved Sophocles." Then he paused. "But you, you who go by the name of Nick, know nothing of that. You know nothing about what I knew and what I studied. I wasn't just some silly old fart who came into your shop because I was lonely. The last thing I wanted was to pick you up. I came in for the books. The books I wanted. And I didn't want your last offering that I bought."

"I apologise," Nick murmured, and he finished his drink.

"Why? You don't owe me. You never really stole from me like the others. You just cheated me once with the Gide, but that's alright. One mistake is alright. But there are others—many others, who have taken me for much larger financial rides than you. A legion of them. All young and delightful, like sickening cakes. I swallowed them all, and I paid for it."

"We are friends," Nick said as if he had to grasp at this description to bring back the Alan he had known.

"I have no friends! You were an acquaintance. That's all. Forgettable."

"Then I had better go."

"Yes."

Alan slumped over the bar again, attempting to grab at the barman, and while he was doing it, Nick got off the stool and left the pub. The light had gone. Among all the lies there had been between them and the sometimes reluctant drinks Nick had had with him, Nick had considered him a friend. But that was a lie. That was the darkness. He had been an acquaintance friend; that garment of human recognition we reserve for people we do not really care about, and in his forgetful drunken state, Alan had perception enough to reveal the hollow nature of their former meetings. Nick felt ashamed—ashamed of his sham acceptance of a man he had not wanted to know, *really* know, and Alan had taken his forgetful revenge and exposed him.

"Am I so shallow?" Nick asked himself aloud. Then, in silence, he walked back to his house.

At a quarter to three, Nick was standing in front of the vast wooden departures and arrivals board at Brighton station. He looked over to the overhanging clock and stared up at it, watching the minute hands slowly trace their way through what we call time. How slowly time crawled, and yet how fast Nick's heart was beating. Suppose Karel had changed his mind or that something had prevented him from coming? All manner of situations passed through his mind, both dreadful and beautiful. He saw the Czech secret service draw up at a curb and pull a frightened Karel into their car. He saw Karel being tortured in images that were too extreme and painful for him to bear, and the clock slowly, very slowly, advanced another minute. No, it was not true, he said to himself. If he does not come, he has met someone in London and has become involved with him, and there will be another letter explaining all this and I will be relieved that the worst has not happened to him. Finally, the black and white clock face said a minute to three, and as he turned to face the platform where the train was due to arrive, he felt a tap on his arm.

"Nick."

The voice! Karel's voice! He looked sideways. Yes, there he was—the thick brown hair, the pale grey almost blue eyes, the skin paler than the eyes, the body thin, tired but beautiful. Yes, he was beautiful, and his mouth was smiling, and despite the visible tiredness, his eyes shone with greeting, the pale grey flickering with blue. Nick reached out and, without a word, held him in his arms.

"My Karel," he said. "My Karel."

They hugged each other tightly, and then Karel released himself and stood back to look at Nick.

"And you? What of you?" he said. "You, my handsome Nick? But there is a look of angst in your face. Tears too in your eyes. What were you thinking?"

"I was looking at that clock and imagining all sorts of terrible and romantic things. I imagined you were prevented from coming and—no, I cannot tell you the rest. It is all melodrama. I almost did not dare to hope that you would arrive safely, and now here you are, safely back."

"But Nick, tell me. What terrible things? And what romantic imaginings?"

Nick steered Karel by the arm, took one of his suitcases, and they began to walk towards the central exit onto Queens Road, that long vista that leads down to the Clock Tower, to West Street, and to the sea.

"I imagined you had been abducted by evil men or that you had fallen in love."

Karel laughed very loudly, and there was joy in the sound.

"Crazy, crazy man," he murmured with tenderness. "Oh, Nick, how I have longed for your words and the way you express yourself, and quite simply, for the way you are. Poet, dreamer and realist all in one! Your mind soars into regions others would not even dream of going."

Karel put down his luggage, and Nick stood beside him, still holding the suitcase he had taken. Superstitiously he had the mad thought that if he put it down, Karel would disappear, and this reuniting of the two of them would have just been a waking dream, a dream induced by looking up at the station clock. The suitcase somehow earthed him.

The day was fine, and the sun was shining. Karel was drawing in deep breaths. A seagull dived nearby, seizing its prize of a stale chip with a fragment of fish attached to it. Karel noticed this act of urgency and gestured with his hand. "The seagull has got what it wants, and so have I."

"It's just sinking in that you are really back," Nick said, "that you are not stuck out there in the heart of Europe and—" he stopped, glancing at Karel's face, which for a moment looked sombre, almost angry. Then the look passed, and Karel remarked on how the town appeared to be its same old self, and that he felt he was home at last. The word *home* struck Nick, and he felt exaltation and pain. Could this really be Karel's home again? Did he dare to hope?

"Shall we get a taxi?" Nick asked.

"No, no, I want to see it all. Immediately. Let me hold the other suitcase as well. It's full of books and records. It must be heavy."

"Certainly not. Walk, we will, and if you get tired, we'll stop and have a good simple English cup of tea."

"In a white mug?" Karel asked, laughing. "In one of those ghastly white mugs? Yes, let's do that."

They walked down Queens Road, and as it was such a beautiful day, tourists were jostling beside them, and one or other of them had to walk ahead. At one busy junction, Nick thought he had lost Karel. He had zigzagged ahead between people, and Nick could no longer see him. He called out Karel's name, and a hand waved at him above the crowd. Nick pushed forward and joined him.

"I don't want you out of my sight for a second," he said to Karel, who gave him a beaming smile. "They will disperse a little at the Clock Tower," Nick added. "Most will go down to the sea, but as for us, I suggest we walk to the top of West Street, then down Duke Street towards the Lanes."

"Fine," Karel said. "It is wonderful here. I am happy. Sincerely happy. And how good at last to get out of London."

Nick wanted to ask why he had stayed there and not come directly to Brighton, but then again, fate, destiny, or whatever you may call it, had given Nick time to notice and read the letter. He was sure more information would come later.

"We are here," Karel said, and coming out of his thoughts, Nick took a few minutes to look at the books outside Hollyman and Treacher. He recalled how he had bought an early William Golding novel on the stall outside. It was a first edition, bought for a couple of shillings and sold for over a hundred pounds. "Shall we go inside?" Karel asked.

"No, Karel, we have so much else to see, and I have some

news about my life that I must tell you. I no longer work in my bookshop. I've found a keen young man to do it for me."

"But why?"

"I wanted a rest. I wanted to write."

Nick did not want to mention breakdown or loneliness or unhappiness. The blue of the sky was too cheerful, and so were the people walking on the pavement near to them. Spring, he thought, must never be defeated by winter in the soul. It is a crime to diminish the light with memories of darkness.

They continued walking down Duke Street, and after reaching Ship Street, made their way towards Prince Albert Street.

"And this young man? Is he gay?"

"I've no idea."

"Then there is no—"

"No, Karel, there's been nothing but amicable meetings about how the shop will prosper."

"I was beginning to feel jealous. I don't want you to have any affections except for me. Let me keep this dream for a while longer, Nick, will you? It became stronger as the train approached Brighton—as soon as I saw the Downs in the distance, and the tunnel, I understood that you and *only* you were waiting for me, and it made my heart beat as fast as the train."

"Exaggeration!"

"No, it's true."

They had reached the end of Prince Albert Street, and the length of East Street faced them.

"Shall we turn right or left?" Karel asked, his voice light with happiness.

"You choose," Nick said.

"The sea. Of course, the sea. We will have tea in white mugs on the Palace Pier and sit facing Kemp Town so that I can see the arches of Madeira Drive in all their glory."

They found a place to sit on the pier, and Nick went to buy tea and a pile of rock cakes. Rock cakes seemed to epitomise

Brighton with their solidness and their thick, salty taste. They were more Brighton than Brighton Rock had ever been. When he returned, he saw Karel leaning back against the glass wall that divided the two sides of the pier with his eyes closed. He was asleep, and Nick, with a mug of tea for him in one hand and the plate of rock cakes in the other, stood and realised that yes, it was love. He loved Karel. He desired him, and he loved him. But to what depths, and even, to what heights did this love stretch? He could not answer the question. In what house of priority within him did Karel exist? He pushed away the thought, and Karel awoke with a start.

"I was dreaming," he said and smiled up at Nick.

"Happy dreaming?"

"The happiest," Karel replied, then glanced at the white mug and the rock cakes. "I can't eat all of those," he said. "I'll get fat if I eat all of those. How did you know I was so hungry? I had nothing on the train. The buffet car was too crowded, and they were all smoking. It was not nice." He stood and took the mug and plate from Nick.

"I'll be back in a moment," Nick replied. "I have to fetch my own drink."

Karel was not listening. He was standing, looking out towards the white houses of Kemp Town, at the dignity and beauty of those majestic buildings, built in an age when beauty and style were all that mattered. He was still in the same position when Nick returned.

"Are you sleeping again?" Nick asked. "Or have you been transfigured into white marble?"

Karel grinned and moved his limbs, and Nick saw that it was with a certain reluctance that he had come back to himself. To Nick, it seemed as though Karel's soul and being had travelled to another realm.

"Where were you?" he asked as they sat down.

"I've no idea," Karel replied simply.

"Well, let us now come back to earth, or rather, these boards over the sea, and drink this tea and eat these cakes."

"Do you believe that we can leave our body?" Karel asked suddenly.

"Karel, no serious questions. I will answer nothing until at least two of these rock cakes have gone into you, and you have slurped your way loudly through that tea."

Without a word, Karel ate and drank, but he was now very quiet.

"I want something," he said at last.

"What?"

"A poem. A poem for me. Now. Now, looking at the sea— the sea new, and yet so old. Write me a poem in your mind now about this."

"But I can't."

"Do it for me, Nick."

Nick closed his eyes, and conscious of Karel waiting beside him, he too tried to slip into a waking dream where he could find the words that Karel wanted, and they came. The words, banal, good, or both, came to mind, and he spoke them, his eyes still firmly shut.

The sun that Homer
lit with bronze and words of silver
shines today:
the cliffs white staring glance
blind at the waves.
This eternal sea.

He opened his eyes, and Karel was smiling. Neither of them spoke, and then Karel stood and offered Nick his hand.

"Come," he said. "Let us pick up the suitcases and walk back to the house."

As they passed through the exit and crossed the road towards the Aquarium, Karel broke the silence and said, "Thank you."

"For what?"

"For this homecoming."

"I did nothing. It was you who chose this."

"Not just the celebratory tea and the poem, but the deep well within that you have dipped in just for me. You lowered your being into that well and have brought back the gift—the finest gift of all, and that is welcome."

"Karel, my romantic Karel."

"No, realistic. I am a realist with love. You know that. I never told you, but when I first met Greg in Chelsea, I could not imagine lovers sharing themselves with others, but when I saw you—"

"Yes?"

"Let's just say, I saw you, and my being changed. I grew strong and had no weakness. I knew the choices we all four of us made were pure. That purity has kept me alive through all the decisions I have made—the dishonesty and the cowardly actions."

"Karel, what are you trying to say?"

They stopped outside the steps that led down to the Aquarium.

"Shall we go and see the dolphins?" Karel asked.

"I am serious. What *has* happened?"

Karel looked at Nick. His sombre expression returned, and the mask that lay beneath his happiness was visible. Another Karel lay behind the Karel that Nick was seeing, and he became afraid of a revelation that he perhaps did not want to hear.

"I have to ask you to do something else for me. It is perhaps not as easy for you as a poem, but it is necessary for me. I want you to promise me that you will never question where I have been or what I have done. I know it will be hard because I understand the temptation of curiosity, but you must never ask me how these past years have been."

"But Karel?"

"I am serious, Nick."

"Why?"

"No whys. Nothing. Do you hear me? Nothing. I am Karel. Not exactly the same as when I left, when I disappeared so cruelly—and yes, I know it must have seemed cruel to you, my leaving. I am not so insensitive. I dispersed all of you with my departure, and I say this with no narcissistic pride or pleasure. I broke up what we had been—the very wholeness and the sanity of it, and the goodness. I am thinking too of Bart, vulnerable in his way, and Greg as well, deceptively strong. It was a crime that I committed."

Here he stopped, and Nick saw tears in Karel's eyes.

"Don't cry," Nick said.

"Nick, take me to the house. Take me there and hold me. Hold me tightly. I feel I am falling apart. The weight is so heavy."

Despite Nick again offering a taxi, Karel remained obstinate. They walked slowly, and tired out, they climbed the hills to what Nick hoped Karel would consider his rightful home.

We can only get glimpses of each other, Nick thought a few days later as he sat alone in the garden of the house. Karel was asleep upstairs, and it was just after eight o'clock in the morning. We can only see each other clearly, briefly. I have made love to Karel, and he has made love to me, but the depth of feeling is no longer there. It was more an act of passionate friendship than love—the same physical desire, and yet we did not *reach* each other. The past was the past, and it could never be recaptured. I cannot go back to those first desires, those first passions, but then again, how much was that intensity was due to the presence of Greg and Bart and the mutual communion we all had, the four of us? Again, the memory returned of seeing Karel penetrated by Greg. The joining of those two had seemed perfect to him, a summit of desire that now, alone with Karel and without the others, he could not attain. Greg was the missing element. Always Greg. And the thought persisted; we can only see each other briefly, only in fragments. Our imagination creates the rest. We should be complete, Bart, Karel, myself and Greg. But what did he even know of himself?

How could there be a clear vision of others when the self is blurred like a mirror covered with steam after a hot bath? And in that mirror, that opaque misted mirror, a face that can not be recognised. Nick drank his morning coffee and heard Karel moving about in the house. I must gather myself together, he thought. I must be complete and try to see Karel as being complete as well. He tried to put the sense of them existing as fragments aside. Years ago, there had been an impression of oneness because the four of them together had sparked, caught flame, and imagination had burned its moulding fire of creation. It had been a consuming fire, with no knowledge that there would be ashes years later. This thought of cold death made Nick tremble, and he longed for the phone to ring and to hear Greg's voice. Perhaps then he would feel differently. It was Greg that he needed to bring life back.

Karel walked into the garden. He looked refreshed and had a smile on his face as he came towards Nick. He bent down and kissed him on the mouth, and Nick's immediate and not very romantic reaction was to wonder if anyone in the houses behind had seen the kiss.

"I hope I didn't do anything wrong," Karel said, looking over at the houses.

"Of course not," Nick said, but still, he thought of it.

"We used to do it *before*," Karel replied. "In fact, they must have had a great view of us sometimes, all playing around in the garden."

"We didn't play around," Nick murmured.

"Alright, showing open signs of tenderness. I remember Greg and I kissing passionately once, and it was mid-afternoon. Bart joined us."

"I'd rather not recall all those details."

"Why, Nick? Because you were not with us?"

"That comment is not worthy of you, Karel."

Karel shrugged and asked Nick if he wanted something to drink. Nick shook his head, and Karel went back into the kitchen, saying he wanted some coffee. Nick got up and followed him in. Compared to the brightness outside, the room was dark, and for a moment, he felt cold.

"Couldn't you sleep?" Karel asked.

"Not very well. Perhaps we went to bed too late last night, and then—"

"—then we made love. Well, I made love. Did you make love?"

Nick, sensing trouble, asked Karel what was the matter and what he meant by saying that.

"I'm sorry," Karel said and made the coffee in silence. He had his back to Nick, and Nick, feeling a sudden sense of sorrow, went and held him from behind.

"No, it's my fault, Karel. I know it is. I have the impression I disappointed you in bed, that I was not as responsive as I should have been. Will you let me try to explain why?"

"It's been a long time," Karel said, turning. "We have not had sex for so long, and to state the obvious, a lot has happened in between."

"Not for me," Nick replied. "I'm just not used to *it* anymore—the act of closeness, of real loving. I've had the very occasional encounter, but that's all." I'm lying, he thought, recalling the desire he had felt towards Nathan, but then again, there had been no consummation.

"Are you sure that's all it is? Perhaps of the three of us, I'm just not the one you miss the most. I have a hunch I know who that would be. Do you want me to tell you, or would that be tasteless? I mean, I have been satisfied by our love-making these past few nights. It may not have been the heights of great passion, but I'm not sure I believe in great passions anymore. Paris kind of took that myth away from me."

"Tell me about Paris," Nick said.

"No, I can't. But I found out that we are fed from birth on the myths of Tristan and Isolde, and all the romantic songs that make us believe love is so much more than it really is."

"And how is it for you now, Karel? Really? After Paris?"

"It's beautiful, and I love you. Please don't forget that. It's just I cannot believe anymore in that immersion in the hot bath of eternal passion. It's for adolescents and fools, and I don't think I am either. Without details, Paris did teach me that there are more important acts in life than the act of love and that we have been indoctrinated, all of us, into the belief that *being in love* is the summit of all experience. I just don't buy that anymore."

Nick saw tears in Karel's eyes. He wanted to kiss them away, but he was afraid to make the gesture. Karel had changed. In what way? He did not know and was not allowed to know. This silence around his going to France and then Czechoslovakia mystified him. And why did he keep referring only to Paris and not there? Nick assumed there had been a life in Prague, or Brno or Bratislava, or perhaps a small town he had never heard of. Why was Karel so silent about the place he had most desired to go to?

"You never speak of Czechoslovakia," he said. Karel wiped his eyes and turned back to finish making his coffee. Nick went around and faced him. "There's too much mystery here. It's stopping us from going deep into the feelings we once shared. After all, then, there were no mysteries." As he said this, the word *fragmented* crossed his mind. Karel was a fragment of his former self. But even then, how real had the fragments been that he had seen and loved? His world slipped a little out of grasp as he thought this, and he trembled, not with the cold of the morning, but with fear. Could no one be known? He wanted to run from the room and from Karel. The fragment he was seeing in him was too painful to bear. "I want to *know* you," he shouted, then apologised for raising his voice. Karel looked at him and sipped his coffee slowly. His eyes were clear and dry now. He looked remote.

"Know me? You do know me. I am not as I was before, but there is still something left of what I was. As for mystery? What do you expect? We are grown-ups. My only mystery is that there are certain things about myself I am ashamed of and do not want to talk about. To be totally honest, I came back *here* to be away from all that I experienced *there*."

"I still do not know where *there* is," Nick said.

"Don't force it, Nick. It is not for you to know. I accept that you are curious—that's a normal reaction. But try to understand that I have no desire to explain what happened to me while I was away."

"Because it was dangerous?" So many scenarios were forming in his head, and all of them were of death, the nearness of death, and perhaps betrayal. The worst of all was that Karel had somehow been responsible for the death of others. Had he been a killer himself? In Prague, or some other place?

After a long pause, Karel said, "Shut up, Nick. I mean, really shut up about it all. If you don't, I will leave, and you will never see me again. Either respect my wishes or accept the consequences. I am capable of leaving. I think you know that."

"Yes," Nick said, and he slumped down on the bench by the long wooden table in the kitchen. "I give up. I give in. I don't want to lose you. I could not endure that."

Karel came over to him and, opening up the dressing gown he was wearing, showed his body to Nick. He had an erection, and Nick again saw the beauty of his penis, the red tip, fierce with blood. Silently, he bent forward and took Karel's cock into his mouth. It tasted of salt, dried sperm and urine, and with intense passion, he sucked on it until Karel had come. The spurt in his mouth of sweet fluid felt like a renewal. This was all of Karel that he needed to know. It was all that was given, and he accepted it, and it was enough. The need to go deeper was no longer required; the surface of this body that he physically loved was sufficient. He accepted, too, the sadness of this realisation.

"Tomorrow," Karel said, "tomorrow, all will be good. Just say this is a bad day for you. I promise you a tomorrow without sombre thoughts—those useless sombre fantasies that poison everything. I was inside you just now. You have my sperm inside you. I am yours. All will be fine when acceptance takes hold, and that is up to you."

"I accept," Nick said.

"Now, take me upstairs and come inside me. I want you inside so hard; it is all that I am, and while it lasts, let me belong to you."

Upstairs, Nick licked Karel's open anus, and then, retreating, caressed it gently with his fingers. He looked at the hole, red and wet, his saliva glistening in the surrounding hair. Yes, this would be a consummation of a kind, but he did not want to see Karel's face. For the first time in their acts of sex, he did not want to see the contortions of expectation and satisfaction on Karel's face. The anus was sufficient to him, and with two quick plunges, he was entirely inside the unmoving body. Karel did not cry out but whimpered; like a child who is oblivious to all but being temporarily fulfilled, Nick thought. And like a child, Nick was aware enough to know that this fulfilment would have a limited duration and that others, after him, would do the same to this body that so readily exposed its entrance to him. He came, and lying back on the bed afterwards, they said nothing and did not kiss or even look at each other.

In the following days, Nick had two phone calls. The first was from Greg.

"Greg," he said simply, silently weeping.

"Yes. Me. I know it has been a while. Can you forgive me?"

"Of course."

"You are crying."

"I am not," and Nick tried to laugh.

"Don't lie. What's wrong?"

"How do you *know*?" Nick asked.

"The other side of the same coin, remember? I could feel your tears in the way you said my name. The emotion was obvious. But emotion about what, or who?"

"You, you idiot," Nick said.

"Love me still?"

"Again, idiot!"

"Alright, so there is something else. You want to tell me, but you don't know how. Not ill, are you?"

Nick paused, thinking, yes, I am ill. Sickened by what I am doing to my flesh, to Karel's flesh.

"Karel has returned," he said simply, and Greg gave out a whoop of pleasure. For a moment, Nick thought they had been cut off.

"Is he there? Really there? With you?"

"No, he is out."

"Fuck, you could have sent me a telegram. Or has he just arrived?"

"No, it's been a week, or is it longer? I can't think clearly, Greg. It's not what it seems."

"Riddles! What the fuck are you talking about?"

"Have you got time to talk? I mean, what I have to say is not easy, and I don't want you to get the wrong idea."

"Nick, stop fudging. I want something concrete. Has he developed two heads?"

Nick laughed. Yes, he thought, Karel has two heads. The one I see and don't want to kiss, and the other, hidden in the shadows.

"I can sense you are in a state, Nick. Just imagine I am there, with you, in the room. Pretend. Shit, I wish you had sent that telegram, then perhaps I would have called when he was in."

"He goes more or less his own way, Greg. He lives here for the time being. Perhaps forever. Who knows? We are taking it day by day."

"You make love?" Greg asked hesitantly.

"You could call it that, yes."

"This doesn't sound right. I mean, you don't sound happy. Am I right?"

Nick felt a pain in his stomach—a savage punch of pain. He had betrayed Greg. He had no idea why he thought and felt that, but he had betrayed Greg. He should have been faithful. Then the explosion in the gut. No one was his lover! Neither Karel nor Greg. He was alone. His mouth was ready to vomit. The explosion was in his throat. The bile was already there, rising inexorably.

"I feel sick," he said to Greg.

"Put down the phone. Go to the sink. Get a glass of water. Drink it slowly. Calm yourself. Whatever it is this sensation, it will pass. Now go and do it."

Nick put down the phone and did as Greg had told him, but he did not sip. He gulped the water down as if he were in the desert and had reached a sudden oasis. He poured another, drank it quickly, and the pain and the threat of vomit diminished. He returned to the phone.

"Greg?"

"I'm here. Better?"

"Yes."

"Now, slowly, tell me what the hell has been happening."

"He's changed, Greg. He is not the same person."

Greg laughed, and Nick wondered what was so funny in all this.

"Trust you to explain it like that. This isn't *Invasion of the Body Snatchers*, Nick. Changed? Taken over by alien forces? Don't go to sleep. Whatever you do, don't go to sleep. You will become like him if you do. No more emotions. No more loving. All gone!"

"It *is* like that Greg."

"Don't be ridiculous. I know we loved old horror films, but please, we are grown up now. He is Karel. K-A-R-E-L," he repeated, spelling out the name.

"But most of him is not here, Greg. Don't joke. It is true. I know nothing about him. He *is* a stranger."

"Nick, now you really are worrying me, but not about Karel. I'm worried about your mind. Was it the shock of his arrival? I mean, it's a shock to me. But to me, Karel is Karel. Full stop."

"I know."

"Well?"

"He is hiding inside himself, Greg, and the outside is just a façade. Even in sex, I don't sense he is really there; the desire yes, the force of passion yes, but not the Karel we knew, the Karel we both loved."

There was a long silence, and Nick could hear Greg breathing. Then, in the background, he heard the sound of breaking crockery.

"What was that?" he asked.

"François in the kitchen. He has just broken something. Now, go on."

"He won't talk about anything. Paris. Czechoslovakia. I have an awful intuition that he has committed some crime, that he killed somebody, that he is in danger and full of guilt, that he is wanted."

"No, Nick, no. Maybe he had bad experiences—life-changing experiences. Your imagination is working too hard. Maybe he suffered or was even tortured. But Karel, a killer? Impossible. More likely there was an attempt on *his* life!"

"Yes, I understand what you are saying, but I feel there is guilt inside him, remorse, a closing-in. He is so empty now of real feeling. On the first day I met him at the station—"

"What do you mean, at the station? Did he ask you to meet him there?"

"Yes, in a letter. The postmark was from London, not Paris. What was he doing in London? He sent the letter weeks before coming to Brighton."

"So he wanted to see London. He may have *needed* the time to get used to England again. Have you thought of that?"

"No."

"Well, do think, Nick."

"I wish you were here, Greg. I really do."

After a long pause, Greg said, "I'm in touch with Bart again. He hasn't changed. Lost his looks a bit, but he's the same clumsy Bart, bumping into life as he does."

"I'm glad," Nick said, but he felt nothing.

"I'll have a talk with him. He's separated from his lover and rather down. He loved Karel too, remember? And then both of us, and maybe François as well, if you don't mind—we can all come to Brighton! I will make Karel *real* again. I promise, but in the meantime, you will have to be patient."

"When?"

"August. I know François can take some time off then. As for me, well, I am a man of eternal leisure, and Bart will make the time. And guess what else?"

"What?"

Greg laughed. "If you can put up with us, we can stay until your birthday! A reunion, you idiot! Think of it."

Nick did. Could he hold out that long?

"But Greg—"

"Doubts?"

"No, not at all. We can all huddle together in this house. The lot of us. Kitchen, floors, living room. I'm not sure about the bedrooms or sex."

"Nick, calm down. I haven't mentioned sex. We will all behave like respectable bachelors." Greg laughed. "Oh, shit, Nick, this is wonderful. Just keep body-snatcher Karel happy, okay?"

"I will," Nick said wearily, but his voice had no conviction.

More words were said, and the call ended again with the promise that Greg, François and Bart, would arrive later that summer.

One evening, while Karel had gone up to London to see an art exhibition by an obscure painter Nick had never heard of, he decided to go out. He went to The Greyhound, which had changed over the years and was no longer that popular. It was nine in the evening, and the place was almost deserted. He asked the barman for a glass of wine and sat in one of the window seats facing East Street. As he stared at the stained glass and the grime on the windowsills, he asked himself, why have I come here? He felt old, which was ridiculous, and the depression that had forced him out only deepened. He realised, now that he was approaching his thirties, that time passes quickly and, cliché though that obviously was, it was still, as it is for everybody, a milestone to pass in life. His eyes were fixed on a red piece of glass, and the red burned his eyes. It became for him a point of meditation, and he saw blood and pain. For a moment, he had a terrible vision of the future and of long years ahead. He saw a furnace burning continuously, and in the fire, bone stripped of flesh, and then the searing flame dissolving the bone until only the dusty embers of self remained. Was it his body in the flames? Was it anyone close to him? He thought of Greg, and the horror of that thought made him pull away from the stained glass. He shook his head, shaking off the brutal vision. It's just the horror of depression, he told himself, and yet the flames had been so real, and it had not only been Greg, or even perhaps Greg himself, but thousands of others, one after another, reduced to ashes.

"I know who I am thinking of. I am thinking of Nathan," he whispered as he drank slowly the wine he had chosen. "I have seen the hell of his heritage."

As he said these words, he had no desire to be confronted by Nathan and to talk again of the Jews and the crimes committed against them, or the crimes some would say they had committed. I have heard it all, he thought. We have avoided each other since our last meeting. Perhaps it is just as well. We have nothing to offer each other despite words of friendship said and an amicable parting.

"May I sit next to you?"

Nick looked up, and the world outside his mind pulled him back into its orbit. A man, probably in his forties and dressed in a grey suit, was staring down at him. His hair was beginning to grey at the sides, but Nick was attracted by the gentle sound of his voice and, above all, to his face. He had blue eyes and black hair, and there was a sharp foxiness in his look that Nick found sexy.

"Of course."

"You're sure? I mean, we are practically the only people here, and it seems stupid to remain at opposite corners of the room."

"I agree," Nick said and then added, "I wonder where they have all gone?"

"Who?" the man replied and sat on the window seat facing him.

"I came here many years ago as a teenager. The bar was full then. Older men, younger men. I expected it to be the same today."

"The choices are multiplying," came the reply. "You can't dance here to the latest whatever, or stare transfixed at the glitter ball and the flashing lights—probably on drugs, and dancing by yourself, even if someone is dancing in front of you."

"I don't go out much," Nick said.

"Whyever not? At your age? How old are you, if I may ask?"

"Almost thirty."

The man laughed. His attractive face creased with laughter and his eyes sparkled. Nick felt his penis harden. He wanted to have sex with this stranger.

"Thirty!" the man said, accentuating the word slowly, and then asked Nick if he wanted another drink.

"Wine. White, please."

"My name is Tom, by the way. But call me Tommy like everyone else. And yours?"

"Nick."

"Nicholas! A wicked sounding name. I forget my theology. Wasn't he banished from heaven?"

"That was Michael, the archangel."

"How knowledgeable you are. I should have remembered. I was going to become a priest, but various people changed my mind, especially some persuasive young men. I'm sure I made the right decision, but enough of my cowardice."

"Why cowardice?" Nick asked.

"I imagined myself at the altar, and beneath my cassock, I imagined my erection as I put the white host into some young man's mouth! An unthinkable thought. I became an estate agent instead."

It was Nick's turn to laugh, and as Tom walked to the bar, he marvelled at his trim figure, his shock of hair and the charming way he had with words. He tried to imagine himself in bed with him, but somehow he knew it was not going to happen. It would not be his choice, but he sensed it would be Tom's.

"Here's to our mutual solitude tonight, and a thank you for breaking it," Tom said, returning with the drinks. He put the glass of wine in front of Nick, then raised his own glass of gin. "So what shall we talk about? Let's talk gay shop, shall we? I mean, the scene out there that you are avoiding, and that soon I will be going onto. Yes, to my shame, I follow youth."

Nick was right. Despite Tom being nice to him, he was too old for this man. To say something, he said, "I don't go out much." He realised he was repeating himself but knew that with the loss of desire, there was also the loss of new words.

"Is it because of the gay lib people? Despite all their pamphlets and bibles, they are depressingly like most of us."

"You seem hostile," Nick replied.

"Indifferent. Why should I be interested? I am forty-four and successful. It's all a load of rot to me. We've got the law on our side now—"

"Partially," Nick interjected.

"Two men in private is good enough for me. All through my twenties, after I decided not to become a priest, I was afraid. Afraid of the law and imprisonment. I was oh, so careful, but I like very young guys. Don't get me wrong, always over seventeen, but it means I continue to break the law. Maybe after I grow up and like men who are over twenty, I will be in the clear, and society will more or less accept me. It's only a matter of time—like trying to get off cigarettes. I'm working on it."

"How hard!" Nick said, his voice close to sarcasm.

"Ouch!" Tom replied and gulped down half of his gin.

"I'm not sure where I stand on gay liberation," Nick murmured, changing the subject away from this stranger's sexual tastes. "It's not for me, for reasons that are not yet apparent, but in a way, I can understand what's happening."

"I can't. They're causing trouble. Bringing lesbians in, who were never imprisoned or fined, plus all the rubbish about communes and shacking up in groups. Consciousness-raising indeed! That's what they call it, I think."

"You're being too tough," Nick said.

"Am I? I don't believe I am. Not for a moment. Not for a jot of a moment. Most of them have no idea what we older guys went through. Plus, it has only been a few years since the law changed in our favour. They do not understand that we are still hurting from the past, where we were *really* persecuted, and they want *more*!"

"Surely some older guys join up with them?"

Tom sounded cynical as he laughed at this and finished off his gin.

"Yes, I suppose some of them may join to look at the young things. Even I have slept with a few. And these liberated boys are hot! Sex, sex, sex. Liberation farmyard I call it. All together and all waving their testimonies promoting change. And sexy as many of them are, they are all too far to the Left."

This last sentence was, of course, the ultimate insult, and with a feeling of disgust, Nick stood up.

"I agree with some of what you say. I agree that it has come very soon after the law giving us semi-freedom was passed, but there is a future, and future means change. I am sure that a lot of gay men in this town secretly admire them for the things they believe in."

"Do you?" Tom said, staring up at him, and it was clear all interest was gone between them. "Well, I will let you into a little secret. This summer, they are going to have the first gay pride march. The public spectacle of our private lives is beginning. We'll see how many of this town's thousands of gay men join in or will secretly want to! Imagine it. Marching, chanting and waving flags with badly written slogans on them. How will the general public like us then? And how soon before the law is set back to what it was? Laws can be replaced by other laws, or didn't you know that?"

"I'm not a lawyer," Nick said. "Clearly you know all about this march. Clearly you know all the *right* people to get this information. At what cocktail party did you hear it?"

Tom glared up at Nick now, anger visible on his face.

"I think you had—"

"—better go? I *was* going! And by the way, just to flatter to your handsome ego, I fancied you. Until that is, I had the mental picture of you hanging around outside Brighton College!"

"Fuck off," Tom said coldly.

Nick walked away, and his depression hit with a vengeance. He had not expected such a war of an encounter. His last thought of Tom was to wonder why he had gone to The Greyhound in the first place. After all, youth had abandoned that pub long before, but then again, perhaps Tom, like himself, was revisiting a place of his past. Perhaps they had that in common. He wondered whether Karel would return that night or stay up in London. His inner world was clashing so violently with the outer world that he felt he could not survive unless he talked to a friend, impartial to the gay arena. He decided to ring Anna. This was something he rarely did, but he needed a sane voice.

"Anna, I have just defended a cause I am not even sure I believe in."

"Right thing to do, Nick. Black is the same as white. Good for you."

He smiled to himself as she said this. Yes, he was both black and white in his beliefs, wary of everything that was too dogmatic and that laid down new *revolutionary* rules—which in his less than perfect understanding of GLF he thought they did.

"I need to talk to you, Anna. My mind is doing strange things. And I feel you are the only person I can talk to."

He heard her cough as if she were claiming time before

replying.

"But Nick," she said at last, "it's late. I would ask you over, but it has not been the best of days for me either."

"I am sorry," he replied. "It was wrong of me to call."

"Hey, hold on a minute, my darling friend, neither of us should ever feel it is *wrong* to call when we are in need. Tell me the gist of it now, quickly, and then tomorrow evening, I will rustle up a meal for us. Potato and tomato omelette with salad. At say, seven-thirty? I'm sure I will be A-1 by then. I am painting now, and it is exhausting, but aside from my own willpower, I have you to thank for starting me off with grey and just that touch of colour. Remember?"

"I am happy you are working. Creating is a remedy for everything."

"And you? What about your poems? Another collection on the way, or is that the problem?"

"I can't write, it's true, and my life has been thrown up in the air by the return of Karel."

She paused, and once more he heard her cough.

"That should be making you shout with joy, but clearly from the way you are presenting it, it is not."

"It's the Czechoslovakia business. He is hiding everything he did there, every detail about his life over the past four years, from me."

"A great deal must have happened to him, and intuition tells me there may be facts in his life that *have* to be hidden. I am not suggesting he is deceiving you deliberately, but perhaps he is ashamed of something. *Crime* is too harsh a word, but some crimes have nothing to do with the law—crimes against the self."

"You mean something he should not have done?"

"Or should have done, but avoided doing," Anna replied. "There are situations in life where we can save ourselves or another and yet fail to do so. Then there is remorse. Perhaps he is deceiving himself and by that deceiving you."

"Anna, this is terrible if it's true. I can't *reach* him. He is not there; the inner being of Karel that *was*, is not there."

"I will think about all this, Nick, and we will talk tomorrow. I assume you have said yes to the omelette and an evening of my company. I also have a Haitink recording of Mahler I want you to hear. Sublime."

"Once again, I am sorry I called so late. You see, Karel is not here. He's in London, and I am not sure whether he will return tonight. I can't confront him. There is no way to do that, and if I try, he threatens to leave and not see me again."

"He said *that*?" she gasped.

"Yes."

"I suggest, Nick, you go home now and that you read your favourite poet. No, read mine, Rilke. I think I gave you *Letters to a Young Poet*, didn't I?"

"You did. I love it."

"It's a slim book. Read it slowly, then read the *Duino Elegies*. I promise you that the nonsense and the cruelty of the world will slide away. You have nothing to fear."

He said he would do as she advised but wondered whether in his solitude, waiting for the sound of a key turning in the lock, he was capable of it.

"Rilke," he said slowly.

"And your own work. Read some of what *you* are capable of writing. Reach high within you. Shut out the rest below where it belongs and try not to think of Karel. It's a mystery to me his behaviour, but like the I Ching says, 'It bears shame.'"

They talked a little more, but this was mainly about how her work was going. He sensed her tiredness and that she was perhaps hiding how unwell she really was.

"I kiss you," he said at last.

"And me you. Read Rilke's letters. Imagine they are to you. Certain passages will hold out a light for you during the coming night. Trust your old friend."

A minute later, the receivers were replaced. Nick walked back to the house, and to his surprise, not once did he think of his meeting with Tom in the pub, and neither did he think of

Karel. As he walked, he pictured himself in the kitchen, with the door open as the night was warm. He would breathe, and he would open the book of letters. He knew already some of the pages off by heart.

Karel did not return that night, and Nick, after reading, slept well. It was past eleven in the morning when he awoke, and he felt surprisingly refreshed as if bathed during the night of all stains and all doubts. He even contemplated writing a poem for Anna but was still uncertain about his ability to put thought and image to paper and did not attempt the act. He stayed all day in the house, mainly in the garden, and he was still, perfectly still. He let the house enclose itself around him like a friend, protecting him from further dark thoughts.

At seven-thirty prompt, he was at Anna's door.

"My darling, come in!" she greeted with a delightful peal of laughter. She was wearing a paint-covered smock and had streaks of green in her hair. Noticing his stare, she waved her hand in the air dismissively. "Yes, I look awful, but does it really matter? I was so immersed in what I was doing, I didn't even have time to take all this off and give myself a wash."

Nick bent forward, gave her a kiss, and then hugged her. The paint on the smock was dry and did not come off on his clothes. She was a walking palette of colour, and he was delighted to see her like this. He had never seen her so excited, so full of visible joy.

"I've worked all day," she said as she led him into the studio. Stacked up against the walls were many paintings, this time facing outwards. Before, she had been discreet about what she was doing, but now she did not seem to care, and he looked from one canvas to another. There were no portraits, only the sea in all its variations, in all its moods from storm to calm. She had put it all there on canvas. She had used acrylics, and the impact was overwhelming as blue tumbled over green and flashes of foam splashed outwards. One picture was a close-up of a rock pool—a world of detail and precision—each small rock, each specimen of sea flower, glittering as if illuminated by the sun. The rock pool was a microcosm of the world beyond it and yet, at the same time, totally detached from it. The pool was itself and itself alone, washed by water and left stranded by water. In the corner of the canvas, a tiny crab reached upwards as if in exclamation at being seen. It was a suspended moment in time; that miracle only a great painting and no photo can depict. She had caught it all. He imagined the tide being far out and this singular universe of form and radiance lasting for several hours before an incoming wave would claim it, hide it and keep it secret. He thought too of the individual self of man, exposed briefly, only to hide again, to be submerged and then revealed again at the destined hour of return.

"You may have it if you like," Anna said simply, brushing at her smock.

"But it's so good—"

"All the more reason. Take it with you when you go. It is one of my favourites, and I don't ever want to give you anything inferior or less than the best I can do."

Nick looked again at the canvas, sensing that over the years, he would gaze into it often, another world opening up to the glance of man.

"Now, stay and enjoy it while I go and change out of all this. But don't avoid the other canvasses. I could have hidden them from you, but like fireworks, I wanted to make a bright display. Form, colour, life—what else can there be to revive the spirit? Even human love is fleeting compared to this, but I do not see it as an extension of myself. The colour is there. I simply use it, unconscious of what I am doing most of the time, and letting the freedom I cannot see inside me dictate what is to come. I try to leave my ego at the door when the process begins. It's the only way to draw out all those inner accumulations of what is seen and felt and restore them to their rightful outer place."

"But love *is* there," Nick explained.

"If you want to call it that, Nick, then it is true. True to you. For me, it is a reminder of separate, singular worlds, where emotion is only felt in stillness. Stillness. I find that is the word I would use instead of love; an acknowledgement that we are *all* fleeting and only revealed in fullness for a moment in the vastness of time."

Anna then left the room, and he was alone with her worlds. He paused before each one, gathering what he could of what each canvas contained—a dash of yellow here, a startling green there, but none of the red that had disturbed him in the stained glass of the pub window. It was as if the fire had to be quenched so the depths could be revealed. Fire sucks inwards and dictates passion, death and annihilation. Red is its emblem, but here she had resisted using it. There was no suffering or extinction of life. Instead, a golden sheen covered one of the paintings as if a veil of gentle sunlight had fallen, not to burn but to illuminate and heal.

"Still looking?" she asked as she returned into the room wearing a long, flowing dress, tender in its shades of muted colour.

"You look beautiful," Nick commented.

"I feel refreshed, my dear friend. Now, sit down with your back to my work, and let me pour you a glass of wine."

She had laid out a small table with snacks and a bottle of wine, and Nick felt a rush of guilt that in his hurry he had forgotten to bring one with him.

"I should have bought the wine."

"Why? Because it is always done that way? Don't be silly and sit down."

They sat facing each other, and for a while, they were silent. Her face was calm and intent, looking at him as if she were trying to read his feelings and thoughts. The wine had been poured, and he held his glass in his hand.

"Did Karel return last night?" she asked, breaking the silence.

"No."

"But you got through the night peacefully?"

"Yes."

"I knew that you would. I won't ask if you read Rilke or your own work. The crisis I think has passed. You look restored, and if it was not in reading or in simply letting go, you have recovered yourself. You are single to yourself, and that is how it should be."

"I really did ring too late last night."

"That is nonsense, and you know it. I am glad that you turned to me. I'm not sure there is anyone else you could have turned to at that moment in time. Solitude is good, but you were in a dark place. I felt it. Perhaps Greg would have been the only other one, but he is not here. I am." She paused then and held out a bowl filled with dried fruits. "Here, take some of these. Delicious."

He took a couple, and they smiled at each other.

"Karel," she said. "I want to tell you what intuition told me last night. He has gone out of your life. He will come back to your house and try to be himself with you, but you must not be fooled. Whatever secrets he has, are for someone else. He may have already met the person, but this person will be the first to hear what he is concealing. I cannot blame him in any way, and neither should you. He believed he came back for you, but he was deceiving himself. There is another waiting. His life will be with him. There. I have said it all."

Surprisingly, Nick felt no emotion. He believed her words.

"I know it is perhaps a private thing to ask, but have you been intimate with him?" she asked.

"Yes."

"And?"

"It failed."

"It had to. The kind of love he was expressing was misplaced. Of course, there is feeling for you. That has not changed. But you are not the person he has returned for. Maybe last night he found him, or maybe it is to come. I cannot tell you which, except that he is in the process of searching. He may not even know it consciously. Yet, you must know it consciously and be patient and distant but kind."

Nick leant back in the chair and stared around the room. What an oasis this studio was to him, and he drank in the sight and smell of the room, wanting to imprint it on his memory so it could be retrieved at a later date. It felt more like his spiritual home than his own house.

"I love it here," he said.

"I know, and that is partly why I wanted you to see all that I have done recently. Everything here welcomes you."

After this intimate talk, Anna opened up other subjects. For a while, they spoke of the Mahler they would listen to after dinner and of what she had seen and done since their last meeting, but there was one issue Nick wanted to talk about, and he knew it risked a fall from the bright heights of conversation they were on.

"Have you heard much about the Gay Liberation Front?" he asked.

She shook her head, and Nick sensed sadness in that gesture.

"I have read a few articles on it. There is a new rush in the world, and it is part of it. For good, maybe in the end, but there is a lot in it that is not good. Undoubtedly, this act of sexual revolution is a necessity—a rebellion against the oppression of ages. Still, they go too fast, and I fear their beliefs will simply be branded, commercialised. Others who have no ideals will take over, and sexuality will be dominant to such an extent that it will kill feeling. A bomb will explode, and they, in their innocent way, will have lit the fuse. I would not want, myself, to see the consequences."

"Do you think more open, more public expressions of sexuality are wrong?"

"Nick, how can you ask me that? I am not of that world. All I know is that indiscriminate sex is a path to destruction. It has to be! Flesh is not meant to crash into flesh in such a blind way. There has to be a balance between the four elements of thought, feeling, sensation and intuition. Sensation and misguided thought, I fear, will take precedence. A crash means accidents of self, destruction of self. But I repeat, this is not my world. Greg would know better than I. He is your darker side, and I feel paradoxically that it is he who will bring you light. More than light! Enlightenment."

"I am tiring you, Anna. I am sorry. It's just this is part of the depression I have felt. After all, I am of that world, and I cannot escape it."

"Neither should you. But detach yourself. Look upon it and see it, but above all, do not be engulfed in this rush towards ill-thought-out freedoms. Choose what is best from it, as you did already when the four of you lived together. Everything was in balance for a while, and pure though it was, it broke apart. Singleness must meet singleness. I do not sense it can be otherwise. Greg too will feel this given time. Single being *must* join with single being."

"You mean the same coin cannot see its other side?"

"What a strange way of putting it. But yes."

The meal was ready, and they went into another room. A second bottle of wine was opened, and Nick became slightly drunk. He laughed a lot, and as the plates were put aside, he told Anna that Greg had rung him and that both he and Bart were returning during the summer and staying for his birthday.

"Bart as well!" Anna exclaimed.

"Yes. It has been so long, and the years have gone slowly."

"No, Nick darling, the years speed by. It seems slow, but what an illusion that is. I am happy. When exactly are they coming?"

"Late July or August. They can both take time off from whatever they are doing."

"I want to see Bart. Be sure to tell him that."

Nick paused for a long while before asking, "Why Bart?"

"I feel he and I need something from each other. He is wounded in some way. I think I can help. Don't ask me how I sense all this. It puzzles me, and I want to know if what I sense is right." She paused and then added slowly, "It saddened me that you did not see how special he is, but then perhaps it was not for you to see it."

"I loved him equally," Nick said.

"No. Delusion. You wanted to, but there was only truly one in your life, and you know it."

Nick stood up and went over to a bookcase. He took down Goethe's *Theory of Colour* and looked at the plates. He had one more question to ask, and he could not face Anna to ask it.

"Will you come to my birthday party? It will be a reunion."

Anna sighed, and he heard her pick up the various pieces of crockery. The sound seemed very loud in the long pause before her answer.

"I have to go away, Nick. I did not want to tell you yet, but you are asking me about October, and I won't be here then."

"Where will you be, Anna?" His voice sounded tight to him, afraid. He gazed at a diagram in the book.

"I've had a stroke of luck, Nick. Last year, when I *disappeared* a while, and you were perhaps just a little angry at me for doing so, I went to the Orkney Islands. Strangely enough, I felt it was my real home—the home I have been waiting for all my life, but I didn't have the money then to contemplate changing my life. But a distant relation, a cousin would you believe, died without close family, and I inherited a few thousand. I realised I could take action, and I went up there again and stayed for one week. Then, as destiny would have it, I found a dilapidated but liveable house in Kirkwall, walking distance from the cathedral. I couldn't believe my luck and bought it. There is work to be done, but fortunately, I do have a little extra money." She said the words quickly, her voice steady, and Nick, his hands trembling, replaced the book on the shelf. "I plan on moving at the end of August," she concluded.

Nick turned and faced her. He had to smile for her. He had to support her departure and not be selfish and dwell on his loss.

"I will visit you there," he said. "I will come as often as I can. You are so precious to me, Anna, and for you, this will be a new life. Is there room for a studio?"

Anna made coffee, and they returned to the studio. She looked around her at the room.

"There is a terrible old bathroom upstairs. I will convert it and have my space to paint. I'll be like Monet doing my versions of the cathedral. I've already made sketches in charcoal. No colour. They are my grand plan for a series of work. I felt such a flow of energy there, Nick, and I don't want to talk about my health, but time is—well, let us say it is passing. This will be my last challenge!"

"You say that as if—"

"—I am impatient," Anna said, finishing the sentence for him. I am impatient to complete my work while the sun still shines and the evening is still some distance away."

Nick put down his coffee and examined each of the paintings against the wall.

"Bring the painting that I am giving to you," Anna said. "Do it now before you forget. I don't think we will listen to Mahler tonight. As you say, I do feel tired."

Nick reached for the canvas, and the space seemed ominously vacant. He saw the room devoid of her colour and her work and imagined another living there, perhaps with no knowledge of what had been before.

"I hope you never sell these paintings," he said. "I want them to remind you of the sea *here*."

"I made them to keep them," Anna replied. "The ignorant think the sea is the same everywhere. It is not. All seas depend upon the light that falls on them, and this part of the world here is blessed with an extraordinary clarity of light. I expect Orkney will have its own quality of seascapes, but for me, the waves that turn upon this shore, along this coast, will always be unique. As I said, I have plans to paint St Magnus Cathedral." She laughed at this as if it were a joke, and Nick smiled his broadest smile.

"I bet you have," he replied, responding to the tone of her voice.

Nick sat down to finish his coffee and realised it would soon be time for him to leave. He had the feeling he would see this room only once or maybe twice before she left, and this filled him with a sense of emptiness, but he could not show his feelings. The canvas was safely at his side. The singular world she had painted with such care: the rockpool coexisting with so many other singular worlds.

"We haven't often spoken about sexuality," Nick said, surprised at his own statement.

"I know," she answered. "I've been reticent about that, haven't I? Alluding to it rather than openly asking or prying. Just wasn't my way, and the years that separate us in age probably explain a lot. Society has been too rigid, and that is why I know change can be a force for good, and it's my heartfelt wish for gay people to grasp this chance of change with both hands." She paused and then added, "But with responsibility. I read several articles on Edward Carpenter recently. In my much younger years, an admirer gave me a copy of *Towards Democracy*. I read it then, of course, but only recently have I understood that he was homosexual and that he lived a complete and full life with another man whom he loved. Many went to him as a sort of pilgrimage, and these pilgrims saw hope for a better way of living. And I think we need, or should I say you and Greg and Karel and perhaps Bart, *need* a new Carpenter. A new model for existence they can visit and be at home with. Carpenter too lived a sort of communal life, but I don't think it resembled at all what this new movement aspires to."

"In some ways, yes," Nick replied.

"If not, then *someone* needs to *make* it happen. Greg I see as a contender."

"The boy from Portslade," Nick murmured. "The complex child of simplicity—and he is both—rich in simplicity, and yet more complex in his actions than perhaps any of us."

"You *do* love him," Anna said.

"I haven't the right to that love."

"What do you mean?"

"He is living with a young man in Paris. He is happy."

Anna leant back and closed her eyes. Her face twitched as if a nerve had been caught. After a short while, she opened them, and there was a look that seemed to deny what he had said.

"I see," she said simply.

"His lover's family is Algerian. I believe they met during a bad period Greg was having in Paris."

"This will pass, Nick. I know it. I am sure Greg knows it, but—"

Nick interrupted and said, "We have had long talks on the phone. He rings me as often as he can. François, the man he is with, knows of our friendship and how close we are."

"And does he know how much you love each other? I think he must be very stupid if he does not."

"Anna, I cannot break it up—"

"It will come of itself. It will happen. Most loves that seem eternal are as fake as the romantic music we listen to. It is all a legacy from Wagner and *Tristan and Isolde*. A *Liebestod*, and yes, there is a death, but it is the death of a wrong kind of loving. How many years and experiences of my own have taught me that? Love is not an aria at the end of an opera, Nick. So many believe it is, only to realise that such emotions have their duration."

"You have never spoken of your relationships." Nick looked at her intently.

"No, and I never will. I ran away too often from them. Was it cowardice? Or was it a sort of deliverance from feelings that would outgrow themselves? This I cannot answer. I know love is a long waiting, and that love as it was held out to me lacked patience." She paused and shook her head. "So long ago," she whispered. "But you, Nick, in your impatient way, have been patient. Look at the past years—this almost monastic life you have lived. It speaks for itself. Greg has been in the lighted shadow of your life. Glimpsed perhaps in a peripheral way, but you have glimpsed, haven't you?"

"Anna, I feel naked with you. How do you see what I fail to see?"

"You came for a good meal and a long talk this evening. It may be the last we will ever have in such depth, and some things you will temporarily forget. But Greg? No. Him you will not forget, nor the way I have juggled the kaleidoscope to make you perceive another pattern. Now it just remains to be played out."

There was silence after this, and Anna got up slowly. She looked as if she was in pain, that the pain had suddenly hit her. She looked startled, and Nick thought he saw fear, but then her features resumed their normal expression of smiles and a need to give.

"I will wrap this canvas for you. Give it to me. I'll be back in a few minutes."

"Anna, you looked as if you were in pain!"

She waved her hand in a gesture of dismissal.

"Of course. I am growing old. What else should I expect?"

"But—"

"No more about it. Now, give me the canvas."

The parting came swiftly then. The canvas was wrapped and protected, and Anna slowly led Nick to the front door. The warmth outside had gone. The night was cold. After they had embraced, Anna said, "You won't forget Bart, will you? I really do want to see him."

"I won't forget," Nick replied, and the door closed. Soon its familiarity would be familiar no more. Strangers hands would turn the key in the lock, and it would be another place. Nick held his painting close to him as if protecting himself from this thought. He knew the vision of the rock pool would have to suffice; her legacy of a world, secret and yet exposed, rich with life in darkness and in light.

It was hard for Nick to come to terms with the *real* world after the ideal universe of Anna's studio. The rock pool was singular, and now he saw it as a person and no longer a cavity in which creatures of the sea mingled and where seaweed glowed even greener beneath the light. He saw this now as the self with its own multiple inhabitants, like change of thought and darting flashes of memories. He saw himself as being that place, open to others but aware that it will be closed over by water. He was not happy about mingling with *other* rock pools, of becoming lost again when Anna had centred him and made him whole. He dreaded the invasion of others and the clash of memory meeting memory and of actions confusing him. But slowly, the centre that he had become with Anna's friendship ebbed away, and it was with resentment that he heard the front door open and Karel call his name.

"I am downstairs," he called back.

"It's cold for this time of year. Are you in the garden?"

Nick did not like being questioned about where he was, where he *exactly* was. No, he was sitting at the kitchen table, at the long table, with a book in front of him, propped up against a white jug. Should he shout these details back? No, he was polite.

"I am—I *was* reading."

"I'll be down in a minute. I feel really cold. Could you put on some coffee?"

"Yes," he said and got up to do so. Confusion descended like a dark cloud. "I am not for Karel," he said to himself quietly. "He is for someone else. Not me."

Karel came down the stairs, and Nick looked at him. He was so handsome in some new clothes (no doubt bought in London) that he felt an itch of desire. He wanted him. He wanted him, and at the same time, he did not want it to be intimate. Like a small ship that has lost its moorings, Nick drifted away, drifted into an ocean of confusion. Karel absorbed his physical desire like a leech. He used this word in his mind and thought of the old horror films he saw when he was young, the vampiric mouth emerging to seduce. These images banged about in his brain and then were brought up short; I love Karel. I am no longer *in* love with Karel, but I do love him.

"You are deep in thought."

Karel came up from behind and put his arms around Nick's waist.

"Where were you?" Nick asked.

"With a Czech friend. I should have rung, but there was no phone in her house. She is paranoid about phones. She has suffered a lot. Don't ask me more."

So when did you have time to buy the new clothes, Nick thought. And wasn't there a public call box to ring from?

"I won't ask anything more," he said.

"Did you worry?"

"Was I meant to?"

"Nick, if you are angry with me. Don't be. I had no thoughts except for her."

"I hope you helped her."

"Are you being sarcastic?"

Nick did not reply, but as his erection hardened, he knew he would give in to Karel and that the need to give in would be futile to resist. Karel would suck his cock into him, enclose it in the narrow channel of his anus, and he would cry out as Nick came. Or would he want to fuck him? Karel had not asked since he had been back, but Nick knew that he liked to fuck. Karel gripped him more tightly, and with a force of will he thought he did not have, Nick moved away from Karel's grasp.

"I can't," he said and sat down again at the table.

"Nick, this is anger. I know you feel it. What did you imagine I was up to in London? That I had shacked up with someone else?"

Turning the pages of his book at random, Nick breathed in hard. There was a suffocating feeling in his chest. He looked at one of the open pages and saw the word *sadness* and loudly slammed the book shut. Karel made his way towards the stairs, and as he was about to go up, Nick called out to him, "I apologise. I have been on edge, and yes, I have been worried about you. You being shacked up, as you crudely put it, was not my main thought."

"Then what was?" Karel asked, turning and going back to the table to sit down beside Nick.

"That you were in danger because of what you've been through these past few years." He realised he was scrambling about for a reason that had nothing to do with jealousy.

Karel reached out for Nick's hands and covered them with his own. "I apologise as well. To be honest, I never thought you would be worried about that."

"But it could have been real, couldn't it? What I felt? What I feared concerning your safety?"

"I can assure you, Nick, I am in no danger."

"I should believe that, and yet—" He stopped the sentence. He knew he should not probe, that he had to accept the silence concerning those years in Czechoslovakia. He withdrew his hands as a sign of retreat. "I must respect your freedom in this house, Karel. I want you to believe that."

"It is strange, isn't it, that word *freedom*?"

Karel looked at Nick intently as he asked this.

"Yes. A heaven or a hell."

"What does it mean for you?"

"Being oneself and being content with the self. Not to cling. Not to be possessive. To cling to anything too hard is a form of slavery, and eventually, there has to be loss."

Karel stood up and went to get a glass of water. He was silent, and turning, Nick saw his back and how rigid he was, as if he were holding something in that wanted to get out. The glass of water was poured, but still, he remained in the same fixed position. Nick wanted to shock him into movement.

"I must tell you something, Karel. Greg rang."

"Oh."

"He is going to come, from late July until my birthday. A reunion. Bart as well. They are still in Paris, but not together. Greg has a lover."

Karel did not reply to any of this and said, "The clouds are clearing. Maybe it will be fine today."

Nick went to him then, and as he reached the sink and stood alongside him, he saw that he was silently crying.

"Are you upset about this?"

"I will be happy to see both of them," and then, moving away, Karel began to pace the room.

"But the tears?"

"Remembering. Lost times. That's all."

"Do you care about them?"

"Yes. Of course I do. My time with Greg in London, and then here in Brighton, and that poem of Bart's about Prague. They will always be enduring memories for me, and to use that word *love*, I still feel it." He paused and then added, "The only thing is, I haven't seen either of them since I left this house. I don't know how they feel about that, even now, years later. I ran away, and I ran from explaining why, only letting you know I was in Paris by letter, not having the courage to ring any of you and tell you. It seems I know how to run away from important loves and important needs."

For a moment, Nick thought Karel was about to open up to him, but after a while, he changed the subject, and Nick knew that he would not. He looked at his watch and asked Nick whether he would like to go out that afternoon. It was midday, and Nick replied it was a good idea.

"The seashore, or shall we take the bus up to Devil's Dyke? I like it so much up there."

"Yes, let's do that," Nick said. "It's especially beautiful on the Downs beneath the open sky and away from the crowds. They never venture far from the pub. It will be good for us."

"I'd better change my clothes," Karel replied. "Put on something warm. Shall we take a blanket so we can sit down somewhere?"

"Fine. There's a spare one in the second bedroom. While you're doing that, I'll make sandwiches and a flask of coffee."

Karel went back upstairs, and Nick heard him go to the record player in the living room. He put on some Brahms—the *Alto Rhapsody*. Nick stood listening to the words:

Oh, who will heal the sorrows
Of he for whom balm turns to poison?
Who drank hatred of men
From the full cup of love!

Nick had always found this to be Brahms' most searing music, as if he had used those words and sounds as a scalpel to open up his inner self. Nick's hands trembled as the music drew to its close, and he cut himself as he sliced the bread. Putting his finger to his mouth, he sucked on the small wound. How right, he thought, that I too should bleed, and how thick the blood feels on my tongue. He longed at that moment to take Karel into his arms, to ask forgiveness for his failure, for his retreat from truly connecting. He searched for a plaster and put it on. After the music stopped, there was silence.

"Why did you choose that?" he asked when Karel returned dressed in black jeans and a dark grey sweater. His face, pale in contrast to the clothes, stared back at him.

"I needed to," he replied simply. "I will tell you why when we are up there on the Downs."

"Can I hold you for a moment?" Nick asked.

Karel approached him slowly, and gently Nick hugged him. He felt a slight shudder go through Karel's body as if he recognised the difference of this embrace and showed it in the reaction of his flesh. Then Nick slowly drew away, and as he did so, he kissed Karel on his forehead.

"That kiss felt like a strange blessing," Karel murmured.

"Did it?" Nick replied.

"Yes. Not a goodbye, but a prelude to a goodbye. Are you letting me go, Nick? Tell me."

"No, just the opposite. To hold you closer. You must know I will never want to say goodbye to you. Whatever happens, we must keep what is between us."

Karel's eyes filled with tears.

"I felt as if some unspoken message was being passed between us, something we could not say with words. I thought of farewell, and you thought of a continuing union. How can both be the same, and yet it appears that they were? Our two messages embracing and being one."

"Love," Nick replied, and the word was so much more. He could not add to it, neither could he subtract from it. He had spoken the word hoping that Karel would know it had a depth and a height that was inexpressible. Karel responded by caressing Nick's cheek gently with his fingers.

"Yes," Karel said and withdrew his touch. As he started to put the food Nick had prepared into his knapsack, he glanced down and saw the plaster on Nick's finger.

"You've had an accident. Not deep, I hope?"

"No, not deep," Nick replied and smiled. "I'm always doing it," he added.

"Are you sure? Did you use an antiseptic?"

"You sound as if you are back working in a hospital," Nick said with a laugh.

"Maybe I will one day. I'm almost ready to return to it. Perhaps it is the real me—to care for those I do not know."

Nick did not answer, and after finding a light coat, he was ready to leave.

The bus to Devil's Dyke was not busy. The weather was too uncertain for that. They sat on the open-top upper deck, and the wind caught their faces. As the bus reached the end of Dyke Road, there was a magical opening out. The Downs unfolded before them, and the impact of this other world, so distinct from Brighton's turmoil and stress, was enough to make them both gasp.

"Why is it always so new, so fresh and alive up here? It's as if everything is transformed. I always feel it, and yet each time I come here, it's like the first time." Karel's face looked ecstatic as he said these words, and Nick, in reply, placed his hand on Karel's.

"We have left it all behind," Nick replied, "like going out onto the open sea,"

"Yes, yes. It is exactly that. The open sea."

Nick watched as Karel opened his mouth, drawing in the air. The wind had reddened his face, and he looked very beautiful.

When they arrived at the Dyke, they avoided the pub and immediately took the chalk path, and after passing through a few gates, made their way along the timeless track. Pieces of chalk were scattered alongside. How long had they been there? Nick always wondered that, as if each rock represented eternity. He knew the answer to his inner question. It was beyond time and would remain for as long as the earth existed. Often he wanted to pick up a piece and take it back, but his instinct forbade him to do so. Their unique selves could not be carried away, and if they were, he felt the stones would burn in his hands until they were returned. He watched as Karel bent down to touch the chalk.

"If we continue beyond the gate ahead, we can turn inwards and find that place which sees neither the Weald nor the sea."

"Yes. It's very special there," Nick said, remembering how on that part of the Downs, in a fold, the view held no other distraction but itself.

Karel straightened up, and they continued walking. Then quite suddenly, as they navigated a narrow point where the path dipped into a hollow, a lark flew up in front of them. It astonished both of them it was so near. They paused, amazed, listening and watching as it rose, its song like no other. Neither of them had ever seen a lark rise so closely. They listened to the complex, entwined sound as the lark, in its polyphony, ascended from grass to heights and then, in circling haste, plunged back down.

"Have you ever—?" Karel began.

"No," Nick said, "never that close. It seemed almost to rise up from ourselves it was so near."

In the distance, they could hear other larks, but it was not the same. The song they had heard had been theirs, and they knew it, and it would probably never happen again. Walking on, they did not talk but gazed about them; at the Weald below in all its fertile richness, and at their destination; that hollow of grass and flowers, where the world of man disappears completely.

"We are here," Karel said with a sigh. "A few more steps, and we will be enclosed in peace."

"Let's make it further down, right into the dip, where everything is open and yet hidden."

They reached the place, and Karel took the blanket and food out of his knapsack, finally the flask of coffee.

"Shall we lie down for a while side by side?" he asked, looking at Nick. "I am not hungry yet. Are you?"

"No."

Karel stretched out and patted a place beside him, and as Nick joined him, they both looked up at the sky. There were clouds passing across the sun, casting shadow over shadow on the seemingly endless roll of unmarked earth. There were no shrubs, no gorse, only meadow. A bee settled close to them, drank nectar from the wildflowers, and then flew away.

"This is what life *should* be," Karel murmured.

"It *is* like this. At its heart, it is. We forget that, back there."

"I don't feel like the same person at all. Nick, it's not us back there, so close to jealousy and conflict, it's not us at all, but two solitudes—oh, how did Rilke put it?"

"*Love consists in this: that two solitudes protect and touch and greet each other.*"

Nick had read those very words from *Letters to a Young Poet* the night he left Anna.

"Yes, that's it. How you remember the important words, Nick. I have always loved that in you. The essential."

For a while, they said nothing. The sun came out, and Karel closed his eyes. Nick, turning, looked at him. He knew he was at peace and that this valley of downland had worked its magic once again. He closed his eyes also. They were surrounded by sound, sounds so pure they blended with the silence without breaking it. Then, at last, it was time to wake from the dream, and Karel gently roused him as if from sleep.

"I was elsewhere," Nick said. "I was inside all of *this*. Were you?"

"Yes," Karel replied, "but now it is time to eat."

They ate slowly and drank the coffee. It satisfied their thirst but was in its way a reminder of the life beyond this space: the life and the ways of men, familiar and yet alien.

"Nick, I want to tell you about the Karel we left behind in that world below. Brahms encouraged me to be brave. That's why I put it on."

"I sensed there was a reason," Nick said. "It is not music that can be played for what the world calls pleasure. It has *meaning*."

"And freedom," Karel added. "It helped give me the freedom to release myself from this cycle of self-loathing I am in."

They lay side by side, and Nick made no comment. He did not want to intrude or prevent that opening up of the self in Karel he was hoping for. It was a few minutes before Karel began.

"I will try to tell you what happened in Paris. There is so much to say, but I will try to be as succinct as possible."

He paused, and Nick heard him take in a deep breath.

"I did not go to Czechoslovakia. I never left Paris."

Nick was surprised and shocked at this revelation but said nothing.

"The day after I arrived at the hotel in Paris, I was seated for breakfast, and a waiter came over to me and said there was someone who wanted to talk to me. He made a gesture with his hand towards a man near the window. I got up and went over, and the man introduced himself. His name was Milan, and after I had sat down, he explained he was the intermediary between myself and those who would get me a passport. He was Czech. He then asked me up to his room and said he would show me his identity to prove who he was and that I was to do the same."

"So they knew what hotel you would be at?"

"Yes, I made contact before I left England. They gave me

the address of the place and told me to wait."

"But wasn't that dangerous? Making contact from here? And how did you do it?"

"I made several visits to London at the time. I cannot say more. I met certain people—"

After this, Karel was silent. Nick raised himself up and looked down at him. "Go on. Please carry on," he said and then lay back again.

"Milan was nice to me and asked various questions. Convinced that I was sincere in wanting to get a passport, he told me I would have a new name chosen for me but that I would not know that name until the passport was placed in my hand. He added that he would be the one to do that."

"How long did it take?"

"I never received it. I will tell you why. Two days later, I did something that was forbidden. I knocked on Milan's door and heard a voice raised in alarm. I have no idea what happened in my head, but I knew I had to get inside that room. So I opened the door. Milan was standing there, and with his back to me was a young man. Milan shouted at me to get out, but the young man, stammering out the words, said it was alright for me to stay, that I should look at him. His English was good, and he had only a slight Czech accent. Milan calmed down, and as the door was still open, he closed it behind me, this time turning the key in the lock."

"Did he leave the key in the lock so you could escape in case of—?" Nick began, then put the remainder of the question aside.

"I didn't think about that. I knew I was safe. I don't know why, but I trusted Milan. I think he was a good man. There was no fear in the situation," he paused, "but there was horror." Karel's breathing suddenly became laboured. Nick was worried and told him not to say anymore if it was upsetting him too much. Karel shook his head and then continued. "The young man's face was scarred. His features were almost totally disfigured. I could also see that he was blind. After a while, he began asking me questions; whether I knew what was happening inside Czechoslovakia and what it was like being an enemy to the regime. Horrified though I was by his face, I replied that I only knew vague details, which was true. He sat down on the bed in the room and asked me to sit beside him. He said to me, 'You have seen my face. This is what they did to me when I was captured. I endured hours of torture. I passed out many times with the pain, and I was unconscious when they blinded me. They did this because I did not and would not betray anyone to them. I did not utter a word all through the pain.' I started to shake when the young man told me this and asked how he had managed to resist their demands. 'By willpower,' he replied to me and then added that he had expected to die anyway. Inwardly, he said, he had felt strong. He wanted to die just to get out of it. We were all silent in the room after that, and Milan looked pale and ill. He kept wiping his forehead, which was covered in sweat. Then the young man continued. He explained they had stopped short of killing him and that for days he was left locked in a room. It was on the fourth day that he was taken forcibly from the room, and someone whispered into his ear, 'You are leaving. Leaving for good.' He then said, 'I thought this man's voice meant death, and suddenly I felt the unexpected. My so-called strength left me. I became desperate to live. I tried to resist. I screamed. They knocked me out, and I remained unconscious until I woke up lying face downwards beside a road. I don't know for how long I was there. Cars sped by. Eventually, one stopped. The driver was a woman, and she told me I was over the border. Was she there to meet me? I will never know. Were the men who came for me torturers or rescuers? Again, I will never know. There are many with divided loyalties in my country.'"

Karel's voice sounded choked, and Nick told him to take his time or to stop. He also said that there was plenty of time for him to continue with this story on another occasion.

"No, let me continue. Then the disfigured man told me more about what was happening in Czechoslovakia. He told me of those thrown alive from windows and of other tortures too appalling to describe. I got up from the bed, muttered an excuse and left the room. Milan called me back, but I was about to pass out and needed a strong drink. In the quiet of the hotel bar, I made my decision to *not* accept the passport or escape from the situation I was in. I was a coward, Nick. I could not face the possibility of torture."

"Did you see this man, Milan, again?"

"No, I left the same day. I had been told in England that if I decided not to go through with it once I was in Paris, that I would never get another opportunity. I would cease to exist for them. I was also told in England that once I had changed my mind, the intermediary, who of course was Milan, would tell others, if asked, that I was in Czechoslovakia. Under no condition would they allow my fears to be admitted to anyone in case it would put others off."

There was a long silence, and the sky above was now covered in cloud. Karel continued to stare up at the sky and then cried out, "Oh, God, I wanted so much to go there, but after seeing that face, I panicked. That panic will stay with me for the rest of my life." Karel turned to Nick and, openly crying, said, "I was afraid. I was afraid of pain I could not have endured. But that young man *had* endured it. It had happened to him, so why not me? Why not me?"

Nick caught him in his arms and hugged him to him.

"I would have done the same thing, Karel. Believe me, I would have done the same thing. I could not have endured the risk of it happening to me. Maybe it is good to be a hero, but what good did it do this young man? Disfigured and sightless."

"He doesn't feel shame," Karel murmured. "He was brave. Only cowards feel shame. And before his eyes were destroyed, he *saw* his native country. Now I probably never will. Or perhaps when I am very, very old."

Nick kissed Karel and told him not to condemn himself.

"You must not feel shame for saying no to something so unbearable."

"Nick, for me, it's the terrible fact of losing the one place that in my heart I feel I could have loved. All because of a reaction of panic and fear. Over and over again, I tell myself maybe I would have survived in Czechoslovakia, that maybe I could have done good. And instead, I deserted. So much effort spent to get contacts, to leave all of you, breaking up what we had to get to my real country, only to run away from it when I was so close to getting my passport. If I had not seen that man's disfigured face, I would have gone, but once seen—eyes empty, a mouth with few teeth, smashed out by torturers. It was too much to see!"

Nick held Karel closer and brushed his lips against his forehead. Then he gently kissed him on the mouth, "It is done, Karel, it is done. You must, in time, release yourself from this guilt. If you continue going over and over this wound, it will never heal. It will destroy you. And you are here now! It took courage to return! You understand that?"

Karel drew away and lay on his back. He laughed. A cold laugh. "Courage? Do you realise how long it took me to return here? I wanted to hide. And I did. I hid away and nursed this terrible shame. I got a job as a waiter in a café by sleeping with the man who owned it. I don't want to go into details. I lived with him above that café, and I was revolted by the sex I had with him every night. I learnt French fluently. I tried so hard to make France a place I could escape into, but then one day, as I was walking along the Boulevard Saint-Germain, I saw Greg and Bart in the distance. I sensed immediately why there were there. I turned down a side street. Promise me, promise me, please, that you will *never* tell them what I have told you. I want them to believe I returned to Czechoslovakia. I don't want them to think they spent so long in Paris looking for me for nothing. Of course, when you see them, they will want to know, and I cannot bear for them to know the truth."

"Isn't that another form of cowardice?" Nick asked.

"No matter. *You* know now, and *only* you must know. I played the *Alto Rhapsody* this morning, and I realised that I could no longer remain silent about it with you, but only you. Don't betray me."

Nick turned to look at him. It was now late in the day, and shadows were forming As he stared at Karel, he thought of Hermann Hesse and *Narziss and Goldmund*. He wanted to say, you have come home, Goldmund. It is time to rest after your journey and your experiences. You have my love, and for as long as you want it, my home. But then again, he thought, the true Goldmund was Greg.

"The last bus will have gone," Karel murmured.

"Yes, I suppose so."

"Can we walk back?"

"It's miles. You'd be exhausted."

"No, really, can we walk back? I want to see the last of the light over the Downs. I can manage it."

"I can if you can," Nick replied and reached out for Karel's hands.

PART THREE:

BART

A week later, Nathan paid a visit. Karel was in the living room listening to music. He had shut himself away for nearly the whole week, not wanting to talk, and when he did, usually during meals, it was of trivialities. He had closed himself off, and Nick was sensible enough to let him be. As Nick went to open the door, he heard Karel turn up the music louder.

"What the hell is that noise?" Nathan asked.

"It's Carl Nielson. *The Inextinguishable*. A symphony."

"Don't know it. Don't like it. May I come in?"

Nick smiled.

"Not before you say *hello*."

"Hello!"

"Would you like me to ask the person playing it to turn it down?"

"You are not alone then?" Nathan questioned, a wary note in his voice.

"No, I am not. But you are welcome."

"I don't want to—"

"Please, Nathan, for God's sake, come in! We will go downstairs. And if you want to know my guest's name, it's Karel. He will probably come down when he wants to."

Nathan's skin seemed darker than ever. His brown eyes smiled, but his mouth did not.

"I made a fool of myself the last time I was here. That's why I didn't contact. I was in a strange state then. I am not now." He paused, then added, "And don't be afraid that I might fall in love with you. I won't."

"Come on down."

"Well, he can't hear us talk above that racket, can he?"

"The music will quieten down. Knowing you, you won't!"

Nathan grinned and, pushing past Nick, went down the stairs first. By the time Nick arrived, Nathan was already making coffee.

"You've only got instant," he said. "But it will do."

Nick sat at the table and watched him move. He was wearing his black boots and tight white trousers, which revealed a lot of what was beneath. Other than that, he wore only a black sweater. The whole effect was highly sexual.

"You look as if you have just come from, or are just going to Duke's Mound," Nick said sarcastically. "I suppose you know where I mean?"

"The bushes? Of course I know it—for frustrated old queens. I can get guys in the street if I want to. I don't have to go there."

"Well, you must admit you are wearing some pretty provocative trousers."

"There's nothing there that other men don't have. I just prefer not to wear underwear in warm weather. I hang better. More freedom."

Nick laughed at this, and with a groan, Nathan made a cup of coffee for both of them. He handed Nick's cup to him.

"Anyway, you've seen what I've got. It's not exactly news."

"*Good* news," Nick commented.

"Don't fucking tease me. I'm not interested anymore in what you think of my body. I came dressed like this because these clothes were first at hand."

"I'll bet."

"Smart arse. Don't flatter yourself that I dressed for you." Nathan paused and sat next to Nick on the bench. "Maybe I'm lying a little. I did feel I needed to make an impression after the way I behaved last time."

"If you go back over all that, I will throw you out."

Nathan paused for a while and then fired a question at Nick.

"Have you heard we're going to have a Gay Pride march here in Brighton? I know your ear is not exactly to the ground on gay rights, but I thought you'd like to know. The date is a secret that I will leave *you* to find out. I want to see you there."

"You'll have to come and fetch me."

"I will." Nathan nodded his head towards the stairs. "Who is *he*?" he asked.

"I told you, his name is Karel. He lived here a few years ago, along with Greg and Bart. He is living here again now."

"Lovers, eh?"

"Not exactly."

"I see."

"No, you don't, Nathan, but it doesn't matter."

"Which one of the three is he? What's he like?"

Nick felt uncomfortable giving precise details. He did not want Karel to be seen purely as part of a foursome. It seemed degrading, and Nathan would look upon him non-objectively. Plus, he knew Karel would hate Nathan thinking of him in those terms.

"He's got a Czech name, so he must be the one that got away. It's him, isn't it? Come on, if I meet him, I'm not so stupid as to say anything. I can be polite, not often I know, but I can be. Try and coax him down. I'd like to see him. It sounds as if that blasted music has come to an end."

"He's been through a lot, Nathan, and likes to be left alone. I respect that, and no, I'm not going to haul him down for you to inspect."

As he finished saying this, they heard the living room door open, and he and Nathan waited in silence to see if Karel would appear.

"I'll stand behind the table," Nathan whispered. "I don't want my trousers to give the wrong impression. I know you think I look like a whore, but I didn't expect you to have company."

"You look very handsome. Now, shut up!"

Karel paused at the top of the stairs, and a few seconds later, his legs appeared. He came down slowly, and as he did so, dressed entirely in black, which accentuated his pale features, Nathan gave a loud gasp. Karel stood there for a while. "Am I disturbing anything?" he asked. He then looked at Nathan and said simply that he was Karel. Nathan also gave his name and went to shake Karel's hand. Nick sensed an electric spark passing between them. Their hands lingered, shaking for longer than was usual, and when released, they looked bewildered, and to Nick's imagination, excited by each other.

"Come and sit at the table," Nathan said, his deep voice becoming softer and more gentle than Nick had heard before. He spoke as if he owned the house and was meeting a guest for the first time.

Nick got up and opened the rear door. He stood looking out at the garden. Bart had had the same look when he first saw Karel. He knew it well and felt suddenly afraid. Of what, he was not sure, but he felt that in some way he was not in control of the situation. He felt like an outsider.

I'm just going into the garden," he said. "There was a strong wind last night, and something blew down."

Neither of them answered back, and Nick stepped into the warmth. The sun was hot that day, almost aggressively so. He disliked the sun and its ability to burn people at will. In recent years, he had dreaded the summer, and yet with Karel on the Downs, he had enjoyed it, watching the sun emerging and then disappearing behind clouds. But there were no clouds today. The pitiless glare made his eyes ache, and he pretended to look for that non-existent something that had fallen down during the night. It was a comedy he felt he had to go through as intuition told him Karel and Nathan needed time together. It was Nathan who called him back in.

"I've been trying to introduce Karel to gay liberation. Seems that he doesn't know much about it." Nathan said, seated next to Karel at the table. For a moment, there was a glance of tenderness on Nathan's face that Nick had not seen before.

"I'm not sure I'm going to be a convert," Karel said, looking at Nick.

"He has to come and see for himself," Nathan interjected. "There *is* an alternative to the gay scene. Sussex GLF meets

Tuesdays, upstairs at the Stamford Arms." Nathan paused and then added, "Preston Circus."

"I know where it is," Nick replied, almost irritably.

Karel asked to be excused and went upstairs, murmuring as he went that he needed the toilet.

"Come back soon," Nathan whispered. It was clear to Nick that Karel would have heard him.

When he had disappeared, Nick said to Nathan, "You like him. It's clear. Clear to me, anyway. Is it clear to you?"

Nathan nodded his head.

"Well, ask him to go along with you. Have a drink. Introduce him to a few people. He really needs to meet others."

"You mean, to end his self-imposed solitude?"

"He has taken to you."

"How would you know that?"

"Because he looked at me in the same way. He chose me with the same expression. And he has chosen you."

Nathan moved awkwardly on the bench.

"I was too busy noticing him to see his reaction towards me." He paused. "Nick, I've been with quite a few guys since we last met—men who picked me up in the street—the standing and looking in the shop window routine! And I can assure you I never felt close to any of them. The sex was neither good nor bad, and as for my emotions, well, they were not involved. But when I first looked at him, there was a lump in my throat."

Nick knew he had to hurry as, in a minute or two, Karel would return. He said directly and quickly, "Don't hurt him, Nathan. I mean it. I have my reasons. Go out with him, get to know him, but please do not have sex with him until you are sure there *is* emotion in what you feel and do. Let's put the word *love* aside. After all, doesn't gay liberation think one to one love is passé?" He laughed as he said this, but Nathan looked at him seriously.

"I am no fool," he said. "He's as delicate as porcelain. He could break easily. Give me credit for some psychology."

The toilet flushed, and a few moments later, they heard Karel's steps on the stairs. Nathan stood up as he reappeared. The dark and the fair—they look good together, Nick thought, and he asked Nathan if he would like to stay for a meal. Nathan readily accepted.

"I'll cook," Karel said.

"No, no," Nick replied, "leave it to me. I won't do anything special. I even think there's a bottle of wine in the cupboard. We have everything we need."

"Yes," said Nathan, looking at Karel.

"But I suggest, while I prepare the meal, that you two get some sun in the garden. The sun loungers are ready to be folded out."

"I'll burn up in these clothes," Nathan said, and I haven't got any shorts."

Nick smiled and said he had some they could use. He took them upstairs. One pair was orange, the other blue. He apologised if they didn't like the colours, but they just grinned. "Who's for blue?" he asked.

"Me," replied Karel.

"Then it's orange for you, Nathan."

As he passed the shorts to Nathan, he realised the colour would accentuate his dark skin, brown eyes, and sexual attributes. It was stupid to feel it, but he still desired Nathan and was jealous of Karel. He was sure they would be intimate before too long and that the intimacy would work.

"I'll undress in the bathroom," Karel said, glancing at Nathan before leaving the bedroom.

"You know what these looks between you two mean," Nick said, "don't you?"

"I know," Nathan replied, taking the orange shorts. He undressed, and Nick remained in the room. He did not think of leaving. It was as if he needed to see Nathan naked for the last time. He watched, as first the shirt came off, and then glanced down at the heavy balls and long cock once they were released from the white trousers. He felt his own cock stir, but Nathan was oblivious. He was soon sitting on the bed in his orange shorts, waiting for Karel.

"You are beautiful," Nick said.

"Too late. I'm taken," Nathan joked.

"Can I remind you, Karel must not be wounded? And I do mean *wound*. The pain would be too much for him."

Nathan stared up at Nick. "I saw him, and I knew I had to be, wanted to be, gentle. I am the lover in this possible relationship, and he is the beloved. Old fashioned language, I know. Didn't expect it to come out of my mouth, did you? I can tell by the look on your face. I *know* wounds! Remember, Nick, the night I cried out for a knife to restore me to the responsibility of being the Jew that I am?"

Immediately regretting it, Nick blurted out, "Karel is Jewish too."

Nathan looked startled. He stood up and went to the bedroom window. He stared down into the garden and, with his back to Nick, murmured, "So what? He is Karel. That is all I care about."

"I shouldn't have said—"

"No, you shouldn't have. He would have told me eventually. It should have come from him."

"I make mistakes," Nick replied. "Far too often!" Why had the words come? He asked himself, and there was no answer. He left the room, letting Nathan follow when he was ready and looking down, he saw Karel standing in the entrance hall. Naked except for his shorts, he looked almost slight compared to Nathan. Nick realised how much weight he had lost over the past few years. Karel looked up and saw him, and without a word, went downstairs and out of Nick's line of vision. "He has gone," Nick whispered. "He has gone from me. That was the last *real* moment between us. The link is cut, the burden and joy of holding a loved one, broken. He is already far away."

Nick entered a brief period of solitude. He tried to write but failed in every attempt. Karel was out most of the time, but they still talked for a while every day, and Nick received Karel's impressions of the Stamford Arms and the GLF group that met there. They sounded friendly, and Karel clearly liked them. Nathan came to the house sometimes, but they were more likely to meet up elsewhere. As far as Nick knew, they had not as yet been sexually intimate, but he did not ask. It was no longer his business. He hoped that Nathan was worthy of trust, and he felt that he was. In no way did Karel look troubled or hurt. On the contrary, his white pallor had gone, and his skin was now quite brown. He had gained strength.

During one of his weekly visits to the bookshop, he was given a note, sealed in an envelope. He asked James who had left it.

"He didn't want to tell me. I did ask." Before Nick could open the envelope, James asked proudly, "What do you think of the shop? I worked hard on it this last week."

Nick put the note down and looked around him. There *was* a change. The most colourful books were in the front of the shop, with the duller ones at the back. James had also transformed the cubby hole, turning it into an antiquarian section. Here he put what he called the *creaky* writers, which included early editions of Samuel Richardson, Henry Fielding and Laurence Sterne. Sir Walter Scott was in a tall pile on the floor, waiting it seemed to be thrown out.

"I agree that Scott can be put into the creaky category, but does he really need to be piled on the floor, looking like junk?"

James laughed. He was friendly, but nothing more. He was doing his job, and financially things were going well. Nick was living on increased earnings.

"Who wants to read *The Talisman* or *Ivanhoe*?"

"Children! Children enjoy Scott," Nick replied.

"Those children are long since grown up," James replied. "Can you see them ploughing through all that unedited prose? And anyway, talking of children, we don't have a children's section as such. Maybe we should introduce one. What do you think? I believe we should attract children. We could have a window of second-hand copies of what they read now."

"I have no idea what they read now!" Noticing the acid in his reply, Nick softened his tone. "Give me time to think about it, James."

"I thought, I mean, I got the impression that I was *first* to choose stock."

"Okay, James, right to correct me. Choose away. Do you *like* children?"

"Who doesn't?"

"Well—"

"I hope to have my own someday," James interjected.

Heterosexuality declared, Nick smiled and changed the subject by returning to various classics in the antiquarian section.

"The only thing I regret is that you have hidden away Richardson. Would you have done the same to Cervantes?"

"Richardson is less important."

"I disagree. *Clarissa* is a great book."

"Have you read it?"

"Yes."

"*All* of it?"

"Once again, yes."

James stared at Nick wide-eyed. Nick supposed that perhaps he was still too immature to surrender to all those pages, You had to surrender to Samuel Richardson, and James did not look the type. Nick then moved to the window.

"I didn't have a proper look at the window display," he said. Inside, he was boiling. What have you done to my cubby hole and to my memories? You are nothing but an immature, heterosexual puppy! He thought of Sarah and wondered what she would have made of all this, and going further back, long before the bookshop was his, he recalled the woman who had first got him his job there. He had already forgotten her name, but he saw her face quite clearly and the way she had seen him getting gay books from that small but significant section, a section which now James had not even thought of including.

143

He stood by the window, and *The Charioteer* came to mind. He wanted that book to be in the shop. He wanted it to be available for people like Nathan to read. He turned and asked James if he had ever heard of Mary Renault.

"What did she write?"

"An excellent book called *The Charioteer*," Nick replied and was taken up by a sudden fervour to explain. "She was a pioneer, way back in 1953, educating ignorant heterosexuals about the normality of homosexuals."

"Oh," James replied. "Did she write anything else?"

"Mainly historical novels, set in ancient Greece."

"Did she write *The Bull from the Sea*?"

"How knowledgeable! Yes, she did. Did you read it?"

"I'm afraid I didn't think it was worthwhile. Someone told me she got all her facts wrong about ancient Greece."

"Maybe she did, maybe she didn't. But she managed to educate many about homosexuality."

By now, James was looking totally bored. He rallied a bit and asked, "What about first editions of her books? Do they sell?"

"To some people," Nick replied.

This last comment prompted Nick to go and look at the first editions. There was now a small section marked *signed copies* within it, and he bent down to glance at the authors. He groaned when he saw Kingsley Amis. The selection was utterly predictable. Instinct told him to go outside to view the window display again. Part of it was devoted to Muriel Spark. James joined him, looking very proud of himself.

"Everything from *The Comforters* to *Not to Disturb*. I got a whole collection only a few days ago from an old woman in Kemp Town who wanted very little for them. It was quite a coup."

"Sounds more like a killing!" Nick said.

"I didn't exactly rob her of them."

"But it sounds as if you didn't give her a decent price. Did you underpay her?"

"Of course. Aren't you happy to have the money in your pocket?"

Nick was suddenly so angry he could not speak. He had always respected the people he bought from and paid them a good price.

"Surely you sometimes told people their books were worth less than their true value," James insisted.

"No," Nick replied, then changing the subject, he asked again about Muriel Spark. "Do you think she will sell?" He had not read her. He knew she was considered *great* by the critics and applauded by the press, but he was suspicious of fashionable greatness.

"Most will, but the Jewish book might be difficult."

"The *what*?" Nick asked, totally ignorant of what James was talking about.

"The longer one. *The Mandelbaum Gate*. Books written by or on Jews don't seem to leave the shelves. It's all the same to me."

"But it *isn't* the same to you, is it? I sense you don't think they have the same worth as other books. What about having a gay section, while we're on the subject of books that supposedly don't sell well?"

James shuffled his feet and looked awkwardly down, noticing a pile of dog shit that had recently appeared in front of the shop.

"I wouldn't know what to buy on that subject. Not many great authors, are there? I've never really thought about it."

"Well, there's Gide and Cocteau. If you like, I could make up a list for you."

"Are you suggesting I make a section?"

Nick ignored this last comment, went back into the shop and picked up the note. He had had enough of James and wanted to sack him. When James came in looking sheepish, almost as if he had been responsible for the shit outside, he stared at Nick and asked, "Have I offended you in some way? You look a bit *off* with me."

145

"You are doing fine," Nick replied icily and smiled.

"I didn't mean to infer that Jews or homosexuals were inferior, but by my experience or perhaps inexperience, I'm never sure what books are written by them or on them. Occasionally an older man may come in and ask where you are, and when I tell him you no longer work here, they look disappointed. They often say that they are looking for *special* books. Do they mean books by or about homosexuals?"

"I have no idea what they mean," Nick replied, the smile still fixed on his face. "Maybe it's books on tropical fish or birds! We did have a nature section once."

"Oh, I see."

"No, unfortunately, you don't, but it doesn't matter. You are doing a sterling job bringing in the money. I must go now. I hope the Muriel Spark books were worth it."

He left the shop with a brief goodbye, and as he closed the door, he heard James call out, "See you soon."

He knew he had to calm down, so he sat in a café along the London Road and ate a greasy meal of sausages and fried eggs. Anger had made him hungry. It was only after drowning this mess with a tepid cup of tea that he opened the envelope. It was Bart's writing. Intuition told him he was in town. He sensed that for some reason he had not dared to come to the house and surprise him. He held the letter at arm's length, not wanting to read the words. He calculated that Bart would now be in his mid-twenties. Why did he recall this so exactly when he never thought of Karel in those terms? Karel still looked so young. Perhaps he would always look young. Karel, the eternal! He read the letter. It said in simple words that Bart had returned to Brighton but that he did not want to impose himself on Nick's hospitality. The message was formal and looked cold on the page. It ended with his address—a room in Upper Gardner Street.

He went there the following day, walking up North Road and then turning right. He passed a former school and knocked on the door of a house that stood a few steps from it. The door opened at once, and there stood Bart, and he had changed. His looks were fading, and he had put on a lot of weight. His face was puffy as if he had been awakened from sleep.

"The house is small," he said without further greeting. "I live in a room upstairs. It's in a bit of a state."

"There was no date on your message. How long have you been here?"

"A while. I can just about afford it. I don't really like the street. There's a market here every Saturday that wakes me up early, but it will do."

They went up a small flight of stairs to a room that faced out onto the street. The windows were wide open, and in the distance an old Beatles song was being played loudly. *I want to Hold your Hand* wailed at them.

"I get that all the time," Bart said, sitting on the floor. There was only one chair, and he offered it to Nick. "You're just as good-looking as ever," he said. There was no expression on his face.

"You too," Nick lied.

"Yes, tell me about it!" He laughed. "I ate a lot of bad food in Paris. Not that I can blame it all on that. Drank too much as well. Talking about drink, shall we go and have a coffee somewhere. There's a café at the end of the road. I eat my meals there."

"But Bart—" Nick began.

"What?"

"Why don't you come and stay with me?" Then Nick thought of Karel. He didn't want to tell Bart about him yet. It was best that Bart continue to think Karel was in Czechoslovakia. To change the subject, as Bart had not replied to his suggestion, he asked, "Weren't you supposed to be coming with Greg?"

There was a long silence.

"He said he would follow on," Bart replied eventually. "He has problems with his boyfriend—the Arab guy, François. François almost never leaves the Barbès district, which, believe me, stinks more than even the worst places in Brighton. This room is luxury compared to what most people have to put up with there. But they have a reasonable apartment. François occasionally ventures into the rest of Paris but soon wants to return to Barbès, where he says he really belongs. His hatred of our so-called western decadence comes and goes. At the moment, he is dreading coming here. He says he knows he won't like it. As for Greg, he is faithful to him, but love? I am sure there is not much left." Bart's hands were trembling. "I need a coffee," he said and stood up.

Nick followed Bart onto the street, and they walked to the place where he had his meals. The coffee was foul, but Nick drank it down. He had no idea what to say to Bart.

"You'd better not come here again," Bart said suddenly. "The guy I share with is not exactly gay-friendly, and he knows nothing about my past."

The words *my past* hit at Nick like a blow. What was he trying to tell him? He drank the dregs from the bottom of his cup and stared at the dark rim around the side.

"What do you mean by your past?" Nick looked up from his cup, but Bart avoided his eyes.

"All that sex stuff. It's in the past." He waved a hand in the air as if dismissing an unwanted fly.

"I don't understand. Have you stopped being sexual, or have you turned to women?"

Bart laughed aloud, and Nick saw that he had two teeth missing from his once-perfect mouth. He was run down, and Nick, of course, wanted to do the *right thing* and step in to help him.

"No. I have nobody. Sex isn't everything, Nick. No one dies because of the lack of it. Food, yes. Sleep, yes. But sex? Have you ever heard of anyone dying because of a lack of sex?"

"You mean you feel no attractions?"

Bart sighed. He looked impatient.

"Nick, it's not simple, but I will try to put it simply. I do not believe in homosexual relationships or their durability anymore. Greg knows this, but I asked him not to talk to you about it on the phone. I wanted to tell you, face to face. I also don't want children, marriage or a wife. I want ideally to be far away, where I can sort out what life really means for me. I want to be apart from this world as much as possible—a bit like François, but I don't have any Barbès to go back to. I want to be in an open space. To be able to contemplate. To meditate."

"Meditate?"

"Yes, Nick, is that so hard to imagine? To be quiet? To be quiet, perhaps until the end of my life?"

Nick paused and then asked, "Do you still write?"

"Oh, yes."

"Poetry?"

"Yes."

"I am glad."

"But they're not for publication. I don't even think of that. I want to get as close as I can to that something else—that something else that is so out of reach for so many people and yet is there."

After a short pause, Nick asked, "Do you mean God?"

"It's a word like *love*. God. Love. Some call it the same. I think they are just convenient words to simplify what is *really* beyond our vision. I don't know as yet what that thing is. Maybe I will never know. I avoid most people because I realise they have no need, no desire to go beyond their flesh, beyond their selves."

"You sound a bit like Anna. She would understand you."

"How is she?"

At the mention of Anna's name, Bart's face came alive. He was eager to know about her. Nick remembered Anna's request.

"She wants to see you, Bart."

"Really?"

Bart leant forward, his head resting in his hands on the table, and gazed at Nick as if Nick were about to open a wonderful door. For the first time that afternoon, Nick saw hope in his face.

"Yes, she asked me to tell you." He then told Bart of the fears he had for her health and how reticent she had been to go into details. Bart looked at him, and his face went pale.

"That is her right, isn't it Nick? All of us have our secrets. They belong to no one but us. I have a feeling you sense she is very ill. Do you mean she might be close to death?"

"I never spoke of death," Nick replied. "I will give you her number—"

"I have it already," Bart interjected. "I'll call her."

Nick wanted to talk about something else as he felt uncomfortable talking about Anna. He had meant to tell Bart that she had bought a house in the Orkneys, but he no longer felt he had to. Anna would tell him if she wanted to, and all the time at the back of his mind was the piercing realisation that Bart had changed! Changed, both outside and inside, and he felt he was now talking to someone he no longer knew. This knowledge bit into him sharply. He had loved this man, or the youth he had once been. He recalled their first meeting at his poetry reading, and the way Bart had come to him, and later how they had gone to a tea shop full of elderly women. The desire had been strong then, and even when Greg returned with Karel and talked about the sexual healing that Karel needed, he had to ask Bart's permission first and consolidate that permission by the four of them meeting up. Anna had chosen Bart then. She had in her own way loved him at first sight. The pieces of the past fell into place like a jigsaw puzzle of destiny completed. Nick withdrew into himself and stared vacantly down at the plastic table and the soiled cup.

"Do you want to walk?" Bart asked.

Mechanically, Nick replied that they could go and sit in the Pavilion Gardens. Without speaking, they walked back along Upper Gardner Street and then on to their destination, where Nick bought them both another coffee from the outside café. They moved away from the crowded chairs and tables and sat on the ground by a tree. It was an awkward spot, but Nick was

150

glad to rest his back against the bark. They stared across at the Royal Pavilion.

"It's a nightmare that building," Bart commented. "A travesty of India on the outside, and a crime against China on the inside."

"It's its own world," Nick replied.

"A pleasure house," Bart said scornfully. "Only that."

Nick noted the censorious tone that appeared to reflect Bart's rejection of sexuality. He wanted to know more. The jigsaw puzzle of his own relationship may have been completed with Bart, but the image was now blurred.

"How did it happen," he asked.

"What?"

"This turning away from human desire, and even pleasure?"

Bart did not look at him but spoke slowly. "I can't be sure. I was in love with a man and went to live with him. His name is not important. He left me, and I was left alone. While I still had my looks, I enjoyed the freedom of having sex with others. And yet, there was a remoteness in what I was doing, as if I were outside myself, watching the sexual act. This sensation or impression, call it what you like, recurred over and over again. I had my own room and a feeling of financial security. On the surface, I had nothing to complain about."

"I stopped sending you money," Nick said, with a sense of guilt.

"As you should have done. No, I had to go my own way. Greg had gone his, and with Karel in Czechoslovakia, I was now alone and responsible for myself. I drifted into jobs, and like a stranger in any foreign land who has no rights, I did the most menial. I cleaned people's houses in places like Auteuil. It was ironic because, during those first months in Paris with Greg, I taught English to a girl called Agnès there. She fell in love with me. Now as I cleaned the floors in her *quartier*, I wondered how she would perceive my situation and why I had chosen to wipe clean the dirt of others!"

"Couldn't you have returned to teaching?"

"No, I wanted to do the simplest of things. When you clean, you are alone with yourself. No one speaks to you. I was just the human object who polished tables and took out the garbage. It is always assumed that this is a woman's job, usually women from foreign countries, but women of wealth like to see *men* do their dirty work for them. They ignored me and watched me, but I became oblivious to their sexual gaze. I went further inwards, and amusing though it may sound to you, it was while scrubbing out a toilet bowl that I thought of retiring from the world. I *wanted* inner solitude. I no longer cared if they observed what they thought was my degradation. I was within myself, and once out of their buildings, my only vice was eating. As I said, I ate bad food because I chose to. I think I had the desire to get fatter, to lose my physical attraction. In this way, I hoped to become even more invisible. I couldn't afford dental check-ups, or rather I chose not to afford them, and I lost some of my teeth."

"But surely something in you cared about this loss?"

"No."

Bart got up and stretched.

"It's terrible to hear this," Nick said.

Bart stood over him and looked down. "Why?" he asked. "By then, I had given up on the gay world. I'd even given up wanking. It was a sign to me that I was finished with my sexual self. But I'm not going to lie. I did see young men I would have desired, from a position even more remote than when I was having sex with them. I looked at them with a lost desire."

Nick shook his head as if trying to deny what he was hearing.

"Only a few years ago, you loved me. You loved Greg, and above all, I think you loved Karel. Did you never think of returning to Brighton and to me?"

"What an ego!" Bart said, and then he laughed with a fierce tone in his laughter. "To return to your cobweb house where all four of us were caught? Caught by the spider of love? No thank you, I did not want to return to that. I had my aloneness. Not lonely. Alone. I looked upon that past we made with—" and here he paused.

"Go on," Nick said, standing and facing him. "With what?"

"Forgive me for what I have just said. There is still cruelty within me, even now. I did love all of you. I did love. I was happy in that cobweb. It enclosed me, and I felt at home in it. I did not see love as being a spider of desire—a metaphorical creature with many legs, just as we had so many legs of love and passion."

"Stop," Nick said, not bearing to hear more. He began to walk away from Bart down the path that led towards the Pavilion. Bart hurriedly followed him.

"Nick, don't run away," he said. "I need to find the peace I know is within me and for it to be complete. Complete as my poetry and as singular."

Nick stopped walking. He was now outside the gardens and facing the statue of George IV. "What do you want of me?" he asked.

"I want you to be here but not to see you too often. I want us to meet always outside, except when it comes to your birthday. I will be there with the others. Until then, no one else must know I am here or how I feel about my life and the dead passions I carry around with me. I hope I have the courage to say as little as possible to them."

"Even to Anna?" Nick asked, glancing quickly at Bart. "We do not change as much as we think, Bart."

"That's your belief. Not mine."

"What about your family?"

"They no longer speak to me. I lost their love while I was in France. Please don't let's talk about that."

"I am sorry."

"Yes," Bart said, and his face seemed to darken. Nick saw his despair. Gently he asked Bart to promise him that they would meet several times before his birthday. "I promise," he said, and turning away, he walked back into Pavilion Gardens.

Nick made his way home and felt a deep sorrow. The

summer and its naked sky overwhelmed him. Once more, the sun had come out. There were no clouds of protection, and yet despite the heat, he was cold.

Soon after, Nick went to London to help James at a book fair. The choice was dull, and they bought very little. He had planned to stay overnight in an hotel but instead returned late to Brighton the same day. As he entered the house, he heard moaning upstairs. It was the cry of sex, and he realised at once that Karel had brought Nathan back assuming that Nick would not return. They had not heard him enter, and the cries continued. His reaction was one of anger and a sense of betrayal. It was a gut reaction, and like all gut reactions, it had an unreasonable aspect to it. He listened, anger mixed in with a desire to listen, to be a part of it. He wanted to hear the sounds of sexual climax. He heard them. Karel shouted out the words "Harder, please harder," and Nick knew then that Nathan was inside him. "Now you. Now you," replied Nathan's voice. Nick felt his own excitement rise and wanted to come himself. He was tempted to masturbate there in the hall, but instead, with a denial that he forced upon himself, he turned on the hall light. He knew they would see it under the chink in the door. They were in the second bedroom, not the main one. At least they had not used his bed. He went into the living room and waited. A quarter of an hour later, there was a knock on the door. Nathan came into the room.

"I suppose you want an apology."

"Is that a question or a statement?" Nathan smiled and said nothing. "No, Nathan. I don't want an apology. I just hope that next time, if there is a next time, you ask me."

"Why?"

Nathan crouched on the floor in front of Nick, who was seated on the sofa. Nick felt that he looked prim, sitting on that sofa and was conscious that his mouth was clenched very tightly. He stared hard at Nathan, who was still smiling.

"You're laughing at me, aren't you?" he said eventually.

"In a way, yes. In the first place, if you had stayed in London tonight as you had planned, you would never have known. In the second place, we are in love with each other, Karel and I, and it is really *our* business to consummate our love."

"But maybe not here," Nick replied.

"Why not here? You have asked Karel to live here. It's his right to bring me back."

"Deceitfully?"

"Only in the sense that he felt he had to, that if he had asked, you might have said no, or that it was somehow tasteless. You've been Karel's lover. He is very aware of that, and also aware that using this house may be some sort of betrayal."

"So, he *does* think it is a betrayal."

"I convinced him it was not. I cannot take him to my home, and why should we tempt fate by making love on the beach or in a park? Those would be the only places we could go. Of course, if you had said no, we would have waited longer. But waiting too long can subdue. The time was right for us. In fact, it has been for a while, and when this opportunity arose, I persuaded him. He dreaded your coldness, your jealousy."

Nick was silent for a moment after this outburst and then asked, "And are you both happy now that you *know* each other?"

Bart stood up.

"Don't be sarcastic, Nick. Don't look at us as if sexuality has passed you by. Sitting there, you are like some dusty book left on the shelf of your bookshop for far too long."

"Well put! Maybe I am. I was accusing myself recently of having assumed a certain primness. Something out of *Cranford*. Have you read *Cranford*?"

Nathan laughed and came and sat next to Nick. "Don't be so smug. Smile, please! Try to be happy for us. We are happy, you know. Don't ruin the feeling between us. We both care enough for you to feel hurt if you are hostile." He paused then and added, "Do you think I'm not intelligent enough to see that you are frustrated sexually?"

Nick felt the closeness of Nathan's body to his. He still desired that body, but nothing Nathan said would make him admit it. Instead of answering this question, he adopted another tactic.

"You haven't hurt Karel in any way, have you?"

"No, Nick. In no way. Neither physically, emotionally, or mentally. Truly we were ready for this to happen. Our feelings for each other are mutual."

"So, why is Karel hiding from me? Why didn't he come down with you?"

"Unlike me, he is having a bath. For some reason, he wants to be clean when he sees you. There is an unspoken anxiety in him that makes him want to be clean for you. As for me, I do not have that anxiety. I am just the same as when we left the bed."

Nick, in his mind, saw the dried sperm on Nathan, and smelled the dried sweat and heat that follows orgasm. He moved away from Nathan and stood at the window, facing the blind.

"Have you noticed," he said without turning to Nathan, "that I have yellow blinds in here? To me, yellow is the colour of clarity, or thought, however good or ugly. Yellow to me is freedom of thought."

"Nick, I am not in the mood to be drawn into pretentious abstractions," Nathan replied.

"Then go down and make us all some coffee. I will join you and Karel, and please ask him not to remain upstairs."

"Alright."

With this comment, Nathan left the room, and Nick listened to him go down the stairs. He told himself not to be a fool and that whatever he felt consciously or subconsciously was not to be inflicted on Karel. He had, in his way, inflicted it on Nathan, but he could not do the same to Karel. The yellow blinds in the house did incite analysis. They did, in a way, make him realise that it was not Karel he desired any longer, but Nathan. Not love, but lust, and the thought disgusted him as well as making him unhappy.

As Nick came down the stairs, Nathan was seated at the pine table with three mugs of coffee in front of him. He stared up at Nick.

"Karel is having a very long bath!" Nick said.

"Don't be sarcastic again."

"Observation." He paused. Then he said quickly, almost unaware of what he was saying, "Now, can we all make peace? You are perfectly welcome to spend nights here together whenever you want."

"When did you decide that? A moment ago?"

"As it happens, yes. If I am in a bad mood or hostile, bear with me. I've had a rough time recently. Bart is back in Brighton. I promised I wouldn't tell anybody, but for some reason I cannot explain to myself, I am going to break that promise to you."

"Did he come with the other one? Greg?"

"No."

"Why?"

"Greg has problems in Paris. My birthday is coming up in a few months, and it was Greg's idea that we should all reunite and celebrate it. I'm not sure how I feel about the prospect of that, but I want to see Greg most of all." He paused at the table, and Nathan handed him a mug of coffee. Taking it, Nick gulped some down. It burned his throat. The coffee was too strong. "I lied," he said. "It's not only you I have told about Bart. Greg knows."

"And Bart?" Nathan asked. "Where is he? Is he coming to live here as well?"

Nick shook his head. "His private life is his own, and he wants to keep to himself, but he has chosen to come to the reunion. We have a friend, Anna, and I hope she will join him too, but I fear that she won't. She's going to live at Kirkwall, in the Orkneys. She has bought a house and is leaving Brighton. I know that when Bart knows this, it will deeply upset him. He is very attracted to her and she to him."

"Love?"

Nick shrugged. He knew Nathan meant well, but he regretted having said anything. "They are special to each other. Let's just say that."

"Are you going to tell Karel?" Nick did not reply to this, and Nathan said, "Don't add anything to what Karel already has to deal with. Let Bart be a surprise at the party. Are you sure Bart has moved on from the foursome you had, or is he still attracted to the memory?"

"He is a solitary person now. It's in the past for him."

Nathan remained silent for a moment, then said suddenly, "I must tell you something. Karel has told me all about Czechoslovakia and his cowardice, which I find ridiculous. I did my best, but I can't change the bruise within him that is still there. Occasionally it shows. He is also bruised from the way he disbanded the four of you, with you being left alone after Bart and Greg left in pursuit."

Nick sat down at a distance from Nathan.

"I too feel guilt—that I did not go as well," he said. I wanted to keep a distance, and in a way, it was I who was the coward. I couldn't bear to be caught up in what I thought was a futile search, although I helped financially. I also didn't want to be ensnared in whatever was going on between Bart and Greg. That's the real reason I hid myself like a monk in the shop. The sudden return of all three of them has jolted me out of that."

"Not completely," Nathan said. "You need someone of your own."

It was then that they heard footsteps on the stairs, and Karel joined them. Maybe he had heard some of this conversation. Maybe he had not. He opened the garden door. Outside, two cats were fighting or having sex. Nick thought of the cries he had heard as he entered the house, but he welcomed Karel with a smile. Karel smiled back, but his fragility showed.

"I wanted to show Nathan my glass collection," he began, "and then, well, you know the rest."

"It's fine," Nick said gently. "Sit next to Nathan. You'll get cold standing there. It's not very warm outside, and we will all freeze if that door is open for too long."

"So we don't have to talk about it then?" he asked, closing the door.

The cats were suddenly quiet, and the night resumed its quiet pace. Nick thought, this night will be slow to pass once I am in bed. I am afraid of what will run through my mind as I lie awake.

"Nick, may we speak of something else?" Karel asked.

"Of course."

Karel came to the table. He looked at Nathan, who nodded his head and seemed to know the subject in advance.

Sitting apart from both of them, Karel began. "It is about what we are," Karel said slowly. "I mean, us both being Jewish. I want you to know that we are confronting the issue together. I owe it to you, Nick, to tell you that. I also owe it even more to Greg, but he is not here. We think it is best if we sort out the various problems we have with being Jewish, together, just between us." He paused as if he was exhausted. "It is *our* question now, and no one else's—what we think of the Holocaust and of the state of Israel. It is *our* responses to each other on this subject that are paramount. I know what Nathan has endured, and he knows what I have been through. People on the outside are just spectators, looking on, either attempting empathy or attacking with pain. Take, for example, you and Greg. Bart too. There is sympathy, and a generosity of understanding. The cruel reality that Jews in Israel can behave badly, can be monsters, only shows how thin our veneer of humanity is, but so is the veneer of liberals who are so open to rage when we behave in this way. It is as if these so-called liberals *want* us to behave in this way." He stopped, and he was panting for breath. "To cut this short, you Nick, and Greg and Bart, are simply not Jewish. Neither good Jews nor bad Jews. Nathan and I are, and our goodness is open to question even to ourselves. For example, how much am I running away from

Israel and the rest of the Jewish community? Am I running away from that in the same way that I ran from Czechoslovakia? Of course, not for the same reasons, but for the urge to assimilate—to be gentile. Don't you *see*?"

"I hope I understand," Nick said.

"I can see Karel is tired out," Nathan began. "Let me explain it in my way. What you know, you can speak of. What you don't know is best left alone. I'm paraphrasing, perhaps badly, words from another Jew. Wittgenstein. These words are right, how ever philosophy interprets them." He paused. "You see, Nick, you can speak to us as homosexuals, but not as Jews. You can speak to us like that because we are all homosexuals. But my Jewish nature and Karel's Jewish nature are different. He and I may disagree or agree on detail, but we are essentially bound to a responsibility towards our race. We have discovered that deeply since we met and loved each other. I believe in fate. Accident caused Karel to meet first Greg, and then you, and Bart followed. But fate is what binds Karel and me. And you, in a complex way, set the scene for our encounter. How can we ever thank you enough for that? I have brought Karel home to himself, Nick, and he has brought me home. We *know* what we are and what our future responsibilities are in a way you never can."

There was little to say after this, and Nick insisted they spend their first night together in the house. He hugged them at the bottom of the stairs, and they left him to think about what they had said. He felt calm suddenly, and despite the cold, he opened the garden door and went outside.

Anna rang about a week later. Her voice sounded tentative, as if she were exploring his reactions.

"Nick?"

"Anna! It's good to hear you. What is that music in the background?"

"Prokofiev. Do you like him?"

"Yes, I think so. I have heard most of his symphonies."

"I never really responded to his music before. Do you wonder why I suddenly like him?"

"Why should I wonder, Anna?"

"Well, it's not what I usually listen to—Sibelius, Mahler, Bruckner. You know."

"I do know, but it seems you think I should be surprised."

Anna laughed. It was defensive laughter as if there were something beyond Prokofiev, something else beyond discovering that she liked him. He felt it was a screen to a secret.

"It's good to discover new things," she said. "But there is something I want to talk to you about, only I cannot do it over the phone. I know this may be unexpected—" and here she paused.

"What is unexpected?" Nick prompted.

"That I should call you so late," and she then sounded distant as if she had put the phone down to listen to something or someone else other than him. Then her voice returned, and the sound of Prokofiev receded a little into the background.

"Are you alright," Nick asked.

Again the laughter. It was like the canned laughter from a television comedy series, laughter that did not exist for itself but for a forced response.

"Anna, that is not your real laugh," Nick said, and she did not immediately respond. Nick heard only the repetitive theme from what was clearly a piano concerto.

"I would like you to come round tomorrow. Not for dinner. I have to explain something."

Immediately, Nick thought of illness. Had she had a diagnosis? He dared not ask. Partly because he feared an answer he did not want to hear. Then he thought of Bart. Bart had called her, and she wants to talk about him.

"There's an urgency in your voice, Anna, that you are trying to deny. Are you feeling your way to some sort of declaration?"

"Oh, you and your active imagination!"

"But aren't I right?"

"It's just that it is eleven o'clock, and I never, ever, contact this late. I am embarrassed, and you may be doing something I am intruding on."

"Like what?" Nick laughed. "I can assure you, you are not intruding."

"So, can you come to the studio around six? That will give us lots of time. I would make food, but it would only distract." Then she contradicted herself, "No, I *will* make food. Piles of sandwiches and a few other plates of tasty things. A trifle too. That's easy."

Nick thought this list was excessive and told her so. He said he could very well have a meal at around five and that he often did so when he needed to concentrate on a book or go to a film.

"I insist," she said. "We can kind of dip into things when we feel we want to."

The triviality of all this was absurd, but behind Anna's voice, he noticed distress, a feeling that she was distracted. The music had reached its climax and stopped, and he sensed she was in some way fearful of the silence.

"I will come promptly at six," he said.

"Good. See you then."

There was the click of the phone as Anna hung up, without a goodbye.

That night, Nick had a strange dream. He was on a bus, and opposite him was this youth who had long, slender limbs and eyes shadowed by fatigue. Nick saw that he was being looked at with furtive longing. When the bus stopped, he got off, and the youth followed him. They had a brief conversation, and then, as dreams do, the scene switched to a room in a nearby house. It was a household full of other youths who walked like pale shadows, grey in form, from room to room. Occasionally he saw one of their faces close up. The same fatigue was on their faces as the youth he had met. The scene shifted again. He was undressed and lying naked on a bed in the youth's room. The youth lay beside him, looking at him with starved eyes, their pale blue blackened by shadows beneath the heavy eyelids. His whole body was languid with exhaustion, and Nick asked if he was ill. "No, it's because of masturbation," the youth replied. "That is my illness, and it will be my death. This will be my tenth time today, my tenth search for someone to share it with me. You will join me, won't you? I cannot do it alone. My cock aches. My heart aches. I want to die of desire fulfilled. Approach me and smell the ancient smell of sperm. I am composed entirely of sperm, wasted and longing to be annihilated. Give me the illusion for the tenth time today that I am still alive. Put your mouth on this cockhead, bloated with blood." And as Nick approached the full thickness of the youth's cock, he awoke. He no longer saw the image of the boy, but he smelled him as if he were nearby, as if he were in bed with him. Sperm and death are indivisible, he thought.

The next day passed slowly. Nick paced the downstairs area of the house, conscious that he wanted to communicate with someone before seeing Anna, but knowing there was no one he could approach. Five o'clock came, and he realised he had not had a bath or changed his clothes. He shrugged the thought away even though he felt scruffy in his corduroy trousers and was conscious that the green sweater he was wearing was dirty.

He knocked on Anna's door, and she opened it at once. He had the weird impression she had been standing behind it waiting.

"Come directly into the studio," she said. She was wearing a kaftan, and her hair, which had grown quite long, was piled up on her head. Even her appearance contradicted what he had known of her before.

In the studio, Nick found Bart sitting on the sofa where Anna usually sat. He looked calmly at Nick.

"Bart!" Nick exclaimed.

"Don't be surprised," Anna said quickly. "He lives here now."

Too dumbfounded to reply, Nick looked quickly around the

room. On the table, he saw sandwiches and a pink-trifle smothered with cream. He felt nausea at the sight of it.

"This is a surprise," he murmured, forcing himself to respond. So Bart was here, he thought. He was here last night when she called. The Prokofiev was his choice, not hers. The mystery of people and how they behaved was, as usual, astonishing to him.

"Can I sit on the floor? Do you mind?" he asked.

Anna smiled at him and nodded her head. She looked as much at ease as Bart did.

"Bart insisted we should tell you like this."

"Tell me what?" Nick replied, settling himself on the floor, lying back and resting his head on a large cushion.

"That Anna has asked me to move in with her," Bart said.

Anna sat beside Bart and looked at his face as he spoke.

"I asked Anna to ring you last night. A spontaneous moment of action. I sensed, if I didn't let you know today, I might leave it for too long. I've left Upper Gardner Street."

"I see," Nick said, but he felt a shock all the same. He turned to Anna.

"Have you thought this through?" he asked.

"Of course. From our first meeting, after he called me, I knew it was right."

"I don't want to pry," Nick replied cautiously, "but why do you believe it is right? Either for you or for him?"

"That is something between Bart and myself. I asked you over to give you the facts. Why we two feel it is right is our personal decision and cannot be explained so easily. It is partly emotional and partly practical. I like Bart a lot, and he likes me. He needs a permanent place, and I have it to offer."

Nick had a déjà vu sensation of being silenced. He thought of Karel and Nathan. Again, he was being excluded from the intimacy of people he had once been close to. An image came to mind. He was to look in through the window and not go in through the door.

"Shall we eat a little before going into details?" Anna asked,

164

and she seemed remote to Nick. He loved her, but she was now remote, almost gone. Only Greg remained, only Greg, but what would happen there? Was he to lose everything? Everything and everybody who had profoundly affected his life? In his early youth, there had been Martin, then Oliver and his mother; now all phantoms who only returned in dreams. Was this now to be repeated in the close-knit fraternity and passionate love that had once been Karel, Bart and Anna?

"I don't want to eat," Nick said simply.

Bart got up and, passing by him without a look, chose a selection of sandwiches. Unkindly, Nick observed that his heavy body would become heavier, and this added sadness to sadness.

"My health is poor, as you know, Nick," Anna said, resting back on the sofa now that Bart was temporarily away. "I know that in all probability I will have increasingly poor health until the end of my life. I need someone dear to me, near me, and Bart is the right person. He is—well, never mind what he is. I don't want to embarrass him."

Why couldn't she have told me this without Bart present? Nick asked himself. He felt angry. Bart, big Bart was in the way. Didn't she realise that, or was that the intention?

"I would like to know what is wrong with your health," he said.

"I know, and I cannot tell you. It's not secrecy, just too private, even for you. I love you very much, Nick, but this, shall we call it, inconvenience to my being, is now between Bart and myself. I can give you a glimpse of what I mean concerning our closeness, Bart's and mine. The other day we read aloud from the *Bhagavad Gita*. It was an illumination, passing to each other that dialogue between Arjuna and Krishna. 'Both renunciation and holy work are a path to the supreme.' How that struck home! Was it Arjuna or Krishna, Bart, who said that?"

"Krishna," Bart replied, still standing by the table of food.

Anna was now almost unrecognisable to Nick. He looked

around him. The paintings were all gone from the studio. Had that blaze of colour and form been diminished? Had it disappeared altogether? There was no smock hanging behind the door, no smell of paint. Maybe she had sent them all on to Kirkwall. He would not ask. He could only draw his own conclusions.

"Absolutely! Krishna," she said, smiling.

But Nick did have to say something, and he turned to look at Bart.

"What relation does Krishna have with Prokofiev?" he asked. "I thought they would be total opposites. There is very little renunciation in his music."

"You misunderstand him. His music is on the surface," Bart replied. "It dances. Krishna is the dance as well. Both Prokofiev's music and Krishna dance in the shadow of death."

"I'm sorry, but I find that pretentious," Nick said.

"Oh, Nick," Anna said, "don't let us argue or disagree. It is because you are so dear to us that we have told you first."

"And are you still going to live in Kirkwall?"

There was a silence when he asked this, and looking from one to the other, Nick sensed awkwardness. It was Anna who broke the silence.

"I will go on as planned. As you can see, there is very little left here. A lot has been sent already. Bart will stay on until after your birthday, and then he will follow me there."

"It's the place of peace I have been searching for," Bart added, coming forward, plate in hand, attempting to gulp down the last of the food in his mouth. "I will write, and I will find a simple job that I can do. Anna will paint images of the landscape, and above all, her beloved sea."

"So you will continue to create?" Nick asked, looking at Anna.

"Yes. Why not? I have created all my life. Do you think pain or discomfort will stop me?"

"I thought—"

"What did you think?"

166

"I saw this studio looking so bare—"

"And you drew the wrong conclusion. No, I am not going to renounce painting. It will be so good to paint what I see in that distant world and to hear the poems that Bart will write. It will be a rest and a beginning for both of us. And Bart is excellent with his hands at repairing things. There will be all sorts of jobs to be done there, and he will do them so well. He will have the adventure of a new house."

Nick saw an image of Bart again cleaning houses and also scrubbing floors.

"Is this what you truly want?" he asked Bart, who nearly dropped his plate.

"Yes."

The answer was brusque and direct. Nick knew that this man who had once been such a sexually passionate youth was seeking to abdicate all that sexuality; throw it to one side as if it were another self, like a snake shedding its skin, in an escape from the pitfalls of emotion and desire, from the whisperings after making love, and from loving making love.

"I think I have to go," Nick said, standing. He felt a burning sensation in his throat. They were beginning to torture him, and he could not bear it. He needed the air of the seafront and the chance acquaintance he might meet there. The aridity of the room was like a desert, and these two so-much-loved people had turned into shadows. He did not want to be in their presence any longer.

Anna stood and looked shocked.

"But you *can't* go, Nick. The evening has just begun."

"I know, but I am very tired," he replied, lying and yet not lying. "I slept badly last night."

"Because of my late call?" she asked.

"No, it's to do with the shop. The man I have employed is doing too much work, and I fear he will fall ill. I may have to go back part-time, and the thought gives me nightmares."

"I don't quite believe you," Anna replied. "Have either of us disappointed you?"

"Not at all, not at all. I just need sleep—an early night."

Resigned to letting him go, Anna stared ahead with a look of extreme sorrow, and in that look, Nick glimpsed desperation. She was fighting hard, no doubt at the physical sickness within, and she *did* need someone to be with her. Bart was her choice, and for whatever confused or clear reasons, Bart had accepted the role of being both her inspiration and her carer. But then, Nick thought, what do I really know?

"Bart is good," he said gently, and he meant it. After he said this, Bart came up to him and kissed him on the cheek. It was a kiss without words, and as Nick looked at him, the mask of years fell away. He saw again the clumsy youth standing before him at the poetry reading. A little shy, a little gauche, but so very attractive. The memory of need resurfaced: the need *for* Bart. But it lasted only for a few moments. It was all a dream now, that past, and he knew that he would only see Bart briefly once more, at his birthday. No doubt Bart would talk to the others who would be there, but he would also be the one to depart swiftly. In his mind, he saw Bart disappear from view.

"I really do have to go," Nick repeated. "I'm sure you will both be very happy up there. I very nearly envy you."

"Yes. A separation from all this—all that is this town of Brighton. A radical change. So much happens here to burn the spirit," Bart said.

"Join us for the holidays," Anna added, and in that sentence, the old Anna returned, the Anna he had known and that he loved so much. Perhaps she was intact after all, and he had misjudged.

"Yes," he replied, "I'd like that." But he knew he never would. The stones of the Orkney Islands, the isolation and the quietness, were not for him. It was their world, or would be, and he would not intrude. The Orkney landscape would be foreign territory to him, alien, with its flatness and ancient burial grounds. He thought suddenly of the Downs. He loved the Downs. Up there, there was always a view of the bustling world below, of the working life of the Weald. True, there was isolation, isolation he treasured so much that he resented the distant bustle of promiscuous Brighton. But beyond that resentment was the knowledge that Brighton was nearby, and once returned to, could be embraced again, however distant and unneeded it seemed up there on the Downland.

He left them. On the street, he gazed up at the window where they were, alone together, but the window was too high to look into. He walked towards the sea.

A few days later, Nick discovered he had Gonorrhoea. After he had left Anna and Bart, he had gone to Duke's Mound and fucked a man in the bushes. In the darkness, he had not even looked at his face. The man could have been any age, there in the night, as there had been no moon, and he had found the man in a particularly dark spot. He only knew that he liked the touch of his skin and that in that touch, he had found him attractive. No words were exchanged, and afterwards, all that Nick felt was that he had affirmed his sexuality and that, in a way, it had somehow been an act of pride against Bart. As he made his way home, he thought of Bart and the absurdity of Prokofiev. Why was Anna listening to Prokofiev? He realised that he was lost in that maze where the loss of people means a misunderstanding of them. He had spent an evening that he had found confusing, despite the apparent clarity that both Anna and Bart had tried to give it. His thoughts were like toothache, persistent, painful and unrelenting. He had dreams of them that night as clowns in costume, humorously trying to entertain a crowd of silent people who applauded at the end but did not laugh. In the dream, Anna said, "We have succeeded, Bart. It is all Maya and illusion, but we entertained them." Nick was drenched with sweat in the morning, then two days later, the ache in the penis and the discharge began. He felt nauseous and went to the clinic. The treatment was not as bad as he had feared, and the staff who attended to him showed no prejudice. They smiled and asked all the right questions and were not at all put out by his description of what he had done. The gonorrhoea cleared up, but afterwards, he still felt dirty and had baths twice a day. This ritual lasted for weeks. It was his first venereal disease, and it had profoundly shocked him. He looked in the mirror constantly, at his face and his penis as if waiting for a transformation. He expected, totally irrationally, to be physically changed by this event. "I will never forget this," he told himself, and like a child who cuts himself for the first time, he was amazed that it had happened and that it had happened to him. The difference was, of course, that the scar was on the inside, and despite searching for it on his face and sex, his persistent thought was that he was changed and that somehow others would see it. He was drained of energy, and whenever the phone rang, he let it ring. He feared it would be Greg with an excuse for not coming to England after all. His mind and body were in total turmoil, and he became a prisoner to himself. Karel was out most of the time and knew nothing about what had happened. Nick assumed he had found another place to sleep with Nathan. He approached Karel and asked him if this was true.

"Yes," replied Karel. "We met a guy in the pub in Preston Circus who has a spare room, and we decided to rent it from him. Nathan's got a job now, and I've been offered one up at the hospital."

"I thought Nathan was living with his family," Nick said.

"He wants his freedom just as much as I need mine. And I cannot keep on relying on your hospitality. You may meet someone—"

"Hold on," Nick replied, his anger visible. "I told you I consider this to be your home as well. If I died tomorrow, who else would I leave it to?"

Karel laughed. "You won't, Nick. You won't. And thanks for the future offer, but hopefully my previous hospital work will put me on the rung to something better, in administration for example. I confess I am a bit tired of all the blood and guts. I would also like to give Nathan a home eventually."

Nick felt faint and asked for a glass of water.

"Have you been ill?" Karel asked and went to get him the water.

Drinking the water down, the greying sensation that precedes a faint receded, and Nick shook his head. He had no desire to talk about what had happened to him.

"It's just a shock, your leaving," he said. Feeling desperately unhappy, he blurted out, "I'm not even sure I want to live here myself. I might as well sell up. I'm beginning to hate this house."

"You can't do that. And certainly not because I am going."

"Too many have gone," Nick said, his voice cracking. "I can't help this. I must tell you. Bart is back. But, he has changed. He won't come to this house, and he's moving in with Anna. Everything has moved so rapidly since you returned. Now, do you see why this house is so empty for me?"

"When did he return?" Karel slowly replied.

"A few weeks ago."

"In what way has he changed?"

"I can't explain it clearly even to myself, but he has turned away from his homosexuality. It seems he loves Anna perhaps more than any of us, and she has asked him to share her life. She was going to leave anyway. I think because of health reasons. So now they are both going to live on the Orkney Islands, in Kirkwall to be precise."

He stopped, shocked at his lack of discretion. Karel did not ask if Bart knew that he had returned. There was a momentary silence, and then Karel said, "I will stay on here until Greg returns. I don't want you to do anything foolish. Nathan will understand. This is all too stressful for you, and as a future professional of our lovely local hospital, I am going to ask you to remain calm and let things sort themselves out. The birthday will come, but can I suggest no party? I don't particularly want to see Bart, especially if he has changed as much as you say. It also might not be good for you."

Nick shook his head.

"No, Karel, I lost my head just now. I will remain here and

calm down as you say, but by myself. As for the birthday, I will keep to the event for Greg's sake. He is bringing his lover, and I want to make them welcome. And you are right to want to find a place with Nathan. He needs you, and you need him. As for this room you are staying in at the moment, I can make things better. I can easily lend you the money to rent a proper flat, and I will not want the money back until you are both firmly established in your work. I assume this man's house is more or less communal."

"Yes."

"All the more reason to have a private flat. You need the privacy it will give your relationship. Secure yourselves together and make a future uninfluenced by others. By the way, I didn't ask, but what is Nathan's job?"

Karel looked amused by the question.

"It's rather banal, I'm afraid. He cuts hair."

Nick laughed. It was a relief to do so.

"See," he said, "you have made me laugh. I am better already." He paused. "Now will you accept my offer? Please say yes, even if it is just for me. I need to feel needed."

Karel hugged Nick, and there were tears in his eyes.

"It is too much, Nick, after all you have done already, but to please you and Nathan, I will accept."

"On one condition though. You must stay away from here. Forget me until my birthday. I *mean* that. Give me space and time to sort all this out. I doubt if I will see Bart again. He is staying on for a while after Anna leaves, but he won't come here and honestly, I don't think I will want to see him. Not until my birthday anyway."

"There's the first gay pride march in July. Won't we see you at that?" Karel asked tentatively, moving away.

Nick shook his head. "I wish it well, sincerely. But I want to remain completely quiet." As he said these words, he knew what he had to do. He would ask James to find another job, and while he was looking for one, he would return to run the shop with him. It would be a sort of therapy and a second home to this now empty house. James would no doubt be upset and might protest, but Nick wanted to take control again. He needed to be among books. To smell them and touch them, and yes, to love them. He smiled to himself at the thought of returning Sterne, Richardson and all the other treasured authors to their rightful place at the front of the shop. He laughed openly at the thought of Muriel Spark and her clever kind, taking a back seat. He would even restore the gay section to a priority spot. In it, he would have first editions, with Edward Carpenter, James Baldwin, and E.M. Forster, and in pride of place, Forster's *Maurice*.

"What so funny?" Karel asked.

"Me. What I am going to do. You are right. Stress needs to be relieved, and my own self needs to be restored. I want the *I* within me back. It has gone astray recently, but I will bring it back and hope for completion."

"Bart and I have upset you. I am sorry."

"Don't be. My surface has been ruffled. That's all. I shall miss all of you, including Anna. But I will let her go without the strain of a parting. You see, I feel she is close to death and does not want to die in Brighton. It's a feeling, not a fact. I don't know for sure, so please treat this in the strictest confidence."

"But—"

"Please, Karel, reflect on this by yourself. She wants to be alone—with Bart."

"Can I say something?" Karel asked.

"What?"

"I'm no longer ashamed of running away, of being afraid to return to Czechoslovakia. By some magic, Nathan has made me lose my guilt and shame of being a coward. Aren't we always cowards when we love something or someone too much? Don't we all panic?"

Nick said, yes, he thought that maybe it was innate in all men and women to panic when love, or what they consider to be love, overwhelms.

"And I don't mind anymore, Bart or Greg knowing how I

stayed in Paris—that I ran away from them when I saw them on the Boulevard St-Germain. I have lost my cowardice about that too."

"It's at moments like this when I hear you talk that I know you are the same Karel I loved so dearly. I am proud of you, and no, not in a patronising way. As Bart once said he had found a sense of finding, I have found a way of healing. And you, too, will heal yourself completely with Nathan. I am sure of that. It will be the same for me when I return to my source."

"Which is?"

"A vigil. A waiting. To see Greg again. Maybe I will never have another opportunity after this next visit of his. And then, when he is gone, I will go back to my work and those beautifully dusty books. It is my way, Karel, and in this talk that we have had, you have made me stronger."

"Thank you for the loan. I *will* repay you, Nick."

"Only when it is time for you to do so. Maybe they are wrong in saying money cannot buy happiness. If a loan from me can make you two a couple with a home of your own, it is worth it."

They said nothing more. Karel went to join Nathan, and Nick pondered how he would tell James of his decision.

PART FOUR:

GREG

Nick needn't have worried about James. He received an offer to work at Hatchards and promptly left for London, giving Nick the space he needed to turn the shop around to how he wanted it.

He did not see Anna again, and was sad about that, but she wrote to him from Kirkwall to say everything was fine and that she loved him. Bart, he did meet a couple of times, but the meetings seemed artificial, as if they were both pretending something they no longer believed in.

On September the 5th, there was a knock on the door. It was late in the afternoon, and Nick had just decided to go for a walk, having shut up the shop at midday for half-day closing. He opened the door, and there was Greg, smiling.

"Well, aren't you going to give me a hug?"

Nick was too speechless to answer, his mouth dry. This *is* Greg, he kept on thinking over and over like a needle stuck in a groove, the one person I have been truly waiting for. "Yes," he murmured and a few moments later, with the door closed behind them, Greg reached out and hugged Nick to him. They remained like that, and Nick's eyes were closed. There would be time enough to look at Greg and to talk with him, but the sudden warmth of this welcome body was enough. He could not break away, and it was Greg who slowly separated them.

"Let me look at you," Greg said.

Nick turned his face aside, his eyes now open. He did not want to see the expression on Greg's face as he stared at him and considered him. He did not want to know what he was thinking.

"You are you! You are just as you have always been."

Nick turned now and looked at Greg's face. Greg had aged, and the ageing was pronounced. His unruly curls had thinned, and the sheen of darkness was gone. His eyes, though, and his mouth, were as they were, and only a few wrinkles showed on his forehead. Greg now looked older than his years, and time had weathered him. The impact of experience, and perhaps even the remains of a horror, showed in his features; an ugly horror that he had seen and had escaped from. What danger had caused this? He stared, and his vision blurred with tears. Greg had been through too much, he thought, and it shows. He looks as if he were almost destroyed but finally escaped.

"Do I really look so different?" Greg asked, his serious face wanting an honest answer.

"Your experiences, whatever they have been, are written on your skin. In a way it suits you. You are more handsome for it, and yet—" he paused and could not say what he thought.

"And yet what?"

"I wish whatever it was, had not happened."

"The same intuitive Nick," Greg said.

"I do not see the boy in you anymore. Where is that face I first saw in St Ann's Well Gardens; that face that flashed lightning at me, crashed into me, and retrieved a football from beneath where I was sitting?"

"It is here. Hidden. You will see it again." He paused, adding, "But is it so important that I remain eternally as I was?"

"No, Greg, no. But I sense the innocence in you has been scarred. Surely it could not have been François who has done this to you."

Greg held out a hand and pressed a finger to Nick's lips.

"Don't search, my darling, don't search. Now, make me feel really at home and get me some tea. I hope you notice I am not asking for anything stronger. I gave up being a hard drinker a while back, reluctantly at first, but now I prefer black coffee and tisanes."

They walked down the stairs to the kitchen area, and Greg exclaimed, "I don't recognise this room. It was always so full of people. I know where they have gone, but where have they gone?" He sat down on the bench and stared out into the garden.

"You said I am as I was. What else do you see in my face?" Nick asked. "And I too want honesty."

"Still physically beautiful, but you look tired, as if you have given up. That's the truth I see, Nick. There are no visible lines on your face. What has happened to you is all within, but you, too, have been through your own war. I am not as intuitive as you, but I would hazard a guess that your war has been solitude."

Nick made the tea in silence and did not answer. He had said what he saw, and Greg had responded with his attempt at the truth.

"Where is François?" Nick asked as he handed the cup to Greg.

"He's waiting in a café near the Astoria. He wants me to fetch him when I am ready."

"But why is he there?"

"He thought we should see each other alone, and he was right. I'll fetch him and bring him to the house in a while. First, I want us to make an arrangement."

"What?" Nick asked tentatively.

"That I sleep in the spare room or down here, and that he sleeps separately. That is if we are welcome to stay."

"But aren't you together?" Nick asked, pretending to sort out a pile of cutlery by the sink.

"We are *with* each other, yes," Greg replied, joining Nick at the sink and then changing the subject. "Has it seemed very long that I have been away? We're not on the phone now. You can turn and tell me face to face. I want to see the look in your eyes as I hear you reply."

Nick stopped what he was doing with the knives, forks and spoons, and for a moment stayed where he was, gazing down at the sink, seeing nothing. He was at a loss for words. Of course it had been a long time for him! Did Greg have to remind him? "I don't know why you are asking me this," he murmured.

"I want to know what time has meant to you. The time of these few, but long years—long for me anyway."

Nick moved away from the sink. He did not look at Greg's face. He was afraid his expression would reveal too much.

"I want to know if you have missed me." There was an almost agonised sound in Greg's voice as he asked this.

Nick turned around then and faced him, conscious that probably all his emotions showed.

"Don't you *know*?" he challenged. "Aren't we the same coin? Aren't we still joined, despite the coin never being able to see its other side?"

"What if the coin has the same image on both sides? Accidents can happen. It has been known."

"Are we an accident? Do you believe that?"

"In the park, all those years ago, when you looked at me, we *knew*. We were not conscious of it, but we were stamped as if by fate itself and then left to discover for ourselves what had happened. Throw me up, and I will fall as you. I believe it is the same for you."

Nick broke out into a sweat. Opening the garden door, he went outside and wiped his face with the back of his hand. Greg was soon beside him.

"Nothing can part us," Greg said, his face flushed.

"I've been alone too long."

Nick wanted to tell Greg to go and fetch François and bring him to the house, but Greg was insistent.

"Have you had many encounters since the four of us separated?"

"Yes, there have been encounters. But with you here standing beside me, they have no relevance or importance. When you and Bart went in search of Karel—when that happened—I kind of fell apart. An inward collapse of feeling is a strange thing. You do not—well, I didn't—feel in the same way as before. With each encounter, your face was branded on my mind."

"You see, I am yours!" Greg cried out.

"Greg, it has been too long. You are with François. You love each other. I have no idea what hell you went through before you met him in Paris, what with losing Karel and the failed passion you had with Bart. I know that François saved you from something more than you could bear. And whatever difficulties you have with him now, stay with him. You owe him that. But it is true, we are one in that image of the coin we've carried with us all these years, but it is *only* an image, despite our desired imaginings. We are two separate people who must follow their own singular paths. And mine, I can assure you, is very singular."

"Beautifully put," Greg said, his voice suddenly very calm. "You are a poet, and as a poet, I think you deal rather badly with so-called *reality*. The truth is we are the same—no metaphor, no desired imaginings—a reality for me."

"Let's stop talking. I am tired out. You and François can stay in this house for as long as you like. I want you to enjoy Brighton and for you to show François the town. I hope he will like it. Now, must I remind you? You are keeping him waiting." He paused and tried to add a touch of humour to his voice. "Or have you sent him into the Astoria to see some flickering black and white film? If you have, he will be disappointed. They don't show the films we liked anymore, but the sweeping staircase leading up to the balcony is still there, the magic of it still intact."

"François doesn't much like our culture," Greg responded seriously.

"But I thought he was Roman Catholic? All of us Catholics, and remember, I am supposed to be one myself, like the extravagant, foolish curves of life's art. It must be in his blood."

"His blood is Algerian," Greg replied in a voice that sounded hollow. "Algeria, and the fragments that Barbès contains of that world, are the only artefacts he recognises as his own."

"And perhaps you have difficulty identifying with that?" Nick suddenly felt a stab of inner pain. He found it difficult to look at Greg's face. He desperately wanted him to go and fetch François. He could not admit it to Greg, but he was in emotional pain in his company, a deep-rooted pain of loss and longing, and he had no desire to comment on Greg's relationship with François. It could not be his business, and yet just a month before his birthday, he wondered how he would tolerate their company. He had suggested that Greg should spend time showing François the town, and he knew he could retreat to the bookshop whenever he needed. "Go and fetch him, please!" he said. "And if you left your suitcases at the station, please collect them before you return. And I do not accept your arrangement. I do not agree with you not sleeping together. You should continue here as you did in Paris."

"We stopped sleeping together some time ago."

Nick sensed he was about to collapse. He felt drained, and knew his expression must be showing that. He said, almost angrily, "Then place yourselves in this house wherever you want. I do not need to know any more. This is all private to you." There was a hardness in the way he said *private* and *you*. He had to make a distance between Greg's emotions towards himself and his emotions for him. François was the measure of that distance.

"Alright, I'll *fetch* him. But I wish you wouldn't make him sound like a fucking parcel." There was acid in his voice. As if he needed some sort of revenge. Revenge towards Nick, and Nick felt it as such.

"We have said a lot, Greg. But before you go, I need to tell you something more. You know Karel has a lover. His name is Nathan. If you bump into them in the street, please don't be awkward about it. Truly, they are happy."

"I am glad," Greg replied.

"It's not only that, Greg. I must also tell you that Karel never went to Czechoslovakia. He was in Paris all the time you were there. He calls it cowardice, but I don't accept that term. He was afraid he would be tortured as so many have been, or that he would disappear, so you can imagine his fear. Don't blame him, Greg."

Greg said nothing. His face was blank. Then he said quietly, after a long while, "I understand fear. I do not blame him for that. But I do blame him for breaking us all up. For tearing me away from what was a good mutual relationship between the four of us." He paused, then added as if it was an afterthought, "Maybe the four of us would have broken up anyway, but later, and at the right time. I would have remained with you. You know that."

Greg then ran out of the garden, clattered up the stairs loudly and slammed the front door.

Greg and François turned up at the house a couple of hours later. They had two pieces of luggage, and Greg entered first, depositing them on the floor. From behind him, François emerged. He was not as Nick had imagined. He was slender with thick and curly hair, similar to how Greg's had been, but darker in shade. His face was a deep tanned brown, but Nick would not immediately have identified him as being Arabic. His eyes were intense, and Nick's impression was that they rarely showed joy. There was a sombreness to them, and they were deep-set as if wanting to disappear inside of him. He was dressed in the lightest of white suits with a pale blue shirt.

"Hello," Nick said and shook his hand.

"*Bonjour*," François replied.

Greg laughed and jokingly commented, "I promise that will be the last of the French language."

"Why?" François asked, turning to him.

"You speak English perfectly now, and you know it."

This brief dialogue jarred on Nick, who sensed the inner combat between them.

"I've made some fresh drinks," Nick said with all the graciousness of a 1950s hostess. "No alcohol, but various juices. We can have them in what I absurdly call the garden.

It's a yard really, with borders of flowers and a wonderful view of the backs of houses."

They went downstairs.

"No trees?" François asked.

"There used to be one in the next garden. I enjoyed its overhanging branches, but a neighbour cut it down. I was unhappy about it for a long time."

François made no reply, and dismissing the room with one glance, went straight outside. There were deck chairs, and he asked if he could sit down. Nick made a gesture with his hand that he was welcome to do so. The drinks were on a round, plastic table that Nick had bought a few days before. Its only redeeming feature was that it was white. François sat down while Greg stood hesitantly by. His face said nothing, neither enthusiasm that they had all met nor any show of feeling. Nick passed François an orange juice. Greg declined the offer.

"We went to a pub before coming up here. I had a real drink. Cognac. François was displeased with me."

"Please don't exaggerate," François said crisply and then added, "At least you didn't buy a whole bottle."

Nick broke the tense silence that ensued by asking François for details of the district he lived in and his job. François responded, with an equal lack of expression, that he now owned his shop and that his fabrics and other goods sold very well.

"I like bright colours," François emphasised.

"I wish we had more colour in England," Nick replied.

"Do you?"

François' eyes showed some life at last. They flashed in the sunlight, and Nick saw golden flecks in their depths. He knew then and there that they would not get on. He considered François was being deliberately cold. His antipathy was clear.

Greg now poured some juice for himself. "I think Brighton has a lot of colour," he said, glancing at François with a look of warning. Then he looked at Nick and smiled. Nick's immediate thought was, he is in my corner. He is with me. Nick left them alone, and as he made his way towards the stairs, he heard what seemed to be the opening of an argument in French. As he entered the spare bedroom to sort out some things, he realised that it was not what François had said to him that was combative, but the words half-hidden beneath. *Do you?* Two simple words. Had he hoped that England would be better to look at? Had he wished for it to be less drab? And what about the train journey from London? The ugly tenement buildings as you leave Victoria Station? The smoke and the everlasting grime? But wasn't Barbès the same? These questions he felt were beneath the surface, and others as well. Yet Barbès-Rochechouart had colour—bright, glorious colour to defy any neglect in housing or injustice or inequality in the district. Barbès hid its grime behind colour?

Greg joined him.

"Why aren't you downstairs with him?" Nick asked.

"He is in a mood. This country has been a shock for him."

"I don't believe he will like it here."

"Will this be his room?" Greg asked, looking around him.

"Have you decided to sleep downstairs?"

"Yes, the sofa will be fine. I am glad you have still kept it."

"There is also space to sleep in the living room."

"Too cramped. I will be comfortable downstairs. You may not know it, but I have slept quite well, even on bare floors. Mind you, that was before I gave up drinking. When you're drunk, it's easier!" He laughed and waved a hand in the air. "And one of the first things I did on returning to this country was to have some of the hard stuff! I promise you it won't become a habit."

"I think you needed it," Nick replied, taking fresh sheets out of the cupboard.

There was a pause before Greg asked the obvious.

"What are your first impressions of him?"

"Physically?"

"Don't shy away from answering. He's good looking. We both know that."

"Yes."

"Then answer my question."

Nick glanced at him.

"Is it so important?"

"It is," Greg replied.

"I find him enclosed. Like a walled garden. I don't think he wants strangers to see what is growing there."

"Nicely put, Nick, but do you like him?"

"Not much, but let's see how he and I get along. Am I right in thinking there may be a bit of jealousy concerning our past relationship?"

Greg shook his head.

"He is indifferent to it. But don't think I am fooled, Nick. Somewhere submerged within yourself, I think there is a touch of jealousy. One day I will tell you about the situation between François and myself."

Nick looked out of the bedroom window in silence.

"Now, please don't give this another thought," Greg said.

After saying this, he left the room, and within five minutes, Nick heard the front door close. He went downstairs and found the two suitcases and a hurriedly scrawled note: *Be back around eight. Am showing François the town.* Nick scrunched the note in his hand and felt worried and disturbed.

Half an hour later, there was a knocking on the front door. Nick was in the main bedroom at the time, resting and trying to restore his energy. His immediate thought was one of irritation and annoyance for not fixing the doorbell, which no longer worked. The apathy of his lonely life accounted for this. Tiredly he went downstairs expecting Greg and François to have returned. Perhaps they have had a row, he thought. François does not want to see the fine, white architecture of Brighton, nor the shadows of its darkest slums. To his surprise, Karel was standing outside.

"I feel guilty. I haven't seen you for a while, and I just decided to call by on the off-chance."

"Come in, but don't look at me. I feel a wreck. Greg and François have arrived. They'll be back around eight. I was upstairs trying to get an hour's sleep."

"Shall I go?"

"Of course not. I want to hear all your news."

Nick knew that Karel had started work at the hospital but had not seen him since he had begun.

"Work is fine," Karel said, then added, "and thanks to you, we have an excellent flat. I am sincerely happy."

Nick took Karel into the living room. Karel sat down and looked awkward. Sometimes the wrong room is chosen for a visitor, and Nick wondered if this was the case today. He vaguely remembered that Karel had never liked the closed-in 'box-like feel' of the living room. He perched on the edge of a chair while Nick flopped down on the floor, rested his head on his hand and looked up at Karel. The same awkwardness was in Karel's voice as he asked, "How is Greg?"

"I am not sure. Honestly, I am not sure."

"I hope he is pleased to see you."

"Yes."

"You are holding something back, Nick. Is it François?"

Quite suddenly, Nick blurted out the words, "I don't like him."

"That sounds definitive."

"I know, and maybe I am wrong. I shouldn't have said it like that. I wanted to take to him, but I knew there was a block between us within the first half-hour, a shutting out, more on his side, I think, but I don't want to apportion blame. We all send out signals. I thought mine were open and friendly, but who knows?"

Karel sighed and asked if they could go downstairs. Nick got up, and silently they went down. Nick brought in what remained of the fresh juices from outside and placed them on the pine table. They sat facing each other.

"I think I heard them rowing in French. I was too far away to hear what they said, and my French is—well, it sounded like a row to me. François does not appear to like England. He hasn't actually said that, and perhaps it's all in my overactive imagination."

"So what if he doesn't? Many people don't. Maybe he doesn't feel comfortable in our messy, raucous land. Not that Paris is immune from noise and mess, but somehow the mess is hidden, and the run-down neighbourhoods are picturesque. Perhaps it all boils down to the fact that he is angry at Greg for bringing him here." He paused. "You should listen to some of the rows Nathan and I have. Epic! But we love each other." After saying this, Karel looked hard at Nick. "Isn't there something else going on there? And isn't that something else going on in your mind?"

"What do you mean exactly, Karel?"

"About how deeply you feel for Greg?"

"Stop it, Karel. I shouldn't have said anything."

Karel reached out with his hand across the table.

"I love you, Nick. You love me. But you are *in* love with Greg. Now throw me out for telling the truth!"

Nick started laughing uncontrollably.

"You are right, Karel. You are right," he exclaimed, still laughing and with tears beginning to pour down his face. "Please stay."

"Nick, please calm down." Like the nurse he now was, Karel went over to the sink and brought back a glass of cold water. "I have never seen you in such a state. Now drink it."

"Alright," Nick replied, gulping it down, but then the explosion of laughter engulfed him again, and to his embarrassment, he brought up the water all over the table. This did calm him down, and he rushed to get a cloth.

"If you are not careful, I'll have to ring for an ambulance to take you to the nearest lunatic asylum."

"Haywards Heath?" Nick replied with a smile.

"I had better stay with you until they get back. After all, I have to see Greg sooner or later. Have you food enough for five?"

"Five?"

"Yes, I want Nathan to be here as well. I'm not sure how I am going to react to Greg and his lover, and unlike you, I'm not in love with Greg."

Nick went to the fridge. He had the worst of food in it, but he had not been expecting company that day or any day. There was a large pork pie, bought on a whim the previous afternoon, and a bowl of potatoes in a white mush of mayonnaise. At the back of the fridge were a cucumber and a beetroot.

"Can I do anything with this? There's also a chocolate mousse hiding somewhere."

"I see it," Karel said. "You should too. Are you going blind as well as mad?"

"I was laughing, Karel, that's all. Don't Czechs laugh?"

"Yes, but we are more subtle, and we don't vomit our water."

Nick flopped down on a cushion on the floor. "Can you make a meal for us all?" he asked.

Karel said that he could, and then began a long monologue about his work at the hospital. After exhausting this subject, he rang Nathan, who reluctantly agreed to come over for the meal.

"Thank you," Nick murmured gently.

"I just want you to be honest with yourself, Nick. The question is, what can you do about it, if anything?"

"You mean about Greg?" Nick shook his head. "I can't break them up, even if it were possible to do so."

"Then you will be doing right and at the same time harming yourself. It is a no-win situation." He then came over to Nick and sat on the floor beside him, and once more, Nick was absurdly convulsed with laughter. To stop it, or maybe simply because he wanted to, Karel pulled Nick's head down and kissed him on the mouth. Nick felt his penis harden.

"You do know what you are doing?" he asked Karel.

"This is strictly medicinal, but I am going to relax you completely. Otherwise the evening will be intolerable. We both have to be utterly relaxed for this event. Remember how long it is since I even spoke to Greg? Never mind the rest that happened between us."

"But Nathan—?"

"Nathan should adhere more to GLF's pamphlets," Karel replied. "Anyway, I am sure he would understand." Then he stood up and drew down the blinds at the windows. "Shall we turn off the light," he asked.

"No," said Nick, and then added, "please take off all your clothes."

"Remember, Nick, we only have an hour."

"I'll keep my watch on," Nick replied, with a forgotten childish streak in his voice. Then he pushed down his trousers to the knees.

"No, that is not enough. If I am going to be completely naked, so are you," Karel said.

"It's more erotic if one of us is semi-dressed," Nick said. "And as it is *my* therapy, I want you naked and me partially clothed." He then edged his underwear down to the same place as his trousers, just below the knees. He looked down at his cock and at the pre-cum at the tip, and then up at Karel, who was by now naked, his cock equally extended. His first instinct was to suck on Karel, but when he asked if he could, Karel said no, and bending down, licked at the juice on Nick's penis.

"Shall we fuck?" Karel asked, lifting his head up. "I would like you inside me."

"I have no lubricant here," Nick said.

"Your cock is wet enough. I can take you. Haven't I before?"

Karel moved back, and lying out on the floor, opened his arse wide. Nick pressed the tip of his cock against the opening and then pushed the full shaft into him in one stroke. Karel cried out and began to thrash with pleasure, and it was not long before they both climaxed. Nick came first, exploding inside Karel, and Karel brought himself off afterwards. They lay back against each other for a while, and then slowly, very slowly, Karel extricated himself and stood up, his cock now limp. He held out his hand to Nick.

"Come on," he said. "Let's take a bath together. Do you feel good after that?"

"Better than a massage," Nick quipped.

"I still desire you," Karel said as casually as possible. "I guess I always will."

"We didn't kiss," Nick remarked.

"No. That was my way of being faithful to Nathan."

Once in the bath, they soaped each other, and Nick could not resist putting his finger inside Karel. Karel moaned again and told him to stop. Finally, they dried themselves and went down to prepare for what was supposed to be a good meal. Karel took out the pork pie and stared at Nick.

"What's the matter?" Nick asked.

"I don't know how you could have chosen it! I guess you will always be a mystery to me." Then he added slowly, "Did you forget there will be two Jews and one Algerian at this party?"

"So what shall we do, Karel?"

"Bin everything that's here. I've got some money on me. I'll go to the fish and chip shop around the corner."

With this remark, he hurried out of the house.

"Has the birthday party begun already?" Greg quipped when he first saw Karel. "Now *that's* what I call a typical English spread!"

"I hope François likes his first taste of fish and chips," Nick said, and despite himself, there was an edge of sarcasm in his voice.

"Well, he nearly threw up when he saw the hot dogs on the Palace Pier."

Karel laughed and came forward. For a few minutes, Greg held him in his arms and then gently kissed him on the mouth.

"Where's your boyfriend?" Greg asked.

"He will arrive any time now."

"Good. I want to meet him. I like a fresh face, so beware!"

"Please don't talk like that," Nick said, feeling disappointed with Greg. Then he looked at Karel, who had clearly taken the remark in good faith, or so it seemed.

"He's Jewish like me," Karel said bluntly.

"So?"

Then François was heard coming downstairs, and all three of them drew as far apart from each other as they could, like guilty conspirators. Which possibly they were, thought Nick. They had, all three of them, been in love with each other, in the distance of time, true, but that conspiracy of loving was still fresh in them. Karel was the first to move forward and held out his hand.

"I'm Karel. I expect you have heard of me."

François smiled at him, and they shook hands. He then stared at the table as if he had seen nothing like it.

"An impromptu meal," Greg commented,

Awkwardly, but with a certain gentleness, the three conspirators drew François into their circle. A good bottle of French wine was found. They toasted each other, and after Nathan arrived, they ate together, or rather François tasted the meal delicately, leaving most of the batter that had surrounded the fish on his plate. Later, Karel piled the dishes into the sink, and they all found places to sit. Greg sat with Nathan, who had been open and friendly during the meal and all too eager to apologise for keeping them waiting. Greg seemed to take to him at once, and Nick watched them both from his beanbag. Karel stayed at the table with François, and they appeared to get along well.

Then a hush descended on the room. The rush of the meal was over. Now was the time to take in the measure of their meeting.

"Three of us here know each other well, and two of us are new to our crowd. I want to be the first to welcome them." Nick surprised himself by saying this, and added, "Welcome to this house, and thank you for sharing this very simple meal. And an especial welcome to you François. This must all be very strange."

François looked down in silence and said nothing. Karel added, "Must have been a hard day for you, François. Is it really your first time in England?"

"Yes," François replied. Then he asked if he could go to bed as he was exhausted. He smiled at Greg and Karel, and then at Nathan and Nick, a smile that asked to be accompanied to his chosen room. Nick led him upstairs and opened the second bedroom door. François looked around him blankly. "It's nice," he commented, more out of politeness than conviction.

"The bathroom is downstairs."

"Don't worry. I will find my way."

"Do you want me to send Greg up?"

"No, of course not." He then bent forward and kissed Nick on the cheeks. "The French way," he murmured. "Goodnight. I hope you sleep well."

"You too," and as he turned to head downstairs, Nick heard François close the door and turn the key in the lock.

"Should I go up?" Greg asked when Nick returned.

"He's locked his door. I think he is overtired and needs to sleep."

Nathan reminded Karel that he had an early shift at the hospital and said it was time they went as well.

"So that is what you have returned to, Karel!" Greg said. "And how is it?"

"Better than before, and my own health has improved as well. Let's just say my heart is beating and is determined to keep on beating."

Nick noticed a wariness in Karel's eyes as he looked at Greg. It was as if he were assessing the visible changes and wondering what had caused them. Greg did not look much at ease either. As soon as Karel and Nathan were gone, Greg asked if Nick could get the blankets for the sofa. He was smiling, but now with weariness.

"This return is—"

"A bit difficult?" Nick asked.

"Yes. I hope we have time, you and I, to talk alone

tomorrow."

"I will make time."

Once Greg was settled and Nick was in bed, he considered Greg's request. He was afraid of what Greg might say. In fact, he was afraid of what they both might say.

It was a sunny September day, and the breeze from the sea was mild. François went out to explore alone.

"He loves water," Greg said. "The seashore here is not exactly Algiers, but it will do."

Nick laughed and looked at his watch. It was half-past nine. The shop was not yet open, and as he had no one else to take care of it, he felt guilty. Greg noticed him looking at his watch and reminded him that he wanted to talk.

"Then come with me, Greg. Come to the shop. See what I have achieved. This house is not my only home. Why should it be? I believe a house should be shared."

"I know," Greg said, "and that is why I want to talk to you, but I will come to your shop. Do I look respectable enough for your customers?" As he said these words, he took Nick in his arms and kissed him passionately on the mouth. Nick broke away.

"Please, Greg—"

"Forget what I just did. It was impulsive. You must know how I feel."

"I'm not sure I do. Or that I can afford the emotional pain of knowing it." There was a long awkward silence between them, and then Nick pretended to look Greg up and down. "You look great today. You know, we have much younger people coming into the bookshop now. Less of the dinosaurs I used to get. That species has more or less died out, and even though I am a good listener, it is no longer a place to drop in for therapy."

"Not even for me?" Greg teased.

"For you, today, I will make an exception. You can play at work and make the tea. James, who ran it for me for a while, wrecked my cubby hole, and it has been hell putting it back the way it was, especially as I now keep my antiquarian books there, and it is even smaller than it was before."

"Well, before that, I will sit in a corner and read. I don't suppose you have any pornography? I read that John Rechy book *Numbers* recently. It's a series of scenes taking place in a Los Angeles park. It didn't have much of a plot. It was simply about sexual encounters, and totally explicit."

"Was it well written?" Nick asked seriously, but instead of answering, Greg came over to him and kissed him again.

"No, not especially. I jerked off to it because I wasn't having sex with François at the time. It did me a lot of good, and I wasn't particularly fussy about the prose."

Releasing himself again, Nick warned him to stop kissing him like that.

"Don't worry," Greg said. "I don't need to talk literature to get into your trousers, but it's not the fucking *Charioteer*! Is that still the kind of reading that excites you?"

Ignoring him, Nick went upstairs to get his coat. Despite the warmth of the day, he felt cold. He wished François were there, not because he had taken more of a liking to him, but to shield himself from Greg's clearly confused needs. He told himself he would not be drawn in by Greg's sexual approaches.

Greg was waiting for him at the door. "I'm sorry for what I did," he said simply.

"At least you swear less," Nick remarked, cuffing him gently on the jaw. "But you are wrong about one thing. About me only liking well-written books. Henry James has been relegated to the back of the bookshop, along with all the other great beasts of literature. You will be surprised to see what's at the front of the shop. I even have the Gay Liberation Front Manifesto. Now *that* should do you some good!"

"Rubbish," Greg said. "It was foreign to me in Paris. Anyway, the French are too intelligent to take it on board without analysing it to death."

They were in the street now, and Greg told him about Jean-Louis and how much he had both shown and given to him. He told him how Jean-Louis had left him the Cezanne in his will and how by some miracle, customs had not found it when he had brought it back into England. Nick was astonished at this and asked him why he had brought it back just for a holiday. Greg replied that he wanted Nick to look after it for him and to keep it in his house, and that he did not trust leaving it in Paris. Nick stopped walking and turned to face him.

"But Greg, it must be worth a fortune. I can't just hang it on the wall."

"Of course, you can. You can put it in one of the bedrooms. If anybody notices, they will assume it's a reproduction. I know it will be safe with you, and I know it will be kept safe for us. Now I want to surprise you with something else. Jean-Louis and others taught me a lot about literature. I've read many books while in Paris. Benjamin Constant, for example, and not just because he wrote slim volumes. *Adolphe* is my favourite. Short, concise, and full of psychological surprises. Among all the *salauds* in that city, I met some intelligent people, and they taught me a lot. Can I show off and recite some Mallarmé?"

They began walking again, and for a while Nick was quiet, and as they approached the bookshop, he said, "You amaze me, Greg. You amaze me with everything you say and do. If I am the passive side of the coin, you are certainly the active one. Now, recite me some Mallarmé." Pretending ignorance, he asked, "Didn't he write *Le Cimetière marin*?"

"That was Paul Valéry," Greg replied crisply. "And as punishment for having put me through that mean little test, I will recite the Valéry as well. I will repeat it so many times that you will see that graveyard by the sea in Sète quite, quite clearly. One day, we should go to see it together."

Nick opened the shop and breathed in the air of the place. Greg laughed and said he was breathing it in as if it were ozone from off the sea.

"Talking of the sea," Greg said, "where is your French section? Do you have *Le Cimetière marin*? I have decided this will be a definite punishment. I will recite it until you are sick of hearing it, *and* I will force you to read the text at the same time so you can make sure I don't get any of it wrong. Deep down, I know you still consider me to be that ignorant boy from Portslade, don't you? Well, I'm not going to let you get away with it."

"You *are* still that ignorant boy from Portslade," Nick said laughing, hanging up his coat. He was talking from just inside the cubby hole. "And maybe, I don't want you to change. I want you to be that boy from Portslade. Let's stop fucking around with Valéry and Mallarmé. It was mean of me to have tested you, but I was only playing. And please remember, I don't want you to change. Honestly!"

With a look of sadness in his eyes, Greg said, "But I *have* changed, Nick. Many people have changed me over there. Some made me better, some made me worse. Jean-Louis was the best. And the worst, whose name was Aurélien—well, I would rather not talk to you about him."

"Why not?" Nick asked, intrigued, stepping into the main part of the shop.

Greg almost shouted at him as he said, "Because I can't! He did me too much damage. And now, find that Valéry poem. I want to prove to you how much I know and how much I have learnt."

Nick, sensing a somewhat dangerous note in Greg's voice, began to look for Valéry's poems which he was now uncertain whether he had. He also noticed out of the corner of his eye Greg fixing him with a look that he translated as both rage and desire. For a while, Nick's attention wavered from the shelves to fantasy; he had closed the shop, and imagined he was giving himself to Greg completely with no one to disturb them. The fantasy was accentuated by Greg's cold command, "Where is that poem?"

"I can't find it," Nick replied.

"*Trouve-le immédiatement!*"

"I will do my best."

Then, by chance, Nick found a Penguin of French verse in

the paperback section and finding the Valéry poem inside, he held it out to Greg.

"I am not reading it but reciting. I want *you* to read it *silently*. Over and over. I mean it. I'm not playing."

Nick recognised there was a shade of intellectual sadomasochism in all this and developed an erection. He opened the book and silently told himself he didn't mind playing the masochist. Then another thought crossed his mind. Why doesn't he just bend me over and spank me hard? What was that Phil Spector song about a hit feeling like a kiss? He wanted to be spanked by Greg. But, he accepted that this so-called punishment was more intellectual than physical and had to be played out in the way Greg had demanded. Looking down at the poem, he glanced at the first line, and as he did so, he heard Greg begin, *'Ce toit tranquille, où marchent des colombes...'* and as he listened, his penis grew harder in response to the sound of the voice, lighter in tone than usual as it intoned the magical lyric of Valéry. Greg recited the poem with a great deal of beauty, and his perfect rendering made Nick's erection harder.

"Greg—" Nick said as Greg finished.

"I said over and over, and I meant it. Don't you like what I am doing to you?"

The words *to you* aroused Nick even more, and he murmured, "Yes, but you don't know how this is affecting me."

"I hope I can guess," Greg replied, and then recited the poem again. After the third recitation, Nick could feel a wet stickiness against his legs. His cock had released itself downwards, out of his underwear, and was dripping with that prelude to a total orgasm. He murmured before Greg began the fourth time, "I can't bear this much more. I am—"

"Shut up. Listen."

This ordered cry only made Nick more excited, and he was precariously close to coming. He closed his eyes, and halfway through the recitation, his leg received the full impact of his sperm. He put down the book and rushed to the cubby hole.

Closing the door behind him and lowering his trousers, he saw the extent of his reaction. He wiped himself clean with some tissues that he kept in the small room and, after adjusting himself, returned. Greg was still standing in exactly the same position as before and had a smug grin on his face.

"Everything okay?" he asked.

"Fine," Nick said, and then put the book back onto its shelf. His hands were trembling, and he knew his face was flushed. He avoided Greg's look for as long as he could.

"Do you know something?" Greg asked, changing both the subject and his expression of voice. "We are both shopkeepers! You turn up regularly to yours, while I just leisurely wait for the bank to let me know how much I have gained from mine."

Nick turned slowly and looked at him. "You make us sound like two bloody capitalists," he said. "The only difference is, I am interested in what I sell, and you are not."

This was intended to be a barbed response for the unexpected torture of silent cries and the inward scream of satisfaction when he had ejaculated, but the aim failed. Greg was indifferent. He walked around the shop and picked out what was being sold as a first edition of Iris Murdoch's *The Bell*.

"I may not care about what I sell, but it seems you don't either. Have you read what is printed inside this book? It says, 'This edition issued on first publication by the Book Society Ltd. in association with Chatto & Windus Ltd., November 1958.'"

Nick felt caught out.

"How much am I asking for it?"

"No price in it. I suppose you make that up when some poor ignorant fool wants the book thinking it is the real thing. Nice work, Nick."

"It's an extension of the first edition. Same year."

"But it *isn't* a first edition."

Greg looked mean and persistent.

"Clever of you to notice. Maybe you could stand in for me

and run the shop now you are so knowledgeable about books. Maybe you could run it even better than me, and you could work again!"

"So you admit you are duping your buyers?"

The vague scent of the sadomasochistic mental game was still there. Nick smelt it.

"Well, don't *we* as individuals pass *ourselves* off as being the real thing as you put it, when in fact it is not our true self at all?"

"You mean when we *sell* ourselves?" Greg responded.

"Stop it, Greg. You've had your fun. I was willing for this extended game, but now it's over. Surely I have been punished enough for testing you in the street."

"Oh, *that*," Greg said, and then added, "and we *are* capitalists!"

Customers started to come in, and during a conversation with one of them, Nick noticed Greg quietly slip out of the door. He did not return.

The following day, Nick closed the shop at midday. He returned to the house, but there was no one there, and he had a feeling of panic. Had they both gone? He rushed upstairs and saw that François' bed was crumpled and his clothing was scattered on the carpet. He hated himself for these fears, but he did have a fear of human disappearance. When he returned to the kitchen area, he saw a neat pile of Greg's things in a corner. He drank two glasses of water and sat down, trying uselessly to empty his mind of all thought. The phone rang, and at first, he did not want to answer it, but it was persistent. He got up and, picking up the receiver, heard Nathan's voice. He seemed to be in a panic of his own.

"I didn't think you would be in. Thank God you are. Can I come over?"

"But—"

"It's urgent. Please. I know you are busy—"

"No, I'm not," Nick replied, and then without further

questioning, he said that Nathan could come over and asked where he was ringing from.

"A call box, not far from you. Are you alone?"

"Yes."

"Good."

"Why good?"

"I'll be over in a few minutes," came the reply and the phone went dead.

Ten minutes later, there was a loud rap on the front door.

"Can't you get your doorbell fixed?" Nathan asked, a look of annoyance on his face.

"I've not been used to company—until this rush," Nick replied, and opening the door wide, let Nathan come in. He was out of breath.

"Those fucking hills," he said.

"Shall we stay up here? The kitchen is a mess."

There was a certain deviance in this request. Nick did not know what time Greg and François would return, and he sensed that Nathan needed privacy.

"I don't care," Nathan said, and opened the living room door.

"You remind me of someone I know," Nick said as they sat down in the living room.

"Who?"

"Greg. When he was younger."

"We're nothing like each other," Nathan replied. "Is he Jewish or something?"

"He is something, but he is not Jewish. Now, what is all this urgency about?"

Taking a few deep breaths, Nathan said, "It's about Karel. He's ill. At least, I think he is ill. He had a sort of collapse at the flat. Felt he was going to pass out. He was white in the face and looked afraid."

"Did you think of calling an ambulance?"

"Yes, but he said he knew what it was. He is a nurse, after all, but then he actually passed out, and it was up to me to bring him around. He's asleep now, and I *had* to see you. You know more about him than I do."

Nick responded with a look that he hoped was one of reassurance.

"He has an ectopic heartbeat. Don't confuse it with a serious heart problem because it isn't, or so I believe, but I'm not a doctor. He had this when he was living with Greg. In fact, he went through a bad patch and was afraid of going out."

Nathan leant forward in his chair and asked if he could have a drink. Any sort of alcohol. It did not matter.

"Like a St. Bernard dog, I have emergency brandy. But please, if you see Greg, don't tell him. It's his favourite drink, and he is supposed to be easing up off alcohol."

"I just feel odd myself," Nathan replied.

"Panic, and these fucking hills, as you put it, that's all it is. I'll be back in a minute."

In the hallway, Nick's first thought was that the past was beginning to recur. He thought of a roundabout that, after having been still for want of people, now had many climbing onto its artificial horses and was about to start turning again. Some of the people had been on it before, and others were strangers mounting it eagerly for the first time.

"It has begun again," he said aloud.

After fetching a small glass of brandy, he opened the living room door and saw that Nathan had his head in his hands. He was crying.

"No, no, you mustn't," Nick said, and kneeling in front of Nathan, pulled his hands away. They were wet with tears. "You really mustn't."

"I thought he had dropped down dead," Nathan murmured, and his moist eyes stared down at Nick. He then took the brandy and downed it in one go.

"I'm not giving you another!" Nick said.

"I don't need it. One does the trick."

"Could you please tell Greg that when you next meet?" Nick asked, attempting a joke to break the tension.

"I feel better."

"It's obvious that you are not. You are frightened, and you have all sorts of fantasies of losing Karel. You have to believe me. He has been in this situation before and, after a while, it passes. It is not, I repeat, this is *not* serious."

Nathan relaxed a little on hearing the emphasis in Nick's voice and leant back. He looked suddenly floppy, like a rag doll.

"I love him."

"I know," Nick replied, "and you did the right thing in coming to see me. It would have done Karel no good to flood him with tears."

"Was Greg stronger with him?"

"I can't remember," Nick replied truthfully, "but they got through it."

"He has been nervous since he started the job. I guess it is all the sickness and the dying. I can't imagine what he has to do, or to be exact, I *can* imagine, and I know I couldn't."

"But then, you are not Karel. He passes his limits sometimes, that's all. And going back to the work he left behind him must have been a tremendous strain. The strain will pass, and if it doesn't, he will find another job."

Nathan added, "We haven't been out for weeks. He says he's too tired, and even on days off, he wants to stay at home. He won't even come to the GLF events anymore. They had a dance, close dancing, and everything, along the London Road. He went to it and loved it, and now he can't face crowds."

"Just be patient," Nick said.

"I must go." Nathan hurriedly looked at his watch. "He will think all sorts of things if I am not there when he wakes up. I don't want him to become more scared than he already is."

Nathan got up like the white rabbit in *Alice in Wonderland,* and in a flash of muted colour, was out of the front door, hurrying down the hill.

That evening, Nick found himself alone with Greg. He told

him what had happened, and Greg's face darkened with concern.

"It's happening again," he said.

"That's what I thought," Nick replied, "but what can *we* do? Or maybe I shouldn't say *we*."

"No, you're right to say we. It's *that* subject I wanted to discuss in the shop and intended to, until you got to my vanity in the street with your stupid test."

Nick looked at him and smiled. They were seated on the sofa downstairs, and the evening was warm and the door open to the garden.

"François came here for one thing and one thing only," Greg said, and Nick thought, he *is* plunging in! He is plunging in, and I do not want to stop him. His hand was close to Greg's, and their fingers were almost touching. He looked down and saw the ten fingers, five of his and five of Greg's. How strange they look, he wanted to say, and yet so beautiful. The roughness and the thickness of Greg's and the slender, more pale ones of mine. Do they want to caress? Do they want their strangeness to marry? But neither hand moved. Then a breeze from outside ruffled the open pages of a book cast aside on the table. The movement obsessed him. Why can't my hand feel that strong breeze and move to close the book?

"François came with me to see if it was possible to renew our relationship, but on arrival, he knew already he had failed."

"How?"

"To put it simply and plainly, he could see you and I were still in love with each other, and we are, aren't we, Nick? Even the sound of my voice can, how shall I delicately put this, excite you? Admit to me that my reciting had a sexual effect on you."

"Yes. But then, the French language has always been erotic, to me anyway."

"Stop kidding, Nick. That's not it. You heard me in a different tone, you heard me in a language that you know something of, and I thrilled you. I was excited as well, and by the time I was halfway through, I wondered if I should stop the

202

game of punishment and come over and ravish you."

Nick got up then and walked around the room. The closeness was too much. Greg had been too quick with what he had to say, too concise. Nick needed and wanted to hear it, but not in such a rush. Greg's impulsiveness made him nervous, and he felt a kind of shock in his body. He heard the sound of youth, the sound of both of their youthful years in Greg's words; direct and clear as if the words were running on legs and the room was the streets of Brighton back when they were no more than children.

"Greg, you speak of François and his feelings. You talk of failure, but he is in love with you and you with him."

Greg replied angrily, "Aren't you listening? I am in love with you. And no, he has made it clear, and it's a relief to me that he no longer loves me." He paused, and then as if it were a throwaway line, said, "He has been having an affair for over two years with a woman. His family knows, and they would like him to marry her."

"What?"

Nick grasped the table. The pages of the book were turning quickly now. The wind from the garden, in its warmth, had strength. He too needed strength.

"You heard me, Nick. He said he was bisexual when we met. He believed, and such is the illusion of so many bisexuals, that his passion for me could make him faithful and that perhaps the heterosexual side of him was a phase he had gone through. But when he met this woman, he was attracted, and his desire for women returned. He no longer experienced much pleasure with me, and quite soon afterwards, I too was looking elsewhere. Not for a perfect partner, only to satisfy the flesh. The partner I really wanted was you. Every time I rang you, I wanted to have you in my arms."

"But what if he hadn't found this woman? Do you think you would have continued loving each other?"

Greg sighed. "Maybe I can't convince you, but my love for him lasted nine months. I counted the months. I hoped, in the beginning, it was the peace I needed, a rest from all the other experiences that had wounded me and that, to use the cliché, it was the real thing. And yes, the illusion lasted for nine months, and then one night while we were fucking I felt only the satisfaction of the act. I had no other feeling but lust."

"Lust can be part of being in love, Greg, as well you know. It often is. And it can last some people a lifetime."

Greg glanced at Nick, and his eyes were fierce. He was struggling to find the correct words.

"It was *only* lust, Nick. That is all I can say. And sexual act after sexual act with François proved that to me. Do you want me to be crude? Do you want the hard core of it?"

Nick saw that Greg's ferocity was increasing. He was leaning forward on the sofa, his hands clenching hard at the piece of furniture as if he were afraid to let his hands loose. He is capable of murder, Nick thought, and the thought appalled him. He could see the brink that Greg was on and how easily he might tip over into extreme darkness.

"Yes," Nick whispered.

"I wanted only the touch of his big cock in my mouth, in my arse, and in my hand as I wanked him off. That was how pure my lust was! My lust remained faithful to his cock, and every other cock I had aside of his was feeble in comparison."

There was silence between them. The dreadful look on Greg's face went away, and he looked like a totally defeated man.

"Has François definitively told you that he will marry this woman? And Greg, please, can we make her human? What is her name?"

"Sara. She is a Christian Arab like him. They have a lot in common and yes, after a couple of days here, in this town that he does not like, and with you, whom he also dislikes, he told me that he had made up his mind to make the necessary arrangements with his family and her family upon his return. They will wed in Algiers, at the Catholic church there. Oh, fuck it, I am too tired to go into details."

Nick wanted him. He wanted him, and he recalled a morning, many years before, after Greg had fucked him violently in St Ann's Well Gardens. He remembered how he had voided his bowels in a public toilet near the seashore, and in the bowl, the white of the sperm mingled with the blood and shit, and then separated itself, opening like a white flower. The distant memory was vivid and clear. He saw only a flower, where others would have seen obscenity, and the violence, even rape, showed itself to him as being pure in that transformation.

"I love you," he said to Greg.

Greg lifted up his head. There was a pleading sound in his voice as he replied, "Take me up to your bed. I am too tired to fuck, but fuck me. No more running away from each other. I want to remain here with you."

Nick went over to Greg and gently raised him up from off the sofa.

"Let François find us together in your bed," Greg said. "That will bring everything to an end. Perhaps he will be less gloomy when he knows it is all settled. He will leave the country with a clear conscience and a single purpose—to return to Sara."

Nick was not convinced it would be that simple, nor was he confident that Greg's version of François' feelings was accurate, but still, he led him upstairs. Somehow he sensed a further act was about to be played out. Once on the bed, he felt Greg cover his body, and after they were naked, Greg bent down and took Nick's cock into his mouth. Satisfied that he had aroused Nick enough, Greg then straddled him and guided Nick's cock into him. He yelled out Nick's name as if calling him from a distance, and continued to cry out as Nick thrust deep inside. Nick cried out with him, and as they fucked, they kissed constantly, cries stifled and then released, shifting position so that their mouths were never too far away from each other. And finally, after their orgasm had passed, they lay still, and slowly, very slowly, fell asleep in each other's arms.

François did not return that night. The sun in the garden the next morning felt and looked autumnal. Nick sat there with Greg, and they had breakfast. They did not talk, and the silence was good. This lasted until the phone rang. It was Nathan assuring Nick that Karel was better and that he had gone to work.

"Who was it?" Greg asked when Nick returned.

"Nathan. A temporary release from the strain of Karel. You must remember how it was for you! Karel has gone to work, but I don't think this is over. I think it is a crisis and that he is desperately trying to fight it off."

"We did not say what *we* would do for them," Greg said as he poured himself another cup of tea. Nick watched the rare and yet familiar act of domesticity with uncertain happiness; after so long, to see this pouring of tea from a cup at breakfast. It had been too long.

"What do you want me to do?" Nick asked.

"Not only you," Greg insisted, "but you and I. I *am* staying, Nick, and if you will have me, I will live here."

Again this impulsive insistence of the youth within Greg. He had made *his* decision, and Nick had to believe that he genuinely meant it. This time, there must be no more escape, no more flight for Greg.

"I'm afraid you will run off again for some reason. Karel left, and you followed. Not only did you follow, but you stayed there, in Paris. I know the situation was exceptional, but I don't want another situation like that. Things happen in life, and who knows what the future holds, but I refuse to be left alone again as I was before. I am too old for it now, and I fear the *us* of us would be broken."

"You have to trust," Greg said, his voice calm. "We are one, you and I. Didn't you taste that, experience that, in what passed between us last night? Has it ever felt quite so right and true?"

The phone rang again, and Greg laughed and said that the house had become already impossibly busy. He smiled at Nick as he said this, a well-worn smile, but it worked. When Nick picked up the phone, he heard François' voice.

"Can I speak to Greg?" he asked bluntly.

"If you hold on, I'll get him."

Greg was already standing in the doorway, and with a long sigh, came forward and took the receiver out of Nick's hand. Nick stood close, to hear what François was saying.

"Yes?" Greg asked.

"I am at the hospital. I was beaten last night. Two men smashed my nose badly. My left eye also. I thought I was blind. I couldn't see until I was in the ambulance. I also hit my head, so the doctors kept me overnight. What a horrible violent town this is!"

"Where did it happen?"

"Does that matter?" François' voice was angry and loud as he replied, and Nick motioned to Greg to hand over the receiver to him.

"It's me, Nick. Karel is working up at the hospital. I think he is on duty. You could tell the staff he is a friend."

"Fuck you too," François screamed at him.

Patiently, Nick continued, "It's just—let me give you Karel's full name. He could help—"

"Shut up, Nick. It's for Greg to come here. I want to talk to him and not on the phone. I am still in pain. They have not released me yet. When they do, I want someone to bring me to the house, and it has to be Greg. Not you. Not Karel. I don't want that—that Yid to touch me."

Too shocked to answer, Nick handed the phone back to Greg and murmured, "You can have him. Fetch him and then find him a hotel for the rest of his stay. Did you hear what he called Karel?"

"Yes," Greg replied. He then spoke to François. "I will get a taxi and be there within the hour. Are you still in the emergency department?"

"Find out for yourself."

The line went dead.

"That was quite revealing," Greg said and returned to sit in the garden.

"Well, aren't you going? I'll call for a taxi. It'll take a few minutes for one to come."

"Let him stew," Greg replied, and then added, "and talking of stew, this tea needs a refresh. Can you make a new pot?"

"But—"

"He can *wait*," Greg said angrily. "The little shit. He never shouted out at me like that before. Maybe the attack has brought out the hatred—hatred I have felt since he met Sara. She is the sort of Catholic who would have started the Counter-Reformation by herself." He paused and stared hard at Nick. "He was a good man when I met him. It *was* real for a while. This is not the complete François."

"Are you trying to condone—"

"No, for fuck's sake, no. The little cunt deserves to be thrown out for what he said, and I don't ever want him to see Karel or Nathan again. But I still believe it's Sara's influence."

Nick shook his head slowly and, picking up the teapot, gazed at its bright sheen of red, glittering in the sunlight. He picked up Greg's equally red cup and saucer. The passion of the colour intensified his anger.

"No, it is not Sara. Hatred like that must have been there all the time. The Jews live in the Marais, don't they? Are they equally in Barbès?"

"How should I know?"

"Because you have just come from there. Surely you are aware of what is around you. Even I know the district is reputed to be full of many different religions."

Nick walked into the kitchen and refreshed the pot. He felt weary. They had only slept for about three hours. Greg came into the kitchen and asked him to try to find a small hotel that provided both breakfast and dinner.

"A gay-friendly one?" Nick asked with a smirk.

"Don't be unkind, Nick. Any place where he can be comfortable. Maybe I should also stay there for a couple of nights while he gets better—in a separate room. I still feel something for him."

"I know," Nick said coldly.

"Don't worry about the tea."

Nick emptied the full pot into the sink. He did not look at Greg.

"I never want to see him here again," Nick repeated. "I know he has had a beating up, and that is terrible, but the unkind part of me, as you call it, says that he deserves it. I cannot tolerate that level of hatred. It is all there in that one word. Hatred for minorities is always best said with one word!"

"Yes, but what words did his attackers use? We don't know, but I can guess. He was probably attacked for the colour of his skin. Some nice Whitehawk boys perhaps, or maybe an ugly-minded kid from Portslade—like I used to be."

"We don't know the colour of his skin was the reason."

"I will find out," Greg said, and without saying more, went upstairs and left the house.

Nick was numb, blaming himself at one moment, then telling himself he was right. The balance hung in his mind and then swayed down on the side of being right. He could not allow François to see either Nathan or Karel again. It was as simple as that, but he wondered if Greg truly understood the reason. He then rang several guesthouses and found one that offered meals. After this, he rang the hospital and left a message with a nurse, giving the address of the hotel and its telephone number. He put down the phone. There was a vacancy in the house again—all presence, other than his own, gone, and the impact of this solitude made him shudder. He paced up and down, and then came the worst thought of all; that not for one moment had he blamed the attackers; the queer bashers (in all probability) that had nearly lost François his sight and had bashed his nose and caused a possible concussion. He swore at and blamed himself. Greg had every right not to want to see him again. The balance in his mind had swung in the opposite direction. He picked up the red, blood-coloured teapot and smashed it on the floor.

In the days that followed, Nick shut himself in the bookshop and read a lot of poetry. It was easier to read than fiction or any other genre. He read Celan and Trakl and Rilke and rediscovered the beauty of Ungaretti. The words washed over him, and yet, many were absorbed within, despite his lack of total attention. He was polite to customers but never encouraged any prolonged conversation. He had placed himself voluntarily into a mental and, in some ways, physical prison. Some nights he went back to the house, but on others, he slept foetal-shape in the cubby hole. He caught a cold and felt ill but still continued with his self-inflicted punishment. He was both torturer and tortured. And yes, he did wonder how François was, and yes, he *did* care. It was a kind older man who heard him sneeze and examined his face closely, who observed that he really should shut the bookshop and give himself a long rest.

"I can't do that," Nick replied.

"Then let me give you something. I spent time in Russia some years ago, and I must say, I found the country incredible, but that is irrelevant. I learned of a special herbal tea that is an immediate remedy."

Nick felt he had heard this before, or had he dreamt the conversation? Fever was perhaps beginning.

"I am Arnold. I have been in here many times, but I don't think you ever really noticed me. I am getting on for eighty, and I have disappeared from the view of many, many people. But there I go again with my irrelevancies—"

Nick smiled at this. His first smile for weeks. How long had he incarcerated himself? Evenings and nights locked away among the dust and spiders of the bookshop.

"I too am becoming invisible," he replied to Arnold. "My name is Nick. I would shake your hand, but you do not want my germs."

"Don't be silly. I am beyond germs. I live nearby, just off the London Road. I will fetch the herbs and the secret ingredient that is so special, and in a short while, I will return."

"What *is* the secret ingredient?" Nick asked.

"I should not tell, but I will. Every *babushka* in Russia would lose all respect for me if they knew, but I will say the magic word." And here he paused as if on the cliff edge of his own self-created surprise. "Care," he said eventually. "Care in its purest distillation. Some have the ingredient. Many do not."

Nick smiled again, acknowledging the wisdom of the reply. "So simple," he said.

"Isn't everything?"

Then the old man bustled out of the shop, forgetting the book he had chosen. It was a book of poems. Nick opened the book and read the poems at random. They were by an author he had not read before called R. S. Thomas, and they had a lucid simplicity about them that for a while made him feel better. He rubbed out the pencilled-in price and replaced it with one that was far below the book's monetary worth. It was a first edition. He didn't want to charge the man at all, but he intuitively knew the man would refuse to accept it as a gift. When Arnold returned, he saw the book at once.

"I thought I had lost it," he said. "Oh, I am so glad I left it here. Forgetfulness! What a thing it is!" He had a flask in his hand and placed it on the counter. "It is full. I want you to drink half now and then the rest later. I will not need the flask. I am always losing them and have about five others in my flat. But you are young. You *will* remember, and I will pick it up next time I come in for a book. No doubt you will remember me then."

Nick looked at Arnold and felt a surge of affection. He hoped he would be like that when he was approaching eighty. He thought of the early decades of the next century, the next millennium. He could not imagine it. Will we be the same kind of people, he wondered, and the emphasis in his thoughts was on the word *kind*.

"Take off the cup at the top and drink it now. You may feel terrible at first. You may believe I have put Hemlock or something in it! But don't worry, it will pass as a lightning flash passes, and then you will feel so much better."

Nick did as he was asked, filled the cup and drank it down. The taste was not good, but he knew instinctively that it would do him no harm.

"Now I suggest you shut the shop for the afternoon."

"I have a small room I call my cubby hole at the back. I will rest there a while, and thank you for being so—"

"So human?" Arnold finished the sentence for him, then picking up the poetry book, he looked at the price and, after searching for coins in his pocket, placed them on the counter.

"I was going to say, thoughtful and generous," Nick said.

"You flatter me," Arnold replied, "but I am as ungenerous as anything. I have led a long life here in this town where I was born, and I was not reputed for my generosity when I was younger. I held myself to myself, and because of that, I am now on my own. I never gave, in the most important way that there is, and I will let your intelligent mind put the dots together. Now I must go, and do remember to drink the rest this evening. Goodbye."

He left quickly, and Nick sensed that Arnold had even now given too much of himself away. A lovable man who has not given love, Nick thought, and the *Alto Rhapsody* came to mind and the words of Brahms' song; the words in that beautiful music of ultimate cowardice. Goethe had written the words. What did Goethe know of this, with all his theories of colour and his book *Werther*? His eyes filled with tears, and feeling unwell, he put up the closed sign and went into his small room.

He was better the next day, and it was a good thing that he was. He had just opened the shop after sleeping in the back and was about to do his accounts when Nathan came bounding in like a dog that had been let off its leash. He was panting as if he had run for miles.

"Stanmer Park again?" Nick asked, smiling.

"Don't be cute! I ran to your place from our place, then on down here. I'm quite an athlete in my own way, or had you forgotten?"

"I've seen your legs," Nick replied wryly.

"So, where have you been nights? We turned up at your house—twice! No one in. And Greg and his frog? Where are they? But most importantly, why are you not there? Karel cares, and so do I."

"I've had stocktaking to do—"

"Rubbish—"

"I have had a lot of stocktaking to do! I have had to make a list of all the books in the shop."

"Don't lie! What do you think this place is, the lost library of Alexandria or something? I presume Greg and François are still in town?"

"In a hotel, I think."

"Don't you know?" Don't you see them?"

"You have used the word *don't* at the opening of a sentence, far too often in succession. It's boring."

"Nick, I am asking, have you seen them?" Nathan's mouth was hanging open, his tongue lolling out, and he looked more like a handsome specimen of a dog than ever.

"It's a long story, Nathan."

"I have time."

"Please, not now—"

"Oh, I can tell by the tone of voice it is one of *those* stories," Nathan said. "Love gone wrong. I won't pry anymore, but I can guess. You are in love with Greg still, and it is not reciprocated, and they have both moved out."

Nick forced a laugh.

"Who are you? Eva Petulengro? Telling fortunes for a living? Are the cards spread out? What do you see? Or is it the crystal ball clearing, revealing truth through the mist?"

"Cute again! I can see you don't look happy."

Nathan placed a book on the counter, marked at tenpence from the stall outside. It was a very battered copy of *Precious Bane* by Mary Webb. Nick stared down at it.

"What is *that*?"

"Mary Webb. Karel reads her. He has got through Thomas Hardy, and now he is on to her. He is just finishing *Gone to Earth* which I bought for him in Duke Street, and before you malign this writer, I agree with you—but Karel likes her, and that's important. I would prefer him to read Dennis Altman, but when he tries, he fails."

"Homosexual and oppression, or something," Nick said, and then added, "Isn't that where you and I came in, as they say? As they used to say when watching double-bills at the movies?"

"Funny!"

"You will be pleased to know, Nathan, that I have read the book. I read it with mixed feelings. It's good, but it will date. We gays are not up to most of its propositions."

"Let's pause on that," Nathan said, then pushed Mary Webb closer to Nick. "So, do I get discount for this?" he asked sarcastically.

"For 10p? Take it. Tell Karel I love him and place the book nicely, and I mean nicely, into his hands. If he has sunk so low as to take on board Mary Webb's contrivances, well, I want you to tell him that I have as well. I confess now that I have read her. She is appropriate for night shifts at the hospital, and I rather guess that is why Karel likes her."

"You've convinced me," Nathan said.

They paused for a long while and looked at each other, and then Nick went to make some coffee for Nathan. When he returned, he asked, his voice now completely serious, "How is Karel now? Honestly."

Nathan sipped the hot coffee. "The attacks are happening again. Less frequent than before, but happening. Even I have come to believe he will have a heart attack one of these days."

"Really, Nathan, you must wake up to the facts. You know what an ectopic heartbeat means!"

"Yes."

"Well?"

"Okay, I know it's not that serious, but it is about the heart."

"And blood will continue to pump in and out until he is a very, very old man. Cheer up, Nathan, and for God's sake, let's close the shop. We can continue talking in my den."

Nathan looked wary. Nick caught the look and laughed. "Don't worry, Nathan. Put away those thoughts. They are disgraceful!"

Together they went into the cubby hole, and Nathan joked that he felt he had gone to earth. "I'm too long-legged for this cramped space. What do you want me to do? Hang upside-down from the ceiling?"

"Once I thought of you as a sexy spider, so try it."

"Then my disgraceful thoughts were right."

"I said *once*, Nathan, once. It seems a long time ago. Now, let's discuss the Altman book, and although I get over-stimulated on coffee, I will join you in a cup."

"Why don't you think gays are up to Altman? Some of us have brains. You, me, Greg and Karel, we *think*."

"It's not just a question of thinking," Nick said, sitting on the floor. Nathan sat cross-legged in front of him. "How many years is it since decriminalisation? Or rather, the *partial* decriminalisation of homosexual acts?"

"A few years."

"Precisely. It is all too recent for this brilliant and frightening attack on heterosexual values. Most gays are still enslaved by these values, and it will take a long time, maybe decades, before they want more freedom or liberation. They, we, are too scarred, Nathan, by long decades of suffering, silence and arrest, to put our heads above the parapet. We have internalised guilt until we have almost drowned in it. How do you put aside the pain experienced, and the suicides, from fear of exposure and prison? You are young, and perhaps among the young—and wiser older men—you will understand a lot of what Altman is saying, but to ask the majority to understand is quite simply impossible. Gays have lived in muted colours for far too long. Centuries too long. And you want them to come out all flaming bright with flashing swords of defiance just a few years, as you rightly said, after an act that has allowed them to *begin* to breathe?"

"You're older than me. Did you breathe?"

"I did. Greg did. Perhaps we were born with armour. I don't know, but even Greg had a tough time dealing with his nature." Nick drank some coffee, then added slowly, "It is hard to put yourself in others' shoes. Because of your age, you did not wear them. Use your imagination. Now, let's change the subject."

"No, I want to talk more about it."

"Nathan, my dear friend, on top of everything else, I haven't been too well. Be good, and let us discuss lighter things. What do you do together, you and Karel, in your spare time? Cheer me up with some small details of happiness. I need it."

Slowly Nathan reached out and touched Nick's hands. "Please don't feel alone," he said. "You are not. Believe me, you are not. Karel and I both love you, and just to raise your ego and nothing else, you are a horny bastard! I bet Greg still feels that. How could he not?"

Nick bowed his head in mock acknowledgement of the compliment. He imagined Greg, Karel and Nathan, entwined together. He revelled in the erotic possibilities for a short while, but then he stood up and said the shop had been closed for too long.

"Time to go," Nathan said. "And when will we see you in your proper place? In your house?"

"Soon, Nathan, soon."

They kissed each other on the cheek, and it seemed to Nick that they did not want to part, and after Nathan had left and the shop door was closed, Nick realised he was ready for strangers.

There were a few leaves tinged with red on the branches. The wind felt fresher and the light in the evenings more golden towards the west. It became a habit for Nick to leave his shop at five, to walk to the Palace Pier, and then along the upper promenade towards the West Pier. He was tired, as he continued to sleep badly in the shop, but he enjoyed the

216

variation in the waves and the drawing outward of the tides when the sands were exposed. He saw himself playing there with Greg, but it was an illusion. He had played on the sands, but long before he met Greg, in those distant, only vaguely recalled days of one's first decade in life. He thought of himself in shorts, running barefoot with a bucket and spade, but this too was false. His mother had been afraid of the water and had forbidden him to run. His dream of himself as a small boy was simply that, a dream, but during these present days of sadness and loneliness, it comforted him to think of his early childhood being otherwise. He did remember his mother, slim then, red in her dress and with a flame of red in her being, standing on the promenade. She had loved the place where the dividing Angel stood, and the bandstand. Vague memories of clutching her hand, and of brass bands playing, resounded in his mind. She was kind to him then, or so he liked to think, and while they stood listening to bad renditions of Strauss waltzes and operatic themes, he would be given an ice cream from a passing vendor, Neopolitan, his favourite, for its varied colour and its flavour. Yes, Nick recalled both true and false as he walked further west towards and sometimes beyond Hove Lawns, following the turquoise and then green railings that separated him from the descent of the beach. When at last he reached his frontier of Fourth Avenue, he would pause and think of the skiff out at sea, imagining again the figure that had seemed to be Oliver. Oliver, so distant in the past. He wondered where he was and what he was doing, and paradoxically at the same time, didn't care about him at all. Then, looking up at the sun, waiting for it to sink, waiting for that explosion that was almost apocalyptic in September, of branding colour spreading across the surface of the sky, burning deeply all before it, until it transformed with such a depth of intensity that it faded in on itself, he would walk back. His walk slowed as the night began to advance more quickly with the year's turning, he cut up to the Western Road and made the rest of the journey back by bus. There was always the same feeling of disjunction from nature when he boarded it, assaulted by the smell of fish and chips wrapped in paper and of stale cigarette smoke. The buses were not often crowded, but Fridays and Saturdays were bad, with youths and their girls, shrieks of expectation and bawdy jokes, plus smoke and all too pungent colognes. He would get off at the Old Steine and stare at the Pavilion, lit so boldly with purples, pinks, and acid greens, all folding into each other and then returning to repeat their colours. He watched this repetition for a while, then stopped at the Astoria to look up at its emblematic name, proud. His palace of dreams returned with monsters on posters clutching scantily dressed females, and stills outside offering tempting images of action suspended, and he would remember Greg. Has he gone? Has he left me, he asked himself, and not once could he make the move to turn in the direction of Kemp Town to the guesthouse to find out. He was afraid of being afraid, and like those frightened figures in the stills outside the cinema, he froze, too scared, lest the monster of truth would catch him, raise him up, and throw him down.

Out of exhaustion, Nick returned to sleep at the house. It was cold, and he felt hatred towards the emptiness of its rooms. He hated the sight of things Greg had touched, hating them as if these objects and pieces of furniture were alive and full of Greg's rejection of him.

On the second morning of his return, he saw a note without an envelope that had been put through the door. At first, he took it for a flyer or advertisement, as the paper was yellow, and the writing (which looked from a distance like print) was bright blue. But when he picked it up, he saw handwriting, wide and expansive, with a strong emphasis on exclamation marks. At the bottom of the one-sided sheet, he saw François' name. He read it slowly, afraid.

Dear Nick!
I must, must see you. Today! After today it will be too late!!!
I will be standing in front of St Peter's Church at 14h this

afternoon! Please be there! I have things I must say.
*   François.*

His first reaction was no. I do not want to see him. Then
slowly, he became more rational. He tried to look at it from all
sides, trying to ascertain the meaning of this request and why
it was François and not Greg. Then his fear grew intense and
rooted itself in his stomach. His stomach hurt, and he rushed to
the toilet twice, hoping that whatever it was would pass out of
his body, but only a dirty, watery substance came forth. He
drank glass after glass of water, hoping to flush the pain away.
Finally, he ate two slices of stale bread covered with honey. The
hard and disgustingly sweet combination did the trick, and the
pain receded. He had a quick bath and put on the first clean
clothes that were at hand. The clock said twenty to two, and
forgetting to lock the front door, he hurried down the hill to St
Peter's Church. On the steps of the church, he saw François
dressed in a heavy black coat with a scarf around his neck.

"Hello," he said tentatively as he mounted the steps towards
the still figure.

"Hello," François replied, smiling, and held out his hand.
After that gesture, there was an awkward silence. Who would
speak first? Nick was hesitant, so François took up the
challenge.

"Can we catch a bus to somewhere quiet so we can talk?"

"Wouldn't you prefer a café?"

"No. I insist. I want it to be a quiet place. Maybe if there is
one outside the boundaries of this town? I want to be in a place
that does not impose itself or shout. The shouting in Barbès I
can tolerate. But not here."

Nick wondered where he could take him and then thought
of the bus that went to Patcham. He had only been there twice
himself but remembered a wooded area facing a peaceful line
of houses, and if he recalled correctly, there was also a place to
eat and drink.

"It will take a while on the bus," he said to François, "but I know of somewhere."

"Good. I have three hours to spare."

They caught the bus after waiting in silence for about twenty minutes. Nick tried to make small talk on the way, pointing out various aspects of the town, forgetting (or did he?) that François had no desire to look at more of Brighton. Patcham came into view, and François' eyes finally showed interest as he saw the upward slope of trees that appeared to be a forest.

"It's beautiful," he said. "Let us go there."

"It's a bit of a climb."

"I'm willing. I want to go into the trees. Can we reach a spot where we see nothing but trees?"

They climbed the rather steep incline, and very soon, they found somewhere suitable. François sat down on the trunk of a fallen and decaying tree. The air was cold, but he was wrapped up. Nick had not dressed so warmly, and shivered as he sat down. François noticed.

"I have a flask of cognac with me. Would you like some?"

"Please."

François put his hand inside his coat pocket and drew out the flask. He handed it to Nick.

"It will warm you."

Nick drank the cognac, more than perhaps he should have. After a while, it made him feel light-headed, and the branches on the trees began to sway unnaturally.

"I haven't drunk alcohol in weeks," Nick said, turning to look at François, who was staring into the green depths. "Now, can we talk?"

"Yes, of course. But first, facts. I *did* have a concussion, and they kept me in the hospital for quite a while. I lost consciousness, and I went into a coma. Although I sensed what was happening around me, I could not see or feel, but I sensed. I heard the nurses and the doctors. I felt as if I was buried alive and that no one would rescue me. It was a very bad feeling."

"I had no idea it was that serious," Nick said, and the feeling in his stomach returned. Fortunately, at the last minute before leaving the house, he had picked up a thick slab of chocolate. He asked François if it was okay for him to eat something.

"But we are far from anywhere—"

"I brought some chocolate. We can share it if you like."

François looked as if he didn't like, and shook his head.

"No, thank you. England is obsessed with chocolate. Is it really necessary for the population?"

He put it so quaintly that Nick laughed.

"It *is* the English vice," Nick replied. "As a child, I was brought up on Mars bars."

François made a face, and this brief, almost humorous exchange brightened the situation considerably. Nick unwrapped the foil and broke off two slabs.

"But it is so heavy!" François exclaimed.

"It's extra thick! Cadbury's make several sizes."

François grinned and exclaimed, "They *do*?"

"Yes, you can break a tooth on them. Children often do! You must have seen we are the country with fewer teeth than anywhere else."

"No," François said, now laughing loudly. "You mean baby teeth or real teeth?"

"The ones for the rest of our lives. We have to smile with our mouths closed."

"Nick, stop. It is too shocking. I eat *le loukoum*, Turkish Delight, but in moderation. There are many sweet things in Algiers, but not the barbaric orgy of choices you have here, not to mention your obsession with terrible cakes. I thought my fellow Algerians were fat, but some of the people I have seen around me far exceed them. I am surprised they do not burst or explode in flames." He paused. "There is some sort of combustion, do you believe it?"

"Blowing yourself up without blowing yourself up? It's what is called an urban myth."

"I see," François replied and pulled a dried twig away from the fallen tree. There was a pause, and Nick munched on his chocolate. Once more, the pain in his stomach receded.

"I am sorry," Nick said, breaking the silence.

"For what?"

"For my reaction to what you said on the phone. The word you used."

"It was an evil word I used. I was suffering, and it came out. Bad words often escape like that."

"So, tell me what happened to you."

François touched him briefly on the arm. "All is well now," he said, and taking the flask out, handed it to Nick. "Come on, drink a little more. Remember how Greg can drink?"

Nick took the flask but did not want to respond to the tentative flag of Greg's name. He drank only a little to warm himself, then looked around at the already deepening shadows casting a thickness of light over the moss and grass between the trees. François, noticing, looked around him.

"It is magical," he said.

"Yes," Nick replied. "I should come more often to these old, old, wise trees, but instead, I go up onto the open spaces of the Downs. Have you been up there?"

"No, and it is too late now." François' voice sounded sad. "But to get back to what happened. I was in the hospital, and after a while, they agreed to release me as long as I had someone to care for me. Greg had been kind and had slept at the hospital, often on a makeshift bed in a corridor. He never left the place, and when I was released, we did not go to that hotel you suggested but to a house in Portslade. I recuperated there, and now I am ready to return to Paris."

Nick caught on to the word *I*. "When do you both leave?" he asked, making sure that he had not misheard.

"I leave tomorrow."

"And Greg?" The question came out half-strangled.

"He is staying here where he belongs."

"But—"

"It is true, Nick, and that is why I wanted to prepare you. He would not like me for doing this, but I chose it. I want to heal some of the wounds, some of the pain I have caused. Like that terrible word I used." He paused. "I said the word to hurt. You see, I was still half in love with Greg then. I was jealous. Jealousy is terrible. But to go back to words—I had words inflicted on me the night I was attacked. They called me a 'coloured bastard' and many other ugly things. One of them said while he was kicking me, 'Take it fudge-face, you won't be fucking fudge for a long time after we're done with you.' And another, said, 'He will miss the brown shit, the arse-fucker. Is it true all you Arabs fuck arse?' I was so full of hatred when I rang you. I was, I hope, not my *true* self."

"I understand," Nick said, and he did. He felt revulsion towards those (and there were far too many) who had so little humanity in them. He put aside all questions of how poverty, how oppression and suppression can do this. He did not want to hear the whitewash of the liberal excuse. He knew those attackers for what they were, lacking in anything that brought hope to the future of mankind.

"Can we kiss?" he asked François. "Can we kiss as brothers?"

François looked into Nick's eyes, and Nick looked into his. A moment of desire? Yes, a little, but more of tenderness and good faith. Nick was the first to move, and their lips met. It was a long kiss and a passionate one, as if they had found each other. François broke away first.

"I want it," he said, "and I think you want it, but it must not happen. I am not afraid of being caught here in the shadows, but it just cannot be. I didn't think we had a desire for each other."

"It can happen that way," Nick replied.

"Yes, but Sara is waiting for me. I have promised to leave my desire for other men behind me for her. She does not know this because she does not want to think about it. It is my own choice. It is best that I am faithful to one sex, and it may be a lifetime with her. I made a sort of vow to not go with women when I met Greg. If marriage existed between two men, it would have happened between Greg and me."

"You loved him that much?" Nick asked.

"More than you can imagine. But after a while, deep down, I realised there was a stronger love than the one he felt for me, and that was for you. I knew then that you and he were married in your *souls*, and I was so furious and jealous I behaved very badly with him."

"And do you believe he still—still loves me?"

"Stronger than ever. As I was recuperating in Portslade, he paced the room like an impatient animal waiting to get out of a cage. He was hungry for you, and he could not eat. I even told him what I saw, and he did not reply, but I knew it was true. He ached with hunger for you, for the sight of you."

"Can I ask you a question? A question I need to know?"

"What?" replied François, looking wary.

"You don't have to reply, but I wish you would. Did you ever in Paris feel that he had been in any sense close to murder or to murdering? Did your intuition tell you he had experienced or been near such a feeling?"

There was a long silence, and the rising wind of approaching evening was rustling in the branches around them. The forest had lost its colour, and all around them was grey shade.

"How could you have guessed?" François murmured. "How?"

"Then there is some truth in what I have sensed?"

"He met someone there. I am being honest because I have feelings for you. This someone brought him to the edge of murder. A cruel, complicated man. He almost slaughtered Greg's heart, and eventually, Greg saw too much of the man's true self. There was violence, to say the least. I rescued Greg from this appalling relationship that, in truth, was not a relationship at all. You see, Nick, Greg is, in his way, a very mixed up being. He is so much of himself that he spills over. It is as if his inner being is divided, or perhaps multiple. Who am I to say, but there is too much within him that cannot be contained. His solid root, his core being, is *you,* and that cannot be split apart, but it seems to me that whatever he has is never enough, as if another self within him is always struggling for more. And then comes, what I call the overflow."

"You know him well," Nick said, "and he will need more than me, despite his fidelity."

"Can you accept that?"

"Yes. I too know a little of how he is. I could have made love with you here this afternoon. You knew that, and rightly retreated. It is not for you that way of existing, but for people like Greg—and yes, me as well, we *need* others in all the senses of the term. I know it will happen again, and maybe soon—"

"What?" François asked.

"This need to reach out, to others, and to love them for themselves, in their flesh as well as for what is invisible within their beings."

"You mean a mutual sharing, with your love for him and his love for you as the core?"

"Absolutely."

François drank the last of the cognac from the flask. His handsome profile could just be seen in the rapidly falling darkness.

"We must hurry," Nick said. "It must be late," and then he laughed again to break up the intensity. "And we mustn't slip down this slope. The last time I came here, I fell, and the person I was with, a sort of Pagan, said a little person had tripped me up."

"A what?"

"Goblins, little green men, call them what you like. People believe they can be found in Sussex. At Chanctonbury Ring, they are supposed to dance in the glades, and if a stranger is receptive, they will reveal themselves."

They had already started the descent, and François stood still for a moment.

"Do you believe they exist?" he asked.

"Why not?" Nick asked. "Are we not strange ourselves?"

Nick knew the hour of the train that François would take but did not go to the station. He did not want to meet Greg in that way, and waited instead at the house in case he came. He waited until nightfall, but still there was no sign of him. Despite what François had said, the doubt returned that Greg had left with him, perhaps deciding to resume his life in Paris alone. It was Karel who came late that night and told him the truth.

"Greg came to us," he said. "He had to talk things out."

"Why to you?"

"He said he felt freer that way."

Nick had been trying to write, to kill time, but writing to kill time produces bad work. He wanted to write a long poem but realised that Saint-John Perse's *Anabasis*, which he had recently been reading, was too much of an influence; that and the stupid thought that the length of a long poem would dull the pain of waiting. The floor of the room downstairs was littered with discarded pages. Karel looked at them, scrunched up into balls, but passed no comment.

"I thought he would come to me. I spent yesterday afternoon with François. We met and went to Patcham because he needed to get away from the crowds in Brighton."

"I know," Karel said and sat down on the sofa.

"So he told Greg? Well, I supposed he would. It was strange but, in its way, it was a good meeting."

"Greg has had a bad time, Nick. I guess you have as well. Nathan noticed how you were when he eventually tracked you down at the shop. He is as concerned as I am about you, and now there is Greg."

"You mean the trauma of the hospital and being out in Portslade with François?"

Karel paused and asked if Nick could make some coffee. He added that he was under strain himself with work and that his nerves were too near the surface, too near to feel secure in himself. Nick did not reply to this but quietly made a couple of sandwiches and a pot of coffee.

"This will keep us awake tonight, but what the hell?" he added as he placed both the coffee and the sandwiches on the table.

"Come on over to the table," Nick said.

Karel came and sat on the bench facing the window, and Nick sat beside him.

"First you, Karel. Is it really not going so well?"

"That's not what I came for—"

"I know, but let's take one thing at a time. I am mentally trying to put Greg on the backburner of my mind. He is not the only priority. You and Nathan. Both of you count."

"You love us, and we love you too," Karel replied and picked up one of the sandwiches. "How did you guess I haven't had much to eat today?"

"Because you look thin and tired, and despite your cool exterior, I have the feeling you are not quite up to this visit. You have been on a bad shift, and you look in need of a meal."

Karel replied with his mouth full, "Nathan wanted to come as well, but I said no. Maybe I wanted you on my own. You are a magnet to all of us, Nick; I hope you know that, and that goes for Greg as well. He is in love with you—deeply in love with you. But I sense if and when he returns to you, and you accept his return, it will be on terms that you might not want—"

"Like what?"

Karel swallowed the last piece of bread and drank from his cup.

"Can I have some more coffee?" he asked.

Nick poured another cup, and Karel leant forward, his elbows on the table, his head propped up by his hands.

"Greg will talk to you about that. It is his place to do so, but I said I would accept. Nathan did as well."

"Karel, *you* must explain. In some ways—and you will probably contradict me—you are the sanest person among us, and before you open your mouth to protest, I think I already know, but I would prefer to hear it from your mouth instead of Greg's."

"Why?"

"Because you are as clear as your beautiful glass collection.

You always have been, and despite your fears which I flatter myself I understand, you are a sensible man. I am not so clear. I am a frustrated poet who cannot seem to put one right word after another, and my mood at the moment is bad. My mind is completely tangled. Unravel it for me. Please."

Karel laughed, and his face became brighter than it had been when he walked through the front door.

"You say you think you know?" he asked.

"I don't often have clarity of mind, Karel, but I do have a large amount of intuition. It is the main function in me. Thinking, feeling, sensation etc. Well, Jung sorted it out, and intuition was the fourth. It seems we are four in all this as well. Am I right?"

Karel nodded his head.

"Four in everything?" Nick asked.

"Yes. But there is something extra—something special that only Greg has the right to express." Karel paused and stared hard at Nick, who had moved away from the table and was walking about the room.

"Do you have any idea what that special something is?" Nick asked.

"It is uniquely between you and Greg."

"Even though the four of us, you, Nathan, Greg and myself are to share everything? Our bodies? Our sexuality? Our meals? And once again, this house?"

"I can tell you that Greg suggested buying a house of his own. It was just an idea."

"Did he? It's a crazy idea! It would be too *fixed* for him. I will do anything for all of you, and I love Greg as if he and I were one person, but this house remains and belongs to all of us. That said, if Greg wants to own a similar house, he has the right to do so. But anything that happens between *us* happens *here*."

"You two. Both of you are so adamant about things," Karel said, smiling. "I came here all tensed up, and now I feel relaxed and want to laugh. I agree with you. This is a home of memories, and they are memories we all should share. Being in a house of Greg's for some of the time would not feel the same at all." He paused. "Greg is a wanderer. Yes, he is happy in this house, but a house is not essential to him. It is the people, and the variety of people who are in it, who are. The difference lies there, in that drift that he can welcome so easily and that you can comply with, but not in quite the same way. You could not, like he did, leave this place and go to Paris. You are part of these walls, and this place is as sacred to you as any monastery. Perhaps that comparison is wrong, but you get the point. Home is a house, and the people are welcome, in sexuality and in love."

"And what of you, Karel? What is essential to you? What is your *function of being,* according to Jung?"

"Feeling. I can feel anywhere. I can feel for many and still have a primary love. That love is now for Nathan. He has the same force of feeling as I have, twinned with intellect, emotion and thought. He can live within any walls. He is like Greg in that, a wanderer in essence."

"We have said a lot," Nick said. "Are you very tired?"

"No."

"Shall we walk a bit? Walk to the sea?"

Karel got up. "Do you need to breathe?" he asked.

"A little, yes. I feel at this moment I want to look at the dark waves. We are so lucky that the promenade is floodlit. It shines on the waters so well—on the foam reaching the shore. It reassures. It too has its home. It never, after all, trespasses on ours."

In a short while, Nick and Karel reached the Palace Pier. The night was clear, and the sea was brightly visible as it pounded on the shore, drawing pebbles loudly from its depths and thudding others back to replace them. The thud and sucking noise of the waves was intense, and the foam sprayed high against the groyne nearest to the pier.

"I love it," Nick said.

"So do I. Aren't you glad that we live here?"

"Yes. Nowhere else." Nick paused and added, "I am very selfish, to want my own four walls to welcome me when this whole town welcomes me as a home."

"Not at all. It is the heart within your heart."

"*You* should be the poet," Nick replied.

"Who says I am not? I write in my feelings. A language hidden, even to me sometimes. Now, come on, let's go down to the shore."

"Okay."

"I will race you."

"Are you out of your mind?"

"Let's have fun. Let's be children again. Race you to the groyne. I want to get splashed by the foam."

Nick cried out as he ran, his voice growing louder as the wind suddenly rose. He took the lead and heard Karel trying hard to keep up, but Nick had a rush of strength. He knew where he was going, at last. He knew there was a destination and a compromise. He wasn't sure he wanted to share Greg sexually, but he knew he would enjoy the love of all of them when they came to his house. The sea in its giving and its eternal taking was symbol enough for him of the truth that Karel had helped reveal. He was the homemaker, and they all wanted him to be that.

He was first to reach the groyne and rested against its wet, hard back. He felt the force of the stone, washed by so many waves, and as he looked out to sea, he saw a massive wave approach. Karel was at a short distance beside him.

"Watch out!" Karel cried, but it was too late. Nick was soaked, and for a moment, he had the feeling the wave would take him back with it. His hair drenched and eyes blurred, he coughed out the water that had filled his open mouth and tried to make out Karel's form. Karel seemed far away in the distance. The wave had indeed almost dragged him in, but in that pause between the withdrawal of one wave and the arrival of the next, he climbed up the incline of shifting pebbles.

"I couldn't see you," Karel shouted.

"It nearly got me," Nick shouted back. The sound of the elements beat like a drum against Nick's ears.

"You could have died, Nick."

"But it felt wonderful, wonderful," and as Nick reached safety, he clung to Karel and then they both fell back onto the bed of the shore.

"We will both be taken into the sea," Karel said, his voice loud and close. He clung to Nick, and there was a sudden heat between them. Another incoming wave splashed near, and they edged their way backwards, out of reach.

"I'm excited," Karel said.

"So am I."

"Let's—let's take out our cocks."

"What?"

"You heard."

"Dirty bastard," Nick laughed, his mouth tasting of salt.

"I mean it. Let's give something back to the sea."

"You won't see anything in this darkness."

"There is light enough."

"You want to? You really want to?"

"Yes."

The wind roared suddenly, and there was violence in it. Nick looked up at the sky. Clouds were skidding across the moon, and shadows glanced and darted across the vast and deeper ocean above. He felt a draw upwards as he had felt the draw of the sea. He wanted to be lost to the earth that bound him to it. To rise or to sink, it did not matter, as long as he could disappear—to be gone from any demand or need.

"Nick, Nick, look at me!"

The familiar voice brought him back to himself. He turned and saw Karel, half-naked on the hard pebbles, a white flash of flesh, as white as the whitest fish thrown up on the shore, and in this whiteness, a darkness; the patch of human hair and the tumescent cock rising proudly upwards. Nick's instinct told him to reach out, and he moved his head forward and took the tip of the penis into his mouth. It tasted hot and as salty as the water that Nick had almost swallowed. Karel groaned and pushed at Nick's head, making him take the full length of the shaft. Nick gagged at first, but then his throat muscles relaxed, and he felt the pounding in and out of the flesh in the same way that he had heard and felt the pounding of the waves, and then a jet of sperm shot into him, which he welcomed and swallowed.

"Oh my God," Karel cried out and lay back panting on the beach.

"I drank all of you," Nick replied.

"What? I can't hear you."

"I said, I drank all of you. I almost drowned!"

Karel heard him and laughed.

"Now, what about you?"

"What about me?" Nick replied.

"Don't you want the same? Come into my mouth? I need it as well. Let us celebrate it. I *do* want to drown!"

Nick lay where he was. Behind him, he thought he saw a couple of people standing, watching, but then, like a mirage, they disappeared. The phantom figures were shadows, more ethereal beings of the wind, making themselves briefly visible in form.

"I saw it," he cried. "I saw what Saint Augustin did not see."

Laughing loudly, Karel cried back, "What was that?"

"The wind! I saw the wind! It appeared in form. It was two shadows. Two curious shadows. Even the wind is interested in us and our needs."

"Fantasist!"

"Of course."

Then Nick pushed down his trousers, closed his eyes and allowed Karel to take him within himself. He felt the caress of Karel's tongue and the drawing inwards of his flesh. He felt the suction of gums, and for a moment, the slight grazing of teeth. He did not feel sexual excitement as such, but a sense of belonging to everything that was around him. He inwardly called on the wind to return and watch, and when he came in a

232

burst of heat, he felt no stronger a sensation than that. Was it orgasm? Could he truly call it orgasm? He knew it only as a flow outwards; a slight eruption of the life force, and it was as good as the rest that surrounded him.

"I took nothing from you that Greg would not have wanted me to."

Karel's words were strange. What belonged to Nick belonged to himself alone. He felt a momentary protest. It had nothing to do with Greg or his permission. Why had Karel needed to say these words? Nick had but given a birth moment to sperm, to flow as the sea flowed and to disperse and become one with the rest as everything else.

"We should go," Nick replied simply, and there was a lull in the roar around them. Nature paused as if to listen.

"Yes," Karel replied.

Greg looked utterly hollowed out when Nick eventually saw him, as if a sculptor had chiselled away all the surplus stone of his face and honed it down to its essential. Giacometti could not have done better. He also had more lines, as if deep cut by the same sculptor's chisel. His eyes appeared larger, more open, and in their openness, Nick thought he saw many things; terror, glimpses of past experience, and a remote withdrawal at the same time. His eyes showed that nothing more could or would remain simple. His cleanly cut lips seemed thinner, and his sharp teeth showed more, as if his mouth would nibble at life now, and not gulp it all in one go as it was used to doing. Nick sensed that the hospital had done this and that those within it had been the artists of his sterner face. And yet, this mixture of stone and flesh had a new smell. Nick drew close and sniffed.

"Cannabis?" he asked.

"Yes."

Nick recalled his distaste for the smell, and Greg, seeing this, grabbed him and shook him.

"What of it? Don't purse your lips like that, questioning me as if it were the ultimate in disgust. It has saved me. Do you hear? Saved me. Your mouth looks tight, like the arsehole of an eleven-year-old boy. Grow up, Nick! This is me, now!"

Nick broke away and, in silence, went downstairs. Greg followed, missed a step and skidded the rest of his way down, his back knocking against the harsh wooden stairs.

"Fuck!" he said as he landed on the floor.

"Let me see your back."

Greg at first protested as Nick turned him over onto his stomach. Nick hoisted up his jacket and his shirt and saw that his back was red and sore, but the flesh had not been broken. "There's no blood," Nick said, and Greg rolled back and sat up on the floor. His face looked even whiter than it had before.

"Shaky!" he said.

"I have some lotion I can rub on it to soothe it later."

Greg got to his feet and waved away the suggestion with a gesture of his hand. "I just need a couple of glasses of water," he said, going over to the sink. He filled a glass, drank it and refilled it. As he held his head back to drink, Nick looked at the line of his neck. It had always been a part of Greg's body that he liked to touch and caress. Putting the glass into the sink, Greg murmured, "Can I lie down on the sofa? I'm worn out. If you are sure the smell is not too much for you?"

Nick made no reply, and slowly Greg lay down on the sofa, his body stretched out. Nick saw and smelled how dirty his clothes were. How long has it been, he wondered, since he has had a change of clothes? I have never seen him like this before.

"I shouldn't have come to you in this state. I should have had a bath, and I forgot how fastidious you can be."

"Greg, I'm sorry—"

"You have a right to be disgusted. I am disgusted with myself at present. It's just I never thought you would be surprised that I smoke. I really did—still *do* need it. It has got me through."

Nick sat down opposite him, and he asked, "Because of François?"

"Yes. No. Things are never simple. I took to smoking in Paris over the past year" He paused. "I loved him. I love him. He chose marriage to a woman, and he is gone. It was an absurd last few months—my increasing hostility towards him, despite what I showed—but I don't want to talk about him anymore. We parted at the station, and we made no promises to contact each other again. I told him to throw away the possessions I left in his flat. The books, the records, the usual clutter of existence. I suppose it is a good thing that I brought the Cezanne with me." He paused again and then said, "After all, in time it all goes, for any of us. All our things end up with antique dealers or junk shops. Flesh burns us into oblivion, and the human jackals disperse our possessions. It is the law of life. Or should I say death?"

"You sound bitter," Nick observed.

Greg stared at Nick.

"Always the observer, Nick, aren't you? Is it the writer in you? Must you dissect?"

"But you have just been dissecting yourself. You have spoken clearly of the process."

"We are the same coin," Greg said wearily and closed his eyes.

There was silence for a while, and Nick broke it by saying, "Do you want to stay the night here? I would like you to. You look as if you need to be cared for, for a while."

"No," Greg said quietly and then moved into an upright position. "I just came to see you, that's all—no intentions behind it. Just to see you. And believe me, I don't want to stink out the whole house."

"You could have a bath."

Greg burst out laughing. "And a change of clothes? Your clothes? And what would we do with these rags I am wearing? I only came back to this country with a few clothes, and none of them have been washed. The hospital smelled of so much decay. My clothes in their grubby state did not seem to matter, adding nothing to the overall stench of urine, defecation, and death. Even Karel did not notice. And yes, he came to see me quite a lot while I was there with François. He was working on a different ward, but all the same, I grew to love him again for his visits." Drawing in his breath, he added, "I began to love him again, full stop. Do you mind?"

"No," Nick replied.

"I am glad," Greg said. "I like Nathan. I desire him, but I don't hunger for him, not in the way that I hunger for Karel." He paused, then murmured, "I love you. You are me, Nick. We are inseparable. But then, you know that."

"We are separate beings," Nick reminded him gently.

"The zoo of our bodies makes us so. That is true. All the little worlds within our individual selves, with their uprisings and their revolts; the zoo within us of microbes, bacteria, and whatever else the doctors could name, each have a claim. They would call themselves individuals if they could, and maybe they do. Have you thought of that? That each rash of Herpes or whatever we get in our groins, or the lumps in our throats, are struggling entities, fighting and warring and sometimes quietly resting. Above all, they *know*, yes know their individual place."

"Greg, you are a poet yourself. Have you thought of that?"

"No. I am not a poet in the way you are, but I was taught in Paris to express what I felt and saw. I had teachers there, and I was *taught*."

"What about the things you taught yourself?"

"Oh, quiet, quiet with these questions. I came to see *you*. I have begun my return. Do you want my return?"

There was an urgency in Greg's voice as he asked this and he leant forward, his face stretched taut, skin tight, eyes glowing as if fervently pleading.

"Yes. Yes," Nick replied and came to him. He put his arms around Greg's neck, kneeling in front of him. He kissed his neck and then reached towards Greg's mouth. Greg backed away.

"My breath. Toothpaste has not been of any concern to me for days."

236

Nick replied to this by pulling Greg's head close to his and pressing his lips against Greg's. Slowly the line of closed flesh opened, and Nick's tongue entered. Whatever taste he savoured, it was Greg's; whatever odour of breath or remnant of decayed food was Greg's. He was kissing him with a passion that wanted to melt all resistance. Then their mouths eventually withdrew, and Greg stared at him.

"We cannot go further than this," Greg said. "Not now. Not at this meeting. I lied when I said I came *just* to see you. I also need to know if it's all alright? If it is alright that Karel, Nathan and I share this house here with you? To make this house a home once more; your house, our home. It is for you to decide."

Nick drew away then stood up. He walked to the window. It was night, and he stared out at the semi-darkness in the garden. It was past nine, and the garden was lit slightly from the bathroom window of one of the houses behind. The opaque glass showed a blurred figure of what he took to be a man. And he saw the gesture of an outstretched arm as it reached for what appeared to be a toilet chain. The light was very strong inside the bathroom, and it cast its glow down onto the centre of the concrete. Glancing quickly, he saw an autumn flower of a colour he could not quite determine, bending forward like an old man nodding his head just before the death that was to come, the end of days after a life of sun and beauty. Then, quite suddenly, the light went out, and both flower and any contour of garden disappeared.

"What are you thinking, Nick?" Greg asked.

Nick remained where he was. And his thoughts were clear. He wanted to reply to Greg, but isn't this a circle? Aren't we going back into the same circle as before? And what if you should leave again and that the others would follow? How could I bear for that circle of assurance and emotional security to break and to suffer as I suffered when you went looking for Karel? The only difference in this new circle is that Bart is replaced by Nathan. Will Nathan, who always seemed to be exclusive in loving Karel, be prepared to share?

He turned to face Greg.

"Is Nathan alright with this? It is new to him. Can you be sure?"

Without any hint of pride or boasting, Greg said, "He is willing. He is attracted to me. He has told Karel that."

"But he would be involved sexually with all of us. Do you really believe Nathan can adjust to such an arrangement? I always thought of him as being exclusive, despite his attraction to GLF and their beliefs." Nick paused, then asked, "What do *you* make of the movement?"

"Do we have to speak of it?" Greg asked wearily.

"Not really. It was just a thought, a question in passing."

"In passing, I think it will open up Pandora's Box. And yet, despite my fears of that, I believe the movement, as you call it, is a justified revolt against heterosexual values. But—" and he paused.

"But?"

"Someone always cashes in on a revolt. Those who cash in on our so-called promiscuous beliefs will make a tidy living by distorting GLF's views. In so doing, the revolt will be neutralised, normalised, when it should be precisely the opposite. Was it Marcuse who said that? I am so confused by the names of these illustrious thinkers."

The words *illustrious thinkers* were said with contempt, and Nick smiled. Greg was still very alive, despite the trough he had been in, the neglect of self and the loss of François.

"Fuck Marcuse!" Nick replied with a laugh. Greg laughed as well, and as Nick embraced the bond of this response, he realised how much he wanted to go to bed with him. However much the smell would repel, it would be annihilated by the need to enter and be entered. Remains of shit, remains of urine, remains of grime or skin, he wanted the flesh he desired. "I've got an erection," he said, and there was still laughter in his voice as he said the words.

"So have I."

"Then stay. Let us go to bed. We want each other."

Greg shook his head, and as the light had been extinguished in the garden, so did the light go out of Greg's response. In a sudden mood swing, he replied, "I have to return to Portslade."

"But why?"

"So many reasons. I said I came to see you. I have. I also had to ask you about the four of us. I have. I have done what I can do, but you and I touching? Reaching inwards? It's just not possible yet. Give me until your birthday. I need that space of time to clean myself outwardly and inwardly. I want to wash out all memories of François that still exist—and yes, I said it was in the past, but the remembrance of his flesh and his desire still haunts me. I have to be entirely alone for that space and time that we have before October the third."

"And how can you be sure you will be ready by then?"

"I trust I will be, and I want you to trust I will be. I want these coming days of aloneness away from you, Karel and Nathan, to restore myself. Oh, Christ, it's so fucking difficult to explain. Can't you feel I am being sincere? That I want the best of our union? And not just this readiness to rut like pigs— and pigs are clean compared to me!"

Nick had nothing to say. He had to let him go. In silence, he made Greg a hot cup of coffee and murmured, "This is to give you strength for the journey. Portslade is far. How will you get there? Should I call a taxi?"

"I will walk, Nick."

"But the distance—"

"Once I am on the Western Road, it is a straight line. I will hold out."

"You are exhausted."

"Nick, enough. I am strong."

"Fine." And Nick looked away from him.

"Nick?"

Nick stared at the floor and asked, "What?"

"Your birthday. Can I arrange it? I mean, you have probably thought of this house and a sort of party for us—but will you allow me to arrange a party elsewhere? It means I do not want you to get anything, just to be at the place I want you to be."

"Which is?" And Nick looked at Greg's face. The white pallor had gone. The flesh looked hot and eager as if already anticipating change and the movement of change.

"I will let you know by a short note I will send in the post."

"This is madness!"

"No, Nick, it is us. The adventurous *us*. Don't you recall the lost days? Our youth? The adventures? More is to come. We are still young. We will *always* be young."

"Alright, Greg. You tell me where and what time."

"Your birthday! Your day, given to you as a present by me. Don't you want that? Isn't it right?"

"Yes," Nick replied, and he meant it.

Soon after this, Greg was gone. Nick stared at the walls of the house, needing their embrace, but the walls did not respond, and on the contrary, seemed to retreat. Night closed in around him, and he hugged himself.

Nick immersed his whole attention on the shop, and the days passed, to his surprise, quickly. Nathan visited once. He wore tight flared jeans and a brown leather jacket and looked different. With close-cropped hair, his face looked older. Nick looked down at his own casual clothes that had, in his opinion, no sexiness about them at all. His simple jacket, white shirt and corduroy trousers were almost timeless, which in the current climate meant bookish and boring.

"I feel like your father," Nick said and grinned.

"In what way?"

"My clothes!"

"It's your style. It suits you."

"A compliment?"

"Yes. We wouldn't have you any other way. You don't have to look like everyone around you. And you don't go out clubbing."

Nick, alerted by the word *clubbing,* asked Nathan if he did.

"Sometimes. Can't always be at GLF meetings and on

marches."

"Does Karel like that?"

"He comes with me, yes. He's not exactly an old man, Nick."

"Meaning—?"

"Meaning he overcomes his fear of panic and attacks. He has even managed to spend evenings up in London with me, doing the rounds."

Nick pretended to be occupied, pricing up some books.

"Where do you take him in London?" he asked casually.

"We did the Chelsea scene, but that seems to be dying, so we have moved on to Earls Court where it is thriving. So many young guys coming out. Much more than in your teenage years."

"—and Karel's teenage years?" Nick interjected.

"Yes, but the young ones like him. They like him more than me. He is very beautiful—lighter than me. I am heavy compared with him. He dances without dancing. I am sort of clumsy. I'm no poet, Nick, so I will end personal descriptions of Karel there."

"Yes," Nick sighed. "Poetry in motion!"

"What?"

"A song from the early Sixties, or was it the late fifties? Back when you were in nappies!" Nick's hand shook as he wrote the sum of seven pounds, and pencil marks skidded all over the page. "Damn," he said.

"Was that my fault?" Nathan asked.

"I guess I was just jigging along in my head to that old song," Nick replied with slight sarcasm in his voice. He wondered how Nathan would really fit in with himself and Greg and Karel in the house. He knew the pace of club and pub gay life was speeding up, and he for one had no intention of going along with it. Would it appeal to Greg? "Have you seen Greg?" he asked, changing the subject.

"No, but I know all about the party for your birthday. He's going to send Karel and me a note saying where it will be and what we must prepare for it. How many candles will it be?" he asked.

"Just put on a hundred," Nick said and slammed the book shut that he had temporarily defaced.

"Nick, is something wrong?" Nathan murmured, and Nick looked at him and saw a very serious young man staring back at him.

"Just call it frustration," Nick said. "I mean, I am in a state of waiting, and I am still young enough to have urges."

"Don't you—well—relieve yourself at all?"

"Nathan, please don't descend into the same coyness as me. No, I don't masturbate, and I try not to read or look at anything that incites me to do so. In fact, if I could stand the prose, I *would* read some of those awful female novelists of the past! But the irony of it is, their coyness only arouses the imagination more. I read a play the other night. Enid Bagnold's *The Chalk Garden*. There's a line in it that says 'even the garden is demented', and I looked down at my pyjamas—yes, pyjamas— and I had an erection! Fuck knows why. There's not even an attractive guy in the play."

Nathan burst out laughing.

"Do you need relief?" he said. Then he put on a camp voice and lisped, "Can I be of any assistance?"

This made Nick laugh, and going to the back of the shop, he made them both a cup of tea. Nathan did not follow him but poked around among the bookshelves. Nick saw him holding up a copy of Nietzsche's *Beyond Good and Evil* when he returned with the full cups.

"Can I buy this?" Nathan asked.

"Have it," Nick replied.

"Thanks."

Nathan put the book in his pocket.

"Have you read Nietzsche?" Nick asked.

"*Zarathustra*. Only that. Does he have more to say in this book, or shouldn't I bother?"

"I'm not an expert on him," Nick replied. "But I do know

about willpower."

They both laughed at this, and just before leaving, Nathan said flippantly, "The four of us are going to be okay. I know it." And then he grinned.

Nick looked at him in silence, and after a few awkward seconds, he blurted out, "Maybe 'Beyond Good and Evil' should be put up as a plaque above the Islingword Street door!"

"See you at the party," Nathan said and left the shop.

The following days passed without incident, and then one afternoon, a schoolboy came into the shop. He was wearing thin grey trousers and had his school blazer slung over his shoulder. He was holding in his free hand a copy of William Golding's *The Lord of the Flies,* which Nick had put outside cheaply as it was in a battered condition. The boy placed it on the shop counter.

"You have priced this very low," the boy said in a posh voice. "I mean, it's a first, isn't it? Even the dust jacket is there, and it hasn't been price-clipped."

Nick picked up the copy. Had he made a mistake? The book cover was slit down the side, and inside he saw that it was not a first edition. There were also water stains, and it was covered with pen notes in the margins of the text. He put the book down and looked at the youth.

"It's really in poor shape—probably not even worth the price I have asked for it. It's also not a first edition."

"My father collects firsts," the innocent face replied. It was then that Nick looked at the face closely. Despite his fair looks and blond hair, the boy looked as if he was from farming stock. The cheeks were full and reddish, despite the overall whiteness of the skin, as if his forefathers had been out in all weathers. He had the ruddy cheeks of a well-off farmer's son.

"You don't look as if you come from Brighton," Nick said.

"I go to school here. You can see on my blazer." He held out the blazer proudly, showing off its well-known emblem.

"I can see that, but still—"

"My family are based in Hassocks. I get the train in the morning."

"Farming?" Nick asked and felt his penis stir.

"Once. Yes. How did you guess?"

Nick made no reply to this, and the boy stared at him in wonder as if he were some sort of clairvoyant.

"I guess I do look pretty healthy," the boy said.

"Yes, pretty," Nick boldly replied, and the cheeks reddened even more. The blue eyes continued to look closely into Nick's eyes. Excitement was beginning to show.

"My name is Edward," the boy said.

"Pleased to meet you, Edward. Are you especially interested in *Lord of the Flies*?"

"I've read it. I read *Coral Island* as well when I was younger."

"How much younger?" Nick asked, and his cock was pounding in his trousers.

"Twelve. I'm fifteen now. I know I look older."

Nick thought, no, you are a strong, handsome fifteen-year-old. There is no real comparison, but Greg was similar to you. Do you, too, have pillars of legs like he had and still has? And do you kick a ball around a field? He then stared down at Edwards's thighs, tightly wrapped in the thin grey of the cloth and saw a distinct bulge. It was the balls and not the cock; the cock was just visible despite the grey covering and was on its own, away from the scrotum, stretching down his right leg. He wanted to unzip the flies and release it. He also wanted to release his own.

"What did you think of Golding's book?" he asked, and he heard his own voice as if it was far away from him. He was not at all concerned about the book or the savage boys in it, but he *did* want to know about this posh boy who he thought, perhaps mistakenly, could never become a savage and bow down in reverence to a pig's head.

"I don't believe in the story," Edward said, a tremor in his voice. Was he following Nick's stare? Did he know Nick's

244

desire? Nick looked away and turned to the battered copy of the book in front of him. He concentrated his mind on what he had read about the book from critics and recalled one that said it was a refutation of *Coral Island* and that the devil does not arise out of cannibals and other such outward visibility of man's monstrousness, but out of the blackness of men's hearts. Was there a blackness, a darkness in his heart with the overwhelming feeling of desire and, yes, sheer lust that he felt towards this boy? Was there an actual bowing down to a pig's head in the book? Or was it just a recall of the book, read years past and now distorted in his memory? All he did know was that he wanted to bow down before Edward's clearly thick penis and adore it.

"Do *you* believe in the story?" Edward asked the question loudly.

"I had almost forgotten the book," he replied, wanting to move out from behind what he now considered his own entrapment: the counter. Would his own erection be revealed? And if so, would Edward believe that primal lust could be revealed, not to kill, but to penetrate? He longed for Edward to show him his arse and to spread himself before him.

"Were you my age when you read it?"

"Yes, I suppose so," and now Nick wanted either to give in to lust or deny it. He felt the battle of sexual frustration wearing him out.

"But in chapter four, a boy pretends to *be* a pig, and the other boy hunters pretend to beat him," Edward said.

"I don't remember that."

"I cannot imagine any of us doing that at my school."

Pushed by a compelling impulse, Nick said, "But surely at your famous school, some of the boys have other savage desires, or if not savage, alien to the society in which we live?"

Edwards, stepping back, turned his back on Nick and looked at some other books on the shelves. His high arse was fully revealed, and Nick's desire was intense.

"Yes, we think of certain things."

"Like what?" Nick asked.

"You really sound interested," Edward replied, his back still facing Nick.

"I am."

"We think of girls a lot and talk about fucking them, but then all boys think of that. We know we won't, or will suppress it, but we also know—" and here he stopped and turned to face Nick. Nick looked down at the length of the cock, and it had thickened. Edward was clearly sexually excited.

"What do you know?" Nick asked.

"That some of us, and I do mean some of us, *want* each other, and that that *is* possible. After all, it's a phase, isn't it?"

"You tell me."

"I think about it."

As he said these words, Edward walked towards the darkest recess of the shop and, as if inviting Nick, placed his hand against his trousers and let the other hand drop his blazer to the floor. Nick went towards him, and his mind raced with fantasies. He saw Edward as a drover on the Downs, a century ago, and how in his loneliness, the youth driving the sheep would pause, unbutton himself and cover the yellow gorse with his yellow urine, and then with easy, rhythmic pulls on his opened-up cock, bring himself to his white climax, spattering the same gorse.

"What are you thinking?" Edward asked. "Are you thinking about—" and he paused, his hand now gently touching the shaft of his clothed penis. Nick watched this gesture, and then he stepped backwards. The word cowardice ran through his mind. If he gave in to his desire for this boy, he would show moral weakness in doing so, but then he thought, after all, would it do the boy any harm? And there was a counterpoint which said, I am a coward if I don't. If I don't, Edward will think his own thoughts shameful, and he will be humiliated. Wouldn't that cause him more harm?

"Have you put certain thoughts into practice yet?" Nick asked.

"Tell me what thoughts. You tell *me*. I promise I won't tell on you. I'm not the sort. I know the punishments of this society. I am not a fool."

"But—"

"Call me Edward," Edward said suddenly.

"Edward, this is not the right place, and maybe not the right time," and Nick paused before concluding, "for any experiments."

"Who says I haven't experimented? There is this younger boy at school. I went back with him. We played around. He has a small one, and it did not satisfy me. I want a bigger one like my own. A man's one."

"You are not yet what the world calls adult," Nick said.

"Tell that to *this*," Edward replied and began stroking himself. "I will only wank when I reach the nearest toilet cubicle. I'm in more danger there than here. Come on. I can sense you want it. Suck me off. I've never been properly sucked off, and I want to see you—" and his voice trailed away in the excited force of what he had just said. The private school mask had fallen. His naked cock needed, fully needed to be bowed down to. Nick's final fantasy saw Edward among the boys on the island, his face streaked like a savage with paint— vivid red paint slashed with yellow.

The cowardly act of refusal was the strongest. Nick turned his back on Edward and moved back to the counter. Then his own savagery took its own special form; he took the battered book and tore it in half, then began to shred the pages with his hands. Edward edged slowly towards him, a look of horror on his face. Nick saw that he thought he was mad and that the boy was afraid of him. He also knew that this act, and this alone, would drive him from the shop.

"Fuck you," the boy said and ran out of the shop, slamming the door behind him. Exhausted, Nick watched him go and put the remains of the book into the dustbin.

"I was a coward," he said aloud as he discarded the last of the pages.

Through Nick's letterbox, on the morning of the second of October, a note in a blue envelope was delivered. He found it on the mat when he came down to have his bath, and he recognised Greg's handwriting immediately. He picked it up, held it for a moment, and felt so emotional that he began to cry. Greg had kept his word, but then, had he doubted him? It seemed so long (which it had not been) since he had been told to expect it, and here it was in his handwriting, waiting to be opened. He went downstairs, placed the envelope on the table and poured himself a glass of water. He drank first one and then two glasses, sat on the bench and gently released the note from its envelope. It was formally written.

Dear Nick, You are invited to—he read on, and after noting the time and place and lingering over Greg's name, he put it down.

"I don't believe it," he said and went back upstairs to run a hot bath. He lay in the water for a long while until it was almost cold, then drying himself off, he wondered how he would pass the time. Should he dress now for the hour written in the note, or should he come back after a walk to change? He decided on the latter. The weather was mild, and he put on a pair of jeans and a black roll-neck sweater, and without bothering to do anything else in the house, went immediately out. He walked uphill and made his way to Queens Park. A couple of men were already playing tennis, and he watched them for almost an hour, hoping it would not embarrass them. They were good at the game, and the sound of their running feet and the hit of the ball against the racket excited him. They were totally involved, and in his imagination, he saw it as a love match. Which of the two would win, the dark-haired one or the blond? He saw beads of sweat on their foreheads and could hear them panting, clearly revelling in the exhausted happiness of being so focused on the ball, of watching each flight of white in the air. Sometimes one of them would cry out. The cry was loud in the morning silence of the park, and other than himself and a few dog walkers, there was no one around. They were still playing when he decided to leave, and he wondered who would carry high the invisible trophy of the effort won.

Walking downwards, he left the park through the archway, and cutting through the narrow streets of Kemp Town, made his way to the seafront. He was full of energy himself, and on impulse, he set himself a challenge: to walk to Rottingdean and back? Full of anticipation for the night to come, he knew he had to succeed; that for him, this journey out and back was important. He told his body that if it failed, he would fail in the new life that was just about to open up for him; a vast sea of time that not only he but also others would try to navigate their way through.

He reached Roedean and stared at the solitary edifice of the school, so proud in its elitism. Then, as he passed St Dunstan's and thought of the blind servicemen within its walls, he wondered how he would manage in such a world of darkness. He considered someone like Greg; a youth called Greg from Portslade, virile and happy before war was declared and then through some chance bullet or fragment of exploded bomb, his life changing forever. He saw this Greg staring sightlessly out of the window, and what of the rest of him? Could he use his limbs, or had they too been taken? Could he lift his hands, or were they no longer there, no longer able to reach for a cup, or in those all too obvious moments of tormented sexual desire, unable to reach down? He saw this Greg walking, holding on to the railing so as not to fall, being led to the cliff face by an attendant to hear the crash of the autumn waves. And he, Nick, stood at the same place he imagined this ex-soldier called Greg would have stood and put his hands to his eyes, covering them. Then ashamed, he lowered them. How could he simulate an action that at its best only partially blocked the visual world? He felt a fraud pretending to an inward loss that he did not have. *He* could see! He could face this self-imposed challenge, this challenge of walking, literally. He moved onward and turned to look at the windmill that had inspired the publishers Heinemann to use it as their colophon. He was tempted to walk over to it and touch it, but Rottingdean was in full view, and he had a straight line to follow.

In Rottingdean, he paused and went to a tea house for scones and tea. He lapped up the last of the cream like a cat and was still hungry to eat more, but instead got up beneath the black wooden beams and paid his bill. Once outside, he decided to visit the church to look at the Burne-Jones windows he had not seen for a long time. But failure awaited him. The door was locked. He could not see the knight in flaming red or the other glorious stained-glass images. Disappointed, he crossed the road and stared at the ducks on the pond. A frog on a wide leaf plopped back into the water as he approached, and the stillness of the village was overwhelming. Few cars passed, and it was as if the beauty of the surroundings belonged to him alone. He sat on the grass and tried to empty his mind of all thought, even the thought of seeing Greg later, of being with him and the others invited, but despite this effort, the thoughts came.

"It is October the second 1973," he said aloud. "I am at the start of what will be my middle age. How will I be in a few years' time? Will Greg still be with me? And the others? How many of them will stay the course and not be tempted to leave the open sea and swim back to the safety of the shore? Loving demands so much, especially when it is in the balance with others and is supposed to be of equal measure."

He picked up a small stone and weighed it in his hand. It was black and white and almost flat, with the same pattern on both sides. He threw it, and it skimmed across the surface of the water, then sank and disappeared. Suddenly he heard a voice behind him.

"You frightened the ducks."

Nick turned around, and a very old man dressed in a heavy coat, with a scarf tightly wound around his neck, stared down at him. His darkly blotched hands clung to a stick that was firmly embedded in the grass.

"Did I?"

"Don't you notice things? I know all the ducks here. You

250

almost hit Gertie." The man raised his stick and pointed to a brown duck in the middle of the pond. "I call her Gertie after Gertrude Lawrence. I suppose people of your generation don't even know the name." His question (or was it a statement?) sounded like a challenge.

"My mother would have seen her," Nick replied, and then standing, he held out his hand. "I am Nick."

The man released one of his hands from his stick and shook the offered hand. Nick noticed how firm his grip was.

"I wasn't young when I saw her. Even back then. Great artist she was. Noel Coward too. Do you know of him? Or is it only John Osborne and his lot?"

"I know about him," Nick laughed, and standing back, he grinned at the man. He saw a fiery youth in the wrinkled features; the fire of endurance, and it made him happy to see it.

"Name one of his plays," the man prompted.

"*Present Laughter*," Nick replied, and the man's face broadened with a smile. He nodded his head, and then as if needing to prove that he did not need it, threw his stick down on the grass.

"Quite right. Good play. My favourite is the musical *Bitter Sweet*—but it is more than a musical! I wanted to be in it, you know. I was young enough for the part, the young lead, but Noel didn't choose me."

"Are you an actor?" Nick asked.

"Was. Too old for it now. And why no revival of *Bitter Sweet*? All this new political theatre nonsense. Won't even mention their names. I read them but won't go and see them. The last play I saw was at the Royal Court. Osborne's *A Patriot for Me*. Considered scandalous at the time. All about the Redl case. The spy. You surely know about the Austro-Hungarian empire?"

"I wasn't taught it at school, but I have read books about it."

"But not *A Patriot for Me*? The only good play Osborne ever wrote?" He paused. "And it's because of him that they have thrown out excellent dramatists like Wilde and Coward and

Rattigan. Not to mention N.C. Hunter. Ever heard of him?"

"No," Nick confessed.

"Why should you?" the man muttered, and then with alarming ease, he bent down and picked up the stick. "I am staying with Enid Bagnold across the way." And he waved his stick at what had been the house of Edward Burne-Jones. "Good friends. Always have been. Beautiful woman. I hope you like beautiful women."

"To look at," Nick said, and then he hurriedly added, "and I know that she writes plays."

"Yes, and novels. Not much read now. How it all changes. How it all flows by—we all become a fashion of the times. You too will be when you reach my age. Guess how old I am."

Nick erred on the side of generosity and said politely, "I am useless at guessing ages, but I would say you are in your sixties."

There was a roar of laughter followed by a sudden burst of coughing. The man brought out an immaculate white handkerchief and wiped his mouth. "I am eighty-nine," he said, choking back another cough. "And you, my young acquaintance, tell little white lies. It's a bad thing to do. It causes misunderstandings, but then, it is all part of *tout vu, tout malentendu*."

Nick did not understand.

"Basic French," the man said. "Roughly translated, all seen, all misunderstood." He muttered the words again, and waving his stick once in the air, turned his back on Nick and walked towards the Burne-Jones house.

All seen, all misunderstood. The words of the nameless old actor kept repeating in his head as Nick made his way back to the coast road. He bought a chocolate bar and set off on the final leg of his challenge. Arriving home, he threw himself down on his bed and slipped into a jungle of dreams.

That night, at half-past eleven, Nick arrived at the appointed place. He entered St Ann's Well Gardens from Furze Hill, dressed, aside from his black coat, almost entirely in white — white suit, white shirt, and grey shoes. When he took off his coat, he felt like the whitest of shadows. In life, the end of one phase and the beginning of another *is* like slipping into a new dimension, and that is how Nick felt. He was ready for any gift, any manifestation. Ahead of him, at the top of a path, the person at the heart of his transition, Greg, stood with a lighted candle in a white glass. Nick put his coat on a bench and moved ghostlike towards him. They stared at each other in silence.

"I am here," Nick said simply.

Greg silently bent forward and kissed him on the mouth. He was dressed in black: a long black coat, black shoes and black trousers. When he stepped back, his face looked translucent in the darkness.

"The others are waiting," Greg murmured, and taking Nick by the hand, led him downhill towards the large square of grass where Nick had first seen Greg playing his solitary ball game. Quite suddenly, he had the peculiar sensation of being back in time, and the football being kicked between his legs. Greg turned to look at him, the candle flickering, and in that slow turn of his head, Nick recalled him vividly, darting between his legs in search of the ball, and then, in an instant, rising up, dark hair damp with sweat,

"I remember," Nick said.

"What?" Greg replied.

"Us."

Nick realised they had arrived at the place of celebration. A white cloth was laid out on the grass, and as they approached, Nick saw Nathan lighting candles to enclose the group. As well as Nathan, there was Karel, and to Nick's surprise, Bart. Greg entered the square first and sat on one of the five cushions that had been placed on the cloth. Nick went to sit beside him. Conversation began, but Nick did not follow it or take up any of its themes. The words sounded like a foreign language he had never heard before. This illusion lasted for a while, and only when Bart stood up and moved away towards the pond did the words become familiar.

"Is this all strange?" Greg whispered to him.

"Yes. It doesn't seem real, Greg. Please make it real."

"The reality is coming," Greg exclaimed, and approaching them was Bart holding a white cake between his big hands. Then, with a slight bow to Nick, he placed the cake in front of him.

"It is almost midnight," Bart said.

Nick looked up at Bart's face, but there was no smile, no intimacy in his voice. This was the new Bart, visiting perhaps for the last time before heading off to the Orkneys to join Anna.

Nick asked quietly, "How is she? How is Anna?"

"She wants you to know that she is with us," Bart replied, then moved away and sat on a cushion that did not directly face Nick.

Greg produced some small candles from his black coat and placed them on the cake. "There!" he said.

After several attempts, Nick succeeded in lighting them all. The others clapped as he completed the task, and then Karel murmured, "It is a minute to twelve, Nick, let us countdown the sixty seconds."

Nick joined in with them as they descended from sixty, pausing only once on thirty for his age, then continuing until zero.

"Blow them out," Nathan commanded, and bending forward, Nick did so and saw the pale smoke left behind drift upwards.

"A knife!" Karel cried out. "Did we forget the knife?"

Bart drew one from his coat pocket and smiled as he handed it to Nick.

"Be generous," Nathan said. "It's a big cake. Big enough for two slices each!" His voice was childlike in its pleasure.

Nick cut the slices, making sure that there was enough for any that wanted more. He knew he would only eat one. When he brought it to his mouth, he tasted sponge and jam oozing out from the centre. It felt like a children's party, and he wondered if another rabbit would be drawn from the invisible hat with a trifle.

"I feel like I am ten years old," he said as jam oozed from his lips."

"I couldn't love you if you were," Greg replied, his mouth full.

Only Bart and Karel asked for more. Greg, noticing this, suggested, "Nick should take what's left back to the house. We can all five of us eat it for breakfast in the morning."

"I'll be on a train by then," Bart pointed out, reminding the four of them that he was passing through.

Nick looked over at him and asked, "Why did you decide to leave on my birthday?"

Bart seemed at first reluctant to reply, then whispering the words so softly that Nick could barely hear them, said, "I wanted to be here, but just for this night. I plan to catch the first morning train—"

"Bart—" Nick began.

"I have to," Bart whispered again. "I just do."

"Are you afraid that if you come back to the house you'll want to stay?" Greg asked, overhearing. The boldness of his question startled Nick.

"Yes," Bart replied.

"Won't you even come back to see the day through?" Nathan insisted, and Nick was equally surprised that Nathan was so concerned.

"I can't."

"Not even to give Nick his gifts?" Nathan continued. "We all have them. I know you do too."

Nick looked at each face in turn. Karel was looking away. Greg was leaning forward, staring at Bart and Nathan, even in this candlelit darkness, they showed a look of disappointment. There was something here among them that Nick did not as yet understand, but he had a moment of fear, sensing there was a fine crack in this bowl of light that he hoped united them all. "I would like you to stay, Bart," he added. "Just for this one day."

"You are four," Bart replied, his voice now clear. "I am a fifth. It was what I wanted, and a fifth is always somewhat apart. That is the honest answer, Nick. Nathan will give you my present for me."

"I don't need a present," Nick said softly.

"It's from Anna as well. We got it jointly."

"I think you're being too hard on yourself, Bart," Nathan said.

There was an awkward silence, and Karel broke it by walking away, up towards the well. Nick watched, fearing he would not return, and turning to Nathan, asked if he was going to follow him.

"It's alright, Nick. Let him be for a while."

Then as if to break the mood, Greg announced, "I have to get something important." He got up and wandered across the grass towards the shadows of the café. Now it was Bart's turn to move. He also got up, looked at Nathan, and made a gesture towards the pond. To Nick, it appeared a silent message, and when he walked away, Nick was about to question Nathan when he too got up to follow him.

"Where are you going?" Nick said aloud, but Nathan made no reply as he went, and for a short while, Nick was alone on his cushion, staring at the burnt candles and the remains of the cake. Already he noticed the night insects moving in on it and knew that by the end of the night, it would be in no fit state to be taken back to the house. He was watching one advance up the side of it when he heard Greg say, "We are alone." Nick looked up and saw Greg standing with two bottles of white wine in his hands, and with what seemed even to him to be a despairing cry, asked, "Greg, what is happening?"

"I did not expect it to be like this," Greg said, and sitting down, put the bottles aside. As soon as he had finished this action, he pulled out a set of paper cups. "My coat pockets are endless. Seems I am to be the magician of the night?"

"Then be a magician, Greg, and sort this out. There's a problem."

"It's not that serious, Nick. Karel and I have already talked about it. To put it simply, Nathan had a sudden, unexpected, and to me incomprehensible attraction for Bart and Bart for him. Bart, it seems, is having his last sexual encounter, perhaps for a long time, with another man, and that man is Nathan. He'll take his train because I know he is determined to start his new, contemplative life and to retire to the Orkneys." He paused, then added, with a note of cynicism in his voice, "Anyway, that is his intention."

"But Karel—"

"Accepts," Greg concluded.

Nick could not accept this conclusion and asked angrily, "Is this another gift for me? To know they are now having sex in the bushes near the pond?"

"They won't disturb the goldfish," Greg replied.

"Please don't be flippant. Has it happened before between them?"

"I don't know, Nick, but Nathan told both Karel and myself of the need for it to happen tonight. He was honest about it."

"Honest? Are we so liberated from all restraint?"

"We are free, Nick. You know we have always lived in freedom. We chose freedom years ago to form a sexual union of four. Bart was part of that four, and now he is going to a new life. Nathan is easing him into it. It is a love of sorts that Nathan is offering. I said I found it incomprehensible, but I regret that thought. I do understand what is happening."

Nick asked Greg to open a bottle, and when Greg had finished the procedure, he drank two cupfuls one after another.

"I want to get a little drunk," Nick said, "and quickly!"

Greg drew close, and putting the cup down, pulled Nick into his arms. "My dear, my beloved Narziss. You must see us Goldmunds as we are. You must tolerate our lapses. Perhaps we cannot always remain in your house, and perhaps we can. Life is a dream, Nick. It is a dream. Like in Shakespeare, we have our crude donkey selves. They too exist in that state of illusion we call dreaming."

"*A Midsummer Night's Dream*," Nick responded.

"It's October now," Greg replied. "We must look towards winter and the warmth it can give. The time of travelling with the sun has gone."

Nick was about to reply when Greg closed his mouth with a kiss and then reached down to caress Nick's penis. Nick let it happen. He reached for Greg as well, and within minutes they were lying back on the grass, masturbating each other, their mouths kissing all the while until they came. Afterwards, they lay side by side and soon they were conscious of Karel standing behind them, looking down at them.

"You are as beautiful as you always were," he said softly, and then bending down, he reached for each of their penises in turn. He touched the cold sperm on their half-uncovered bodies and brought some of it to his lips. Nick stared up as he watched Karel lick his fingers.

"We are safe in our loving," Karel murmured. "This is a night to celebrate. This sperm is the joy of your flesh, and it is my drink, my wine."

"I love you both," Greg said, looking first at Nick and then at Karel.

"I too," Nick added, and lifting his head, he offered his mouth for Karel and Greg to kiss. Then Nathan and Bart appeared, adjusting their clothes.

"We must all kiss," Nathan said, sitting down beside the still half-naked flesh of Nick and Greg. Tenderly, he touched them both and did the same as Karel had done, gathering the last of the sperm to his mouth. Then the four of them kissed, passionate kisses that Bart, standing aside, watched. He watched, in the hours that followed, showing no signs of tiredness, these long embraces that lasted until the first glimmer of light in the east.

"It is almost dawn," Bart reminded them. He was, it seemed, their watchman. The four looked at him, and in their looks, they let him go. They all knew he was welcome in their home any time he wanted but sensed that he had already entered another sort of world in the Orkneys.

"I will miss you," Nick said. "You are my poet, Bart, and always will be. I want only one gift from you."

"What is that?" Bart asked gently, his head still turned towards the vague eastern light.

"A poem."

"Now?" Bart asked, kneeling in front of the entwined four. "Do you want the last poem I wrote before this act of leaving?"

"I will listen, I will learn it, and I will treasure it," Nick said.

Sitting cross-legged in front of them, his face seemingly transformed into its younger self, Bart began to recite his poem. It was a poem of loss and goodbyes. Nick took in the words. They seemed to have been written just for him, for his inner self, and it was as if it was of no concern to the others. Then Bart got up and began to move slowly from them. He walked towards the exit beyond the pond, and as he walked, he waved as they watched him go. Then he disappeared, and the light broadened in the east.

"Is he a coward to leave?" Karel asked.

"No," Nick replied. "It is brave to go where he is going and to resist desire. Could any of us do the same?"

"How could we?" Greg asked. "We are at home with each other. He has chosen his way, and we have chosen ours." He paused, then added, "All five of us have our unique kinds of bravery."

He then got up, and the others followed, and when they were all standing, Greg gave his big boyish smile, surprisingly bright in this advancing light, and whisking up the white cloth, he cried out in triumph, "And now for the last act of the magician, I bring on the strength of the day!" And in that whisking gesture of flashing white, it seemed to Nick that they all disappeared, white into white, enclosed within their love for each other.

*****

Thank you for reading *Love and Cowardice*.
Please share your thoughts and reactions with others.

Have you read the other adventures of **NICK & GREG?**

COMING SOON **GREG AT THE STATION**

Sign up to receive information about these and other titles
from Wilkinson House: http://bit.do/gayreads